I0690756

Darkwalker

by

Kat de Falla

Book Two:
The 7 Archangels Series

This is a work of fiction. Names, characters, places, and incidents are either the product of the author's imagination or are used fictitiously, and any resemblance to actual persons living or dead, business establishments, events, or locales, is entirely coincidental.

Darkwalker

Cover Art by *Debbie Taylor*

The Wild Rose Press, Inc.
PO Box 708
Adams Basin, NY 14410-0708
Visit us at www.thewildrosepress.com

Publishing History
First Black Rose Edition, 2016
Print ISBN 978-1-5092-1002-2
Digital ISBN 978-1-5092-1003-9

The 7 Archangels Series
Published in the United States of America

"Split up!" Lucas called,

charging left with three monks on his heels. They went head to head with the ground minions. Seamus and Dean went right, staying close to the two monks.

Lucas was surrounded. Three winged beasts swooped in trying to snatch them up, but Lucas and the monks managed to foil their attempts. The monks were ramming their heels, knees, elbows, and fists into any attacker in their way. Lucas drew his Wakizashi swords and began slashing demons, spilling their intestines, and severing heads from bodies. The scene was reminiscent of a Middle Age killing field. He knew he needed to gash open a pathway like a maggot eating its way through flesh to find the demon leader.

Wiping the crimson life-forced infused fluid off his face, Lucas cast a quick glance at Seamus and Dean to see if they were taking advantage of the blood soaked opening he was creating.

A winged demon snapped the neck of one monk and tore the jugular out of another with his teeth. They were dying out here in the open, like a rabbit in an open field caught in the eyes of a raptor. Casualties amid clouds of black dust continued to litter the field.

"Move under the pillars," Seamus yelled.

Lucas pulled back so they would be protected by the roof and support columns surrounding the grassy courtyard.

They regrouped. "Let's harpoon that mother fucker and pull him down to us," Lucas pointed to the black-horned demon he'd identified as the leader. "If we can take him down, we might stand a chance."

The hoard moved in like the fog off a stormy sea.

Dedications

Thanks to my editor, Lill Farrell,
who is an amazingly beautiful woman
on top of being an incredible editor.
Once again,
I thank everyone at The Wild Rose Press, Inc.
for believing in my work.

~*~

Thanks to Rachel, Bruce, and Heidi.
And to my one and only,
my soulmate and my eternity…Lee.
I walk in the truth and light because of you.
Thanks for saving me.

Nothing is so dark that the light can't penetrate it...

Adrienne Perdu has lost her parents and herself. Residing in Paris, she merely exists without living. To fill the void, she turns to a self-help group preaching isolation and self-preservation. Too late, she finds out the group is a cover for Darkwalkers, searching for relics that angels have spent centuries guarding.

Seamus Bron has spent his life guarding the religious relics that have been in his family for centuries. Constantly on the move, he's had no real place to call home and little interest in finding one.

Thrown together by circumstances beyond their control, Adrienne and Seamus find they share a mutual attraction. With the help of angels, a semi-reformed demon, and others met along the way, they work together to keep the relics from falling into the wrong hands. They may have a future together but first they must save lives, including their own.

Chapter 1

Wauwatosa, Wisconsin

The chime attached to the door of the bakery jingled. Calise Rojas and her best friend, the angel Ellen, stepped into the October sunshine toting day-old French bread. The semi-stale crusty snack was a favorite of the mallards and wood ducks waddling in the grassy fringe of the Menomonee River Parkway. Calise's son, Michael, and cousin, Max who waited beside the river with their dads waved at them with big smiles. She couldn't tell if it was a greeting or if she was being told to hurry up, but she smiled and waved back anyway.

"I forgot Michael's birthday present in the car. Not every day your little man turns five. I'll grab it quick." Ellen dug in her purse to retrieve her keys.

"No problem. Want me to wait?"

"No, I'll just be a second." Ellen said.

Cradling the long sticks of bread, Calise held up one finger to her husband, Lucas, who gave her a thumb up. He lounged on a blanket under their favorite willow tree, while her brother Dean chased Max and Michael in a game of tag. A warmth spread through her. She twisted her wedding band before pushing the walk button, then shifted the bread to her other arm and laughed watching Michael chase their dog, Stogey. The

1

loveable mutt had more gray around his nose than the brown he'd sported in his youth, but there was still a bounce in his step, especially whenever Michael wanted to play. Was it her imagination or did the sun shine a little brighter and the sky grow a little bluer every day?

Maybe because for the last five years, all had been quiet in her crazy world of angels, demons, and seers.

The walk signal began to flash a few seconds after the light turned red. Stepping into the road, she paused in confusion when Stogey broke free from Max's hold and charged right for her. It had been years since she'd seen him move so fast, he darted toward the street, barking and growling the way he used to when he saw a…

Tires squealed. Calise turned her head, but it was too late. A vehicle ran the light and was heading straight for her. In the front seat…three sets of red, demon eyes.

****

Shane *would* stop Nara.

He had to.

He played through every scenario in his head and in each one, he stopped her. It was inevitable.

When his demon girlfriend, Nara, learned his ex, Calise had escaped the Russian orphanage with her life, burning rage had consumed her every waking thought, day after day, year after year. Shane did everything in his power to be the demon husband and father Nara wanted. But he could only placate her for so long.

Suppressing Nara's fury and buying Calise more time, he lied, promising his demon wife that when the time was right, and his demonic powers were stronger, they would exact their revenge together. After five years, he'd run out of time. Nara's wrath could no longer be contained. Her one goal: take their sweet time carving up Calise and everyone she held dear.

Nara wanted blood. Calise's blood. Shane just wanted Calise back.

Somewhere deep inside him, he was convinced she held the power to save him. But how could she do that if she were dead?

The icy cold void of living without the warmth of the Creator's love pricked his soul like knives second after miserable second.

He'd failed to change Nara's mind on this matter. Because he was weak. His only strength had ever been Calise.

Was there still time to win her back?

En route to Calise's apartment via North Avenue in a stolen black pick-up truck, Shane's five-year-old daughter, Melki bounced happily on Nara's lap. The vehicle's owner lay dead in a way station bathroom on Interstate 94—collateral damage.

He convinced himself to work by any means necessary on his slow nail-clawing climb from the sewers of hell. After brushing the cigarette butts and used food wrappers onto the floor, Nara slid closer to him on the truck's ripped bench seat. She turned up the radio which was cranked on Gun N' Roses *I Used to Love Her*.

"You finally ready to do this? Once and for all?" Nara asked. Her eyes sparkled with rancid hate and her black aura pulsed, enveloping his daughter who clapped in delight absorbing her mother's icy odium.

Poor Melki. Born and raised in Nara's clutches. Shane loved the little girl, even while he felt himself pulling away from her. *Her loyalty already lies with her evil mother and today, he'd use her as his pawn to bargain for Calise's life.*

"I want it to be over as much as you do." Shane said, staring straight ahead. He gripped the steering wheel tighter until his knuckles turned white. "We kill Calise. If Lucas or their kid gets popped off too, that'll be an extra bonus." *I hope she believes me.*

The only thing stopping him from leaving Nara before today was Melki. But he knew the only way to save his daughter was get her away from the wicked one. He curled a black lock of her hair around his finger. She giggled in contentment.

Shane coveted one thing: Calise's unconditional love. Second best would be the same from his daughter. But she was already a disappointment. Damn demon offspring.

He needed his daughter alone, away from Nara, so they could find their way back to the Creator. *If he redeemed his child's black soul, would he retrieve his essence?*

After today he would have no problem abstaining from the seven deadly sins until he was redeemed. If Calise was his again, envy, anger, and lust would dissipate like frost on a spring morning. The rest: pride, gluttony, greed, and sloth she would help him with as well. But he needed *her*. She had to understand that.

Nothing he'd done since that day at the orphanage had given him even temporary respite in the hollow cavern of his heart. He fell from grace right in front of Calise when she rejected him. He was a demon and Calise was his only hope of salvation.

His mind replayed his plan while driving down

North Avenue—overpower Nara with brute force, take his child, reclaim Calise, and run like hell.

It had taken years to come into his full demonic strength. To know he could defeat Nara.

Now, he was ready. He vowed to be at peace after today was over, one way or the other.

Then there she was…in the middle of the road. Calise!

Nara and Shane saw her at the exact same moment. Red light. He lifted his foot off the accelerator, but Nara stomped her left foot over his right one and screamed, "Hit her!"

She held a long bundle wrapped in a blanket—*her angel son?*

He jerked the wheel to swerve but Nara anticipated and countered the move, holding the wheel straight and pushing harder on the gas. He slammed on the brakes with his left foot.

The tires squealed.

"What are you doing?" Nara wailed.

No. No. No. This isn't happening…

He wanted Calise back, not dead. She was his savior. He knew it!

His eyes locked with those of his true love and in those fractional seconds, he registered her one emotion—*pity.*

In the face of her demise, she showed mercy. In her final moments, her human eyes held unmistakable compassion. Then metal connected with flesh and bone and launched her limp body into the air. He thought he heard a dog howl in the distance.

She landed with a sickening thud, like a slab of meat slapping against the pavement.

Time stood still.

Like the hearing loss he used to experience at the end of a drum set with his band, he registered noise and movement around him, but couldn't hear any of it. A calmness overtook him. He shifted the truck into park and opened the door before his auditory senses switched back on.

Nara *demonstrated*, showing off her true demonic-form—a sign she was pissed. "If you get out of this truck, you will NEVER see your daughter again," she shrieked at him. "Don't you dare go to *her!*" Her grip on their child made python-like.

His daughter blinked, registering no emotion. Her black locks haphazardly fell around her porcelain face and her eyes, glowing like a ruby sunset, sent daggers into his heart.

With one step onto solid ground, the crooked world righted itself. Everything made sense. The long-consuming emptiness dissipated. He put one foot in front of the other and fought his way to Calise.

She lay in the road, Lucas cradling her limp body and a dog licking at her cheek.

Nara slid into the driver's seat, jerked the truck back into gear, and sped away.

A child cried nearby—Calise's child, alive and well in Ellen's arms. The spilled bundle in her arms was bread.

When Lucas saw Shane, he cried, "What have you done?" he snapped.

Shane had killed his only chance at salvation. That's what he'd done. So he did the only thing he could think of.

He turned and fled.

Chapter 2

A few weeks later…

Lucas Rojas awoke with a jolt from a series of loud beeps. The smell was all wrong. He wasn't at home. He blinked, still groggy and took a few staccato inhalations before allowing the grim reality of his surroundings to seep back in.

Hospital Bed.

ICU.

A nurse reset an IV and then slipped out of the room.

His beautiful wife, Calise had tubes down her throat and needles stuck in her arms. They were hidden by tape but still there. Monitors with flashing numbers surrounded her, and machines beeped unceremoniously at the worst possible intervals.

The low fluid in the IV bag is what had jerked him awake. He must have nodded off using the metal railing on the side of Cali's hospital bed as a pillow.

He was still holding her hand.

Damn Shane. Damn him to hell. The fact the former angel was already damned to hell wasn't even a splinter compared to the pain Lucas would inflict on that asshole if Calise didn't wake up.

Wake up.

Who was he kidding?

The leaves brushing against the second floor window had already begun to change color. Emerald summer leaving without a fight. Green leaves changing to hues of crimson, ginger, and gold before they fell to the earth escorting in the cold of winter.

Life happy to usher in death.

And here he sat...helpless. Unable to help his wife—his soulmate, the mother of his child and his other half. Being tough in a physical fight hadn't given him any advantage in this battle.

Nearly brain dead. That's what the doctors told him. An emergency surgery after the accident had relieved some of the pressure on her brain. Her heart seemed strong, but there was very little brain activity.

Alluding to the fact there was no hope and she'd never recover, he'd have to pull the plug.

Not happening. He'd said no. And he'd keep saying no. Day after terrible day. Week after miserable week. Thank goodness Ellen had convinced them each to fill out a medical power of attorney after Michael was born. Without it, Lucas wondered how much say he would have had in his wife's medical care.

Lucas had no way to fix this and it was killing him. No angel of virtue had shown up and held a flashlight of inspiration over his head.

The gray curtain squeaked when it was pulled back. "Hey, Lucas."

"Hey, Dean." Calise's brother had been there every day. And every day he told Lucas the same thing. *Take a break. Eat something. Leave for a while, I'll sit with her.*

But no one could or would make him leave her side. The dark side of him said the plug would get pulled and he wouldn't get to say goodbye.

He grasped her cool, limp hand and kissed it for the billionth time.

"Still waiting for that miracle?" Dean asked.

Lucas suppressed the desire to beat the shit of him. He did need a miracle. So he bowed his head, still holding Cali's limp hand, and prayed for just that. A hand squeezed his shoulder.

"You need to take a break. Get some air. See Michael."

"I'm not leaving her side. Even for Michael. He's fine with your mom and you know it." Lucas tucked Cali's hand back under the blanket. Was she getting colder?

"I'll stay with her. I won't even sleep. Just take an hour break. The boys are with mom at my house. I'll give you a key. Take a shower. Take a nap. Go in the hot tub or something. You aren't doing Calise any favors if you don't take care of yourself."

"Everyone else before myself," Lucas whispered under his breath. His Dad used to say that. A man who was entirely selfless, until...

Until his world crashed in around him, much like Lucas' had.

Shit.

He'd vowed never to end up like his father. Never be a prisoner to sorrow. Yet here he was sitting in a puddle of his own remorse, self-loathing, and agony.

He pointed his finger at Dean. "If you so much as take a whiz, you better call me to come back. Don't let anyone inject anything or check anything besides her vitals, or come too close, or—"

"I've got it, Lucas. *When* Cali wakes up, you don't

want to be stinking up the place. You smell stronger than hospital stench. Got me?"

"I'm counting on you."

Dean let his cocky attitude fall away. The look on his face told Lucas the jokes, as usual, were only a cover. "I've got your back. And you know I have Cali's. Now scoot." Dean pushed him out the door.

One hour. A shower or maybe just a dip in Dean's hot tub. Chlorine couldn't make him smell worse and maybe it would kill all the other bugs hospitals can harbor.

He passed the nurses' station with a wave. All angels. Thank God Ellen had some clout here. The charge nurse, Lily looked up from the round desk situated in the center of the circular band of ICU rooms. She was a kindly woman in baby blue scrubs who'd been Cali's nurse on the day shifts. Lucas swore she lived on peanut butter and soda. "Heading out for a bit?"

Still trusting no one, he couldn't help but lie. "No, just getting a drink and using the bathroom. I'll be right back. Cali's brother is in there. No other visitors, okay? No exceptions."

"Not a problem, Lucas. You know those are the house rules anyway. I'll keep an eye on her, you know it."

Lucas nodded and headed for the automatic doors leading to the east elevator bank. The place smelled of death and he was not going to let Calise become another one of its casualties. Inside the elevator stood three hospital employees chatting amongst themselves. His germ phobia kicked into overdrive having to stand next to people in scrubs, hair and shoe covers.

What did this death house have inside of it to make people cover up their street clothes?

The demon Nara dispensing invisible flesh-eating bacteria here sent a shiver down his spine.

The words coming out of the workers' mouths were Greek to him, probably because most medical words derived from ancient Greece anyway.

Stepping off the elevator in the brightly lit foyer, Lucas rushed for the entrance and almost smacked into the person heading right for him…Ellen.

"Lucas! I'm glad to see you. Can we talk?" Tears rolled down her cheeks as soon as she began to talk. "Any change?" Tears began to run down her cheeks. "I should have been with her. I just went to the car to get Michael's present and I never thought—"

Lucas squeezed her shoulder. "It's not your fault." For an angel, Ellen looked like hell. Dark circles under her eyes, hair unkempt, hands shaky, even her pumps were mismatched. One was navy and the other black.

"I'm not sleeping, or eating. Look, you need to know," she swiped at her face smearing her black mascara, "We're running out of time."

"What do you mean?"

Ellen couldn't keep his gaze and looked away. "I can hold the ethics committee off for maybe two more weeks, tops."

"What's an ethics committee?" he asked.

"It's complicated."

Lucas didn't like where she was going with this.

"If she is declared brain-dead and you won't agree to take her off life support, the ethics committee may pull the plug without your consent. If the swelling goes down, they'll wean her from the vent because the hospital needs the room. The committee is not made up of all "friends" if you know what I mean." Ellen squeezed Lucas' hand and leaned in for a sympathetic hug.

He pushed her away. "I don't want your sympathy. I want Calise back. I won't let her die. Give me other options." He held her shoulders and searched her face. "Ellen, give me hope."

Looking into her eyes, he knew she had nothing to give.

****

Lucas would never understand why anyone chose to remain in a place with winters so brutal it hurt to take a deep breath outside. And winter was well on its way. With steam and mist clogging his immediate field of vision from the October air, he tried to relax in Dean's hot tub without success.

Stagnant frothy hot water was no respite for a haggard, sleep-deprived, heart-broken man. His soulmate may never wake up. And he was sitting in a hot tub? *Absurd*. He needed to get back to Cali's side for when she woke up.

The alternative was unthinkable. *Think, Lucas. Think!*

Damn Nara and Shane to hell.

Consumed by regrets, he lay his head back and closed his eyes trying to unwind. Five more minutes then he'd towel off and head back to the hospital. There must be some way—something in his arsenal—but he and his aunt had been over everything and had come up with nothing. Apparently, being from the line of the biblical Nicodemus and protecting artifacts used to fight demons for over two-thousand years didn't have any advantage when it came to saving his wife's life. Being a seer of the angels and demons walking the earth did him no good today.

His Aunt Carmen was his only surviving family member. His years of hiding in Costa Rica might have been peaceful and uneventful, but he'd never trade finding his soulmate for anything, no matter how short their time together on earth. And then for them to have a son, and not a human son…but an angel! But every uneventful day they had spent together over the last five years only made Lucas more paranoid something bad would happen. And now it had.

Cali's mom was taking care of their son, Michael, since the accident and brought him to the hospital to visit each day. Lucas relished those minutes even though they brought him pangs of guilt. Was he greedy to hold his son to absorb his angelic calm? The waves of peace Michael gave off were part of what kept Lucas going.

The patio door slid open and Dean appeared with two Spotted Cow beers. "Here." His words lacked their usual sarcasm.

"You promised you wouldn't leave her!" Lucas stood up with a splash and reached for his towel.

"Relax," he said. "My mom stopped by the hospital with the boys. You must have just missed them. She sent them with me so they could play here and Michael could spend a few minutes with you outside the hospital."

"Fine," Lucas nodded, waving off the alcohol. "But I'm not drinking."

"Suit yourself." Dean flipped off the cap with a bottle opener and tucked the bottle cap in his pocket.

"You like the hot tub?"

Lucas waited while Dean took a long swig of the beer. "It's a welcome change but I'm preoccupied with Calise regaining consciousness."

Dean gave him the *look*. The same look replete of hope Ellen used outside the hospital. "I want her to wake up, too." He plopped down in a patio chair and took another swallow. "Uh...I know this isn't the best time to talk to you, what with Cali in the hospital and all, but I've been having some really weird dreams— about our time in Russia. At the orphanage."

Shit. The last thing Lucas needed to deal with right now was Dean remembering snippets of the horror they lived in Russia. Was Ellen's mind erasure weakening? What would happen the day Dean woke up and realized he'd killed his demon wife, fought in a battle with dozens of demons, and witnessed the archangel Raphael swoop down and save the day? That would be fun.

"What aren't you telling me, Lucas?"

"There's nothing to tell. Ask Ellen."

Dean chewed his lip and sipped his beer. "She's not talking and I'm starting to think you're both full of shit. If Cali wakes up, we're going to sit down and talk. Agreed?"

"*When.* When she wakes up."

"I'll go wrangle the boys." Dean went back in the house, popping the cap off the beer he'd brought outside for Lucas.

Even though he wasn't drinking—he couldn't, not when Cali needed him—he had to admit a beer sounded good. He'd like a cool, icy drink right now. Many in fact, to dull his pain.

Drink.

Drinking.
Cup.
The angel Raphael.

What did his Aunt Carmen say? The other guy, Joseph someone, kept different artifacts than Nicodemus. Lucas' family had thorns from the crown of Jesus, and fragments of the cross, as well as vials of the myrrh and aloe used to prepare his body. The archangel Raphael had told him the descendants of Joseph kept something else…a cup. The cup had touched Jesus' lips while on the cross. "The cup. I wonder…," he said aloud.

"No need to wonder. The cup would wake her."

The silky voice made him jump from the hot tub and splash water over the concrete patio. "What the…Who are you?" He drank in the tranquil beauty of the angel in front of him. She was tall and slim with flowing black hair and innocent eyes. She wore skin-tight white leather and her angelic aura shimmered like diamonds in the fading sunlight.

His life experiences left him cynical and untrusting of angelic help. He'd already met angels who broke their word, like Raphael who'd all but abandoned him once the angel was reunited with his paired essence, Anna, who was trapped in hell. Although he did show up in Russia, he hadn't heard a peep from him since. Likely, he was still obsessing over how to get Anna out of hell.

"I'm your guardian angel, silly. If you find the other set of artifacts—which includes the cup—you could awaken your wife. And the truth to their location has already been made known to you, hasn't it?"

"My father, before he died…"

"Lucas, please know I will be with you the whole way. I thought it was time I finally made myself known to you. My name is Asmoday." The angel smiled.

"Why now?" Lucas asked.

"Because now is when you'll need me most. You are alone and vulnerable. Your path is fraught with danger but for the sake of your true love, you must not fail." The angel spoke with a quiet urgency.

"Are you sure the cup will work?"

"Yes. The cup of everlasting life is protected by the descendants of Joseph of Arimathea. If Calise drinks from the cup, she will awake and come back to you."

"My father…My father told me where to go," Lucas said, closing his eyes to recall his father's deathbed words to him. When Lucas opened his eyes, he felt the calm, drug-like effect angels can project. Asmoday's body shimmered and she drew closer.

"It is time, Lucas. I am always watching over you and will be there if you need me. Just call my name. Where did your father tell you go?"

"Gl—," Lucas was interrupted by the creak of the sliding glass doors. Dean ran out, yelling, "I remember!" followed by the boys.

When Lucas snapped his head back around, the angel was gone.

"An orphanage! I remember something about an orphanage," Dean cried.

Now was not the time to deal with his brother-in-law's fractured memories. Besides that, his son and nephew were dangling balisongs, or butterfly knives, between their fingers trying to flip them open. "What the hell are you boys doing with those?"

"Uncle Lucas, these are sweet," said Max. "Can

you teach me how to use them?"

Lucas swung his legs over the end of the hot tub and yanked the knives away from the boys. "No. You both know better than to dig through my pockets."

They shrugged their shoulders and exchanged guilty looks.

"Michael…?" Lucas asked, knowing it wasn't in his capacity to lie.

Michael hung his head like a scolded puppy. "I just wanted to show Max what you used to fight the bad people, Dad. He didn't believe me, so I showed him." He fumbled with the strings of his sweatshirt.

Lucas corralled the boys inside the house. "Max, go get me a towel, would you?" Max scampered off happy for only a verbal admonishment. He sank down in front of his son. "Michael, what do you think you know about bad people? And what makes you think I fight them?"

"I have dreams, Dad. I know I'm not like Max. Sometimes, I see the bad people in my dreams. I fight next to you and Mom." He blinked, with a calm acceptance of all he could not yet understand.

Lucas drew him close and held him tightly. Remembering when he was Michael's age, he too had wanted nothing more than to train and fight next to his parents. Look how that turned out. Both slain by demons. "If I have anything to do with it, I won't ever let a bad person get close to you. That's my job, you know…" he ruffled his son's sandy blond hair, "…to protect you."

Michael spoke into his father's ear. "You can't protect me. I was born to fight. And I can feel it. The fight builds in me every day."

Chapter 3

Wauwatosa, Wisconsin

There's nothing better than a first kiss. The body's slow deliberate movement forward, the man's hand cradling her face as though she were the finest china— the wild anticipation and hunger of possibilities. When it's only two people and they find out in one instant they cannot live without each other.

My sinful drug desire is adoration. It is blasphemous because I am an angel of the Lord, but since my best friend has been in the sleep of death, it's all that's sustaining me.

Doctor Ellen Engel caressed the shoulder of the man gently snoring next to her. Thank Father she hadn't slept with him. But she'd thought about it. Was even in his bed partially undressed. *Who am I? And what is happening to me?*

After that tender first kiss, she'd had the overwhelming desire to have him hold her. She wanted to freeze this moment in time, because she could feel the earth shifting and changing. Something about the upcoming change scared her to death.

She covered his eyes with her hands and spoke in Angelical language, "Forget Me" then slid out of his bed and got dressed. As soon as she spoke the words, her failings gathered around her again like static-charged cloth. They covered her with grime that couldn't be washed off.

Calise was in a coma because of her. But the years of living in peace had made her complacent instead of staying by Calise's side that day. She regretted not being vigilant. She could have protected her! But no...she'd failed her best friend and the guilt was too much. Dulling the pain with alcohol proved to be her worst decision yet.

It was supposed to be one drink with her old college friend, Sarah. Sarah was supposed to be consoling her. That was the plan. But then everything went to shit. Sarah's one drink turned to six, she hooked up with a stranger and left crying on his shoulder.

Ellen should have left, too. *Why didn't I?* For every waking second since the car accident, guilt had consumed her like a straightjacket. The drink with Sarah was supposed to buy her a few hours of empty consolation. From the moment she allowed a smidgen of her angelic light to show to the human man, she regretted it.

Her whole life, nay, her whole purpose in this life was to *watch over* humans. Direct them. Guide them. Protect them. After her colossal failure, she found herself drowning in an intense desire for someone to comfort her. Just this once.

Until tonight, Ellen had considered herself a law-abiding angel of the Lord who'd always followed the letter of the law. But tonight, she couldn't help thinking...where had that gotten her?

Before Calise was rendered comatose by psychopathic demons, Ellen had never let a human man get close to her, knowing their imperfect lust would only distract her from the righteous path.

But my path is lost now…

Allowing human adoration was not permitted, but the look of wonder on the man's face the moment before he kissed her, reminded her of how Calise looked at her.

For the last five years, she'd been addicted to it.

And without it…well…

Last night, Ellen hadn't given the man's apartment a second glance. They'd headed directly for his queen-sized bed with flannel brown and green striped sheets. He pulled the blinds and killed the lights and she let herself shine onto him.

He probably didn't know if he'd been drugged or was in the midst of a spectacular hallucination, but Ellen projected her warmth and beauty so it seared his mind and body. He couldn't get enough of her to touch or murmur enough words of adoration.

He held her. And when he tried to do more, she sent him into a deep and peaceful slumber and allowed herself to lie in his strong arms.

In deceitful comfort. Then she drifted off to sleep herself.

Now, in the light of day, she picked up her clutch and jacket and realized the apartment was no more than a single man's hovel. Stepping over piles of dirty laundry, she picked her way to a bathroom whose sink was decorated with razor trimmings and a toilet seat that needed to be put down for her to pee. She made a mental note to send over a cleaning service for him every two weeks.

Before leaving, she cast one last look at the man. A nice human—good-looking enough with thick brown hair and a smile which was slightly crooked on one side. She was wrong to have let her aura seep into him last night. He was instantly smitten, believing she was the only woman in the world for him.

Never again.

This was an accident. A onetime mistake.

But she was angry at Father. Trained in modern medicine, a healing angel of the Lord, and yet she'd done nothing but watch when the car slammed into Calise. So many years of doing Father's will and now, it felt like He'd turned on her.

Punished her.

Lying in the man's arms did not have the intended effect. It had dulled her pain for a mere blink in time. She was stronger than this. *Remember the higher purpose.*

Never again would she use human men's adoration to distract from her own pain and inadequacies. The lure of being able to walk in anywhere and pick out the man of her momentary desire had lost its thrill.

I need absolution for my transgression.

Burdened with guilt, she sneaked out of the apartment and gently pulled the door shut behind her. What was Father's limit? Would forgiveness be bestowed simply because she asked for it or would she be punished with His retribution for her crime?

Of course other angels had done worse. But she knew, in her essence, she did not want to be like the other angels that wandered the Earth: Passive. Selfish. Dishonorable.

Saint Jude's church was four blocks to the east. The autumn day held a blustery chill. *Poor Lucas.* Yesterday, Ellen hadn't bothered to tell him Calise's brain function wasn't improving. In fact, the opposite was true. She'd known it wouldn't do any good. He refused to see the truth.

The stale smell of leaves and brush burnt in a backyard fire left a smoky taste in her mouth. Broken twigs and leaves crunched under her feet as the season let out its final respirations before nature's asphyxiation. The earth headed into the sleep of winter, like Calise.

Lost in her neuroses, she rounded a corner and smacked right into him. Literally smacked into the one being who deserved The Father's wrath heaped on him like no other—the demon who was the reason Calise lay comatose in a hospital bed right now.

Shane.

****

Ellen felt the rage she'd suppressed for so long, ripple through her body. "*You.* Everything would be better if your existence was erased! How do you live with yourself? I hate you. An emotion I should know nothing about."

Tears filled Shane's eyes, he dropped to his knees right there on the sidewalk, grabbed her by the back of her legs, and bowed his head. "Is she dead?"

"Not yet," she said.

"I deserve everything you say to me. You can only punish yourself so much and then you need help. Punish me, Ellen. Kill me. I'm too much of a coward to take my own life."

She wanted to punish him. Worse, she wanted to make him pay. Ellen had *warned* him to stay away from Calise in college. Now her friend was a in a coma, Lucas was alone, and Michael might never know his mother. She jerked her body away from him. "Get up, you fool. Someone will think you're proposing to me instead of begging my forgiveness. I'm still an angel, but I carry no sword of justice. Justice will be given to you by Father." She forced herself to walk away from him. "I'm going to church, but I won't be praying for you."

She could hear his hurried steps thumping the pavement behind her.

"Good. If we are in Father's house, maybe you'll listen to my side of the story."

Her face burned. "What side? You tried to kill her. Because of Nara's jealousy? Your own? I really don't care. Leave me alone. You've shattered countless lives, including mine."

Ignoring her, he fell in step behind her and followed her through St. Jude's heavy, wooden doors.

The ornate carvings of the Stations of the Cross and the penance worthy wooden pews gave her a semblance of peace. Even as an angel, she knew this was simply a *place* to worship, but she waited to *feel* Father's warm love here, wanting the familiar waves of calm to wash over her vile indiscretions.

Still, Shane was right about one thing. Inside these sacred walls, she had no choice but to listen to him as she would not disrespect a house of worship with a fight, verbal or physical.

After making the sign of the cross with the holy water at the back of the church, she headed to the front pew and knelt down to pray. They were alone in the church. Where were the familiar smells? The lingering incense. The aromatic oils of freshly polished pews. The confessional door stood ajar but no other parishioners were ahead of her waiting for the confessional. Where was everyone?

She didn't feel Father's presence like she usually did. Was it because she was now among the flock of sinners? Or because…

Once she settled back in the wooden pew, Shane tapped her on the shoulder. Sliding out of his reach, she mentally counted her sins and hoped Father would release her of them in exchange for forgiveness.

Another tap on the shoulder.

Resting an elbow on the backrest, she glared at him, "What? What could you possibly have to say to me?"

He avoided her gaze. "I want forgiveness, too. But I didn't come to a church pretending to be a human entitled to absolution."

Angels had no free will in heaven, only on earth. Upstairs, they followed orders. Now here was the real test. A test she was failing.

Here on the firmament, no one really knew how it worked. Did Father absolve earthly angels when they deviated from their path or would he deal sternly with them once they were back in heaven? Her experience was with a loving Father who allowed mistakes in exchange for true remorse and a change of behavior.

"You're not actually going in that thing?" He motioned to the confessional. "Give me five more minutes to explain…"

"No." She began to rise, intending to make her way into the confessional, but Shane held her in place.

"El, it wasn't supposed to happen. We were going to Calise's so I could kill Nara and escape with my daughter. I swear. I'd held her off as long as I could.

You have to believe me. Calise happened to be crossing the road. She wasn't supposed to be there. It was an accident." His words rang sincere. "I left Nara. I've left the path of evil. And I lost my daughter and probably killed Calise in the process."

Ellen sat back down.

"As soon as I saw her in the street, I took my foot off the gas. But Nara slammed her foot down and hit her."

"What is your daughter's name?" she asked, still not convinced of his authenticity.

"Melki, born a demon to Nara's delight. All I ever wanted was someone to love who'd love me back. Now that will never be Calise. And I thought I could save my daughter, but now I'll never see her again. Nara will make sure of it," Shane said.

He was telling some truths. She could tell. "You damned your own child to help Calise?"

He nodded.

"Wow." It was all Ellen could think of to say. The pain he bore almost touched her essence. Deep down, she did pray he would be able to find Melki and save her.

"Um, we're in church, El. Maybe I will use that confessional when you're done. No amount of Hail Mary's and Our Father's will give me absolution though. I'm damned."

Ellen felt the same way. An angel luring a human to comfort her for selfish reasons. Big no-no. Was she any better than the fallen angel she hated? How easy would it be to continue down a road devoid of righteousness out of anger toward Father?

Shane's big mistake was opening his heart to a

human who did not return his love. Maybe Ellen's mistake was never letting anyone in at all. Why was he worried anyway? Obviously he was a *transitor* again, or how would he have followed her inside a consecrated church?

She closed the confessional door behind her. This box was a claustrophobic sinner's worst nightmare. She made a mental note to send fresh bouquets of flowers for service on Sunday. The scent, even inside the tiny cubicle was that of rotten flowers. The flimsy panel between the booths slid open and she could see the shadow of the priest's garb behind the crisscross opening. "Hello, Father Greg. It's me Ellen."

"Father Greg is on sabbatical and I'm his replacement. Feel free to confess anything and everything to me, my child," the voice said.

"All right," she agreed, eager to get this over with. "Last night, I went home with a man I didn't know and spent the night." After expounding on her deluge of last night's sinful behavior, she sincerely hoped she wasn't scaring the new guy to death or worse yet, turning his celibate self on.

When she finished spewing her near-whorish ways and abundance of sinful thoughts, sans the "I'm-an-angel and I-erased-his-memory and God-doesn't-allow-human-adoration-of-angels" part, Ellen expected the requite forgiveness and penance of saying a few prayers and trying to do better. Something about confessing to a stranger made her entirely uncomfortable.

The priest was quiet.

Far too long.

"How many humans have you slept with, angel? I'd love to be added to your repertoire." The voice was smooth and sinister.

A demon.

Ellen never hesitated.

She punched both fists through the paper-thin lattice and lunged for the imposter priest. Her fingers found his neck. She squeezed, anger coursing through her essence. *How dare some demon trick me into telling him these things?*

He ripped her hands off his neck like they were paper napkins before he *demonstrated* to show his true demonic form. A dozen horns pushed out of his bald head like a spiked Medusa. His forehead ripped into two sides, each with a large, outward protrusion. He smiled at her with jagged teeth behind leathery skin. "That all you got, sister?"

"Not even close," she spat back before jabbing his eyes with her fingernails.

Screeching, he flailed wildly through the torn grid finding a handful of Ellen's hair. He slammed her head into the wood-lined wall again and again. Repeating only loud enough for her to hear, "My eyes! You stupid bitch!"

She pressed her back to the opposite wall, seeing double from blurred vision.

Before she could charge him again, the priest's door was pulled off its hinges and Ellen caught a glimpse of a massive *demonstrated* Shane shining like a blood red sun. "Time to do some penance, asswipe." His eyes flicked to Ellen before he grabbed the faux priest and vanished.

Forced to hold onto the wall for balance, Ellen slid along the wall to the church office. Shane had *not* transitioned. He was still a demon! Angels and demons walking the earth could fall or rise depending on their actions. Shane, born an angel, had become a *transitor* before turning his back on Father and becoming a demon. But great acts of righteousness could save him. Too bad leaving Nara and his daughter hadn't counted in his benefit.

Once outside the confessional walls, it was all clear. Someone had lifted the church's consecration. How could she have missed it? How? And more importantly…why?

She'd have to deal with her violent headache later. She needed to find Father Greg first. Inside the orderly office, the church secretary was typing on a computer with a vacant look on her face.

"Carol?" Ellen interrupted. "Can I ask you a quick question?"

Carol never looked up. Ellen walked around behind her and touched the woman gently on the head to remove the blinding illusion the demon had held her with. Her computer screen had the same three words typed over and over again: "God doesn't exist." Her senses dulled to the point that these were the only three words repeating in her head.

While the woman rubbed her forehead and moaned, Ellen reached over her shoulder and hit the delete button on the computer file. Carol swiveled her chair around to face Ellen.

"It is okay, Carol. I'm Dr. Ellen Engel. Remember me? I delivered your daughter a few years back."

The woman nodded slowly as if waking from a long dream. "Yes, doctor. I remember. Did you ask me a question?"

"Yes, Carol," Ellen spoke slowly. "When did the

new priest arrive?"

"This morning. I never got a chance to say good-bye to Father Greg. Father Damien met me outside. He instructed me to remove the altar stone with the relics of Saint Jude in them and…" her face clouded over, "…and I can't remember what I did with them." Her hands trembled and tears began to roll down her cheeks. "I did something terrible, didn't I?"

Ellen couldn't tell her the truth, so she tapped her temple to erase her memories of this morning. "You needed to leave early today and go get groceries. You did a great job at work today and Father Greg will be here in the morning," she said, cementing the false memory.

After Carol cheerfully gathered her things and left, Ellen headed for the sacristy, which had a private entrance on the side of the main church altar. The priest's vestment robes were laid out as if he was prepared to dress prior to administering the sacrament of Holy Confession. A whimpering sound came from a huddled mass in the corner.

Father Greg, eyes wide and body paralyzed with fear, sat on the floor with his arms wrapped around his legs, hyperventilating and rocking back and forth. Ellen could see the illusion the demon had implanted to torture him: the holy man, surrounded by those he'd buried, rotting corpses pointing their fingers at him and blaming him for damning their souls.

She touched his head, dismissing the illusion.

The poor man jumped straight up in the air. "Where did they go? They were just here! It was my fault. I'm a failure! I've damned them all!" He released a blood-curdling scream and began looking under tables, in closets, and behind doors for the vengeful dead.

Ellen caught him and held his hands allowing her calm and warmth to seep through the frazzled Father. Then, she let out her aura for the pious man to behold. "Relax, Father Greg. You know me as Dr. Ellen Engel from your parish. But I am an angel. What you were seeing was an illusion."

Father Greg let his tears fall freely. "You are beyond beautiful. I believe!"

Ellen smiled patiently. "You've always believed, Father. Now concentrate. I need your help." She released his hands. "A demon entered your church this morning at great personal risk. Do you know why?"

The old man's eyes went wide as he dropped her hands, scrambling toward his altar. "The relic! Where is the arm?" She trailed behind him to the altar, where he lifted an intricately stitched turquoise cloth covering his simple wooden altar. He disappeared beneath it. "It's gone!"

St. Jude's contained a third class relic attached to the underside of the altar. A first class relic was part of a Saint's body, and a second class relic was something the saint owned or an instrument of torture used against them, while a third class relic had merely touched a first or second class relic or a tomb of a Saint. Father Greg could obtain another third class relic without worry. "What's the problem? What arm?" Her heart dropped. "You can't mean…"

He made the sign of the cross. "Yes, I do. We had the arm of St. Jude Thaddeus on loan from Chicago for a special service. Who would have taken it?"

Ellen bowed her head. An infinite loss. The arm of

St. Jude was the largest first class relic of an apostle located outside Rome. The Saint's forearm, fingers outstretched was encased in a silver reliquary and was given to the Dominican Shrine in Chicago in 1949. It was priceless.

Most churches had some kind of relic kept under the altar, which consecrated the church. Veneration of the relics was not worship though. The practice started in the early church in Rome during the persecution when Christians met in the catacombs housing the tombs of martyrs. Mass was celebrated on these tombs and the practice continued to have relics present in churches under the altar as a reminder of Father working through their lives and their deaths.

She didn't know how the priest would react to what she had to tell him. "A demon took it. And right now, your place of worship is exposed. With your permission, I will reconsecrate the church."

"Will that protect us?" the priest asked.

"I don't know," Ellen answered honestly.

Chapter 4

Paris, France

The angel Gabriel relished his first bite of a chaussons aux pommes, letting the delicate sweetness wake up his snoozing taste buds. The French did make a great apple turnover. Sitting on a wooden bench, he watched tourists amble through the massive arches of Cathédrale Notre Dame.

First Friday of the month.

His monthly trip to Paris for the veneration of the Crown of Thorns. The Crown supposedly held seventy authentic thorns from the crown placed atop Jesus' head by Roman soldiers to mock him before the crucifixion. According to the church...all authentic, all priceless. It was sad, really. People paying homage to pieces of bundled twigs held together by gold threads. The crown was marched through throngs of believers on the first Friday of the month and every Friday during Lent. What they didn't know was that the only thorns with true divine power, the ones that had pierced the Lord's skin, were safely guarded by the angel Alejandro and himself. Alas, just another fake relic on parade.

The same painful smile crossed his face as he took in the majesty of Notre Dame. He remembered the men who built the church. Knew most of them by name. Men who hammered out religious statues with their fervent belief driving them to go without food and rest for days. He'd liked listening to them while they chiseled away. Those days were long gone.

They'd been real religious zealots. *Lightwalkers.*

So few walked the earth anymore. So few humans were truly selfless now or devoted to being God's servants for the betterment of humanity. Strategically bred out of existence in the last few millennium by demons. *Pity.*

And replaced with drone-like *darkwalkers.*

He debated even staying for the ceremony. He wasn't needed here. Angels swarmed the place like mother hens making sure no demons tried anything funny. Heavenly host perched on the rooftop, while others swooped over the unsuspecting humans. Gabriel waved to Remiel and Verchiel who led the Principality and Powers angels, respectively.

Lucky angels. After a quickie assignment, they could go *home.*

I miss home.

And he didn't mean the Glastonbury, England home where Seamus eked out his reclusive existence. He meant heaven.

Being chosen to guard the descendants of Joseph of Arimathea was an honor, but the truth was…he was bored. Sure, he'd had the occasional messenger gig sprinkled in the last two-thousand years. But for the most part, his bread and butter was keeping his ward and progeny alive and the family's artifacts out of the hands of demons.

Done and done. And if Seamus didn't procreate soon, there would be no line of descendants to protect anyway. Maybe then he could go home? Was it so horrible to want Seamus—and with him, the undiluted two-thousand year old bloodline of Joseph of Arimathea—to grow old and die?

His job would be done.

Tourists streamed out of the church indicating the ceremony was complete. And without incident. The thorns would be returned to its reliquary in the Sainte-Chapelle a few blocks away. The angels vanished one after another. Gabriel took to his regular stroll along the Seine, crossing the river at the Pont Saint Michel and heading right on the Quai des Grands Augustins.

Over the last few decades, Gabriel could *feel* this world dying, and he couldn't be happier. It was all so meaningless, anyway. Over two-thousand years, living alone among unthinking humans, with no concrete timetable from upstairs—the last blip in his angelic existence was like a game of war with a never-ending deck. He was tired.

His only joy came from his favorite *holy* pursuit. Converting *darkwalkers.* In fact, everywhere he went, it seemed they were multiplying.

Darkwalkers left fractional dark silhouettes of themselves in their wake, like the after image from staring at the sun and then blinking, where the sun shape still lingers behind the eyelid.

Selfish humans, out for their own best interests. Gabriel wondered when science would figure out it was dark matter, the karma of the universe. He listened to the thoughts of the humans around him. Why did they all sound more and more the same? Heads held high, repeating a mantra in their brain dead minds: "Why shouldn't *I* be happy? No matter the cost?"

The downward slide of humanity disgusted him.

Skim a little off the top here, hire a few foreigners there, evade some taxes here, make a little more money there. Everyone was at least a little crooked. Even the demons he came across weren't *evil* enough to really worry about. Not in Europe anyway. Maybe it was this particular century? Selfish humans seemed to make happy humans.

More. More. More.

Want. Want. Want.

Mine. Mine. Mine.

Still, the nagging darkwalker movement tugged at his subconscious.

Humans, he shrugged. He never understood why Father created them. Probably would never figure it out...until it was too late. *But really, why do I care?* To Gabriel, end of days, schmend of days.

Not. His. Problem.

In fact, if Armageddon came, that would let him finally get out of his prison guard shift for the seers and artifacts and return Home. He'd be relieved to go back to the other side and start taking orders again. The angels in the heavens had absolute knowledge but no free will, which he found overrated.

So they were given a choice. Live one early life to experience the gift of free will. As Gabriel saw it, being an ethereal being had its perks and humans could keep their "gift." Free will led to inner conflict, which led to guilt, which led away from Father's light.

Then he saw her.

The most beautiful *darkwalker* he'd ever laid his eyes on. Too bad she was damned. Maybe he could change all that. Elegant long legs ending in black patent heels clicked on the boardwalk. A skin-tight dress hugged a body with curves where a woman was meant to have them. Pristine straightened blonde hair danced with her every step. And that was only from the back.

Today is her lucky day.

She left the main drag and followed a twisted, narrow street before ducking into a quaint hotel with a yellow overhead banner. The hue of black smoke, the sign of a darkwalker, trailed behind her like a heavy mist.

Gabriel opened the front door of the hotel and mouthed to the clerk, "Where's the girl?"

The clerk immediately jutted his thumb over his shoulder into the courtyard. "Pauvre fille," he mumbled under his breath. *Poor girl.*

"What do you mean?" Gabriel asked in English, turning up his glow factor. The male clerk swooned and gave Gabriel his undivided attention. Any information might assist in her redemption, he reasoned.

"Oh, she was a graduate student renting a room here while she finished her thesis. Her parents' plane went down over the Atlantic on their way to visit her," the clerk answered in flawless English. "She's never left."

"Merci." He tossed one-hundred Euros on the counter. "Bring us coffee and leave us alone."

The clerk pocketed the paper and held open the door to the courtyard for Gabriel.

"One more thing, my friend. What's her name?"

"Adrienne. Adrienne Perdu," he answered before returning to his post

The angel wasn't lying to himself. His actions weren't very angelic anymore. That ended fifteen hundred years ago. Now, he only saved beautiful women. Maybe because the angel could sense the end of days were fast approaching. Selfish or stupid, Gabriel wanted only the most beautiful women with him upstairs.

The open-air courtyard hidden in the middle of the small housing complex. The Paris air was warm and the courtyard was bathed in sunshine and sheltered from the wind. Four wrought iron tables with accompanying chairs sat in conversational posts along the stucco yellow walls. Potted plants stationed at regular intervals gave the place a homey feel. The girl sat tall with her lean legs crossed, holding a small hardcover book in her left hand. Propped open with her thumb and pinkie finger, she brought her right index finger to her mouth and licked it before turning the page

Her stick-straight dark blonde hair was parted in the middle and punctuated with highlights. Her long face and angular jaw highlighted eyes set too far apart for Gabriel's liking. Poor dear was pushing thirty. Gravity wouldn't be far behind.

He sat at an adjacent table. At first, she acted indifferent to his presence.

But Gabriel would change all that. His fulfillment would culminate when he lifted the *darkwalker* cloak off her shoulders. Yet again, who was he to determine who should be saved and who should perish?

Before he could answer his own thought, the clerk appeared in the patio door. "Cappuccino?"

"*Oui, s'il vous plaît.*" She said without looking up.

"How kind, I'd love one as well." Gabriel said.

She huffed at his response as if his very presence disturbed her.

Every minute movement left trails of darkness

behind her. Gabriel wanted to clap his hands in glee. He almost couldn't wait to unravel her perfect little world of self-obsession.

Pulling his angelic warmth and the divine light around him, Gabriel approached the table. "May I?"

She closed her book and set it on the table.

Taking that as a "Yes," he pulled up a chair. "What are you reading?"

"My bible," she answered without thought. "And you didn't wait for an answer. Which would have been 'no.'"

He ignored her. "Don't use the word 'bible' for that filth. Covering 'The Satanic Bible' with brown leather doesn't make it any more worthy to be held by your beautiful hands." Gabriel let his index finger skim her hand.

"How do you know what I'm reading? Look, I don't know you. Please go away and stop *bothering* me." Her eyes were dead and her soul asleep where it could be numb and forget her pain.

Gabriel retracted his aura from the tart. He'd win her back old school. He had time and pity seeped inside him at what he knew would be her shitty hell-after-death. "I'm not saying I don't believe in Satan." He held his hands up defensively. "I do. But if you believe in him," he pointed to the concrete stones at their feet, "then you *must* also believe in Him." Gabriel pointed upwards to the cornflower colored sky.

"Fuck you, your righteous prick. I'm in a public place and I've asked you once to stop bothering me. If you don't—"

"*C'est une belle journée pour café dehors au soleil, oui.*"

"*Merci*, it is a beautiful day," Gabriel thanked the man and took a sip of the warm drink.

The woman pushed back her chair and carried her beverage to another table where she resumed reading.

Sipping the frothy velvet brew, he watched her, reflecting on human faith. If God just poofed out proof of his existence, angels would be entirely bored on earth and demons would lose. Free will—the best and worst gift bestowed upon His favorites, humans.

He tilted his head letting the warmth seep inside him. She wasn't the first *darkwalker* he'd seen since arriving in Paris this visit.

Maybe with the exponential increase in scientific knowledge comes more reliance on self and less on faith. The gross excesses of this generation was nauseating and one way to console themselves was to follow ideals that sanctioned—nay encouraged!—indulgence and self-gratification.

Most *darkwalkers* didn't even know what they were. Yet demons everywhere were sucking them in with their lies. Luring them deeper into the abyss.

Gabriel studied the woman. Her parents had died needlessly. Her prayers and grief went unanswered. The only way she could see to bandage the wound of her raw pain was to retreat into the darkness of pleasing only herself.

Why couldn't humans understand?

Gabriel sighed. She was his mission now. But pulling her back to the light might not be as easy as he'd thought.

Chapter 5

Wauwatosa, Wisconsin

Shane dragged the faux priest to the church's back alley, far away from prying eyes. "You can't attack an angel in public," he said.

The demon cowered, crossing his forearms over his face. "Sorry, sir. I just got here this morning. Yes, sir...I mean. I should have known better. It won't happen again."

What the hell is going on? To risk exposure was never a part of the plan. If demons were exposed, then God would gain infinite strength and be accepted. It was human free will that evil fed on to force feed lies, hatred, and distrust. Even though Shane wanted to kick the demonic shit out of this guy, he needed answers first. "I'm your relief. How far along are you on accomplishing your mission?"

The demon peered through his arms, his fear radiated outward in concentric blue circles around his aura. "I'm...I'm done sir. I was just having some fun before I left. How would I know a slutty angel would come in and give confession?" The demon smirked.

At the mention of Ellen, Shane delivered a thrusting front kick to the gut sending the demon stumbling backwards. "You fool."

The demon groaned, clutching his belly. "What

was that for? The arm of St. Jude is destroyed. I checked first. It's not here, so I burned the relic, as I was told. Can I go now?"

"Checked the relic for what?" As soon as the words were out of Shane's mouth, he knew he'd made a mistake.

"Who are you?" The demon stretched to his full height. "If you don't know what I was sent here to do, we aren't working for the same side."

In a flash, the demon attacked, but Shane was ready. He sidestepped the charging demon and threw him to the ground, then rammed his knee into the demon's back grabbing his arm and putting it into an arm bar, pausing for a moment before breaking it. "I asked you a question. Now answer it. Checked the relic for what?"

Screaming in pain, the demon worked himself loose with a violent roll to get out of Shane's grasp. "You know nothing of the true purpose, rat. If you aren't with us, you'll have to die." He pulled out a gun with his good hand.

Shane saw the piece before the demon could cock the weapon. A swift outer crescent kick to the demon's wrist made the gun fly out of their reach. Grabbing the now empty hand, Shane pulled the demon and swung him around wrapping one arm around his neck. With his free hand, he twisted the demon's head until it gave a sickening crack. He let the lifeless body fall to the ground.

With a cloud of black dust…the demon was gone.

Shane pocketed the weapon and went to look for Ellen. Demons always had some grand master agenda or plan, but something about this demon, in this church, right now, felt very wrong.

What could be hidden in relics demons could want badly enough to risk their own skin? Was Nara involved? Another faction?

All Shane knew was if he and Ellen didn't figure this out, something would go terribly wrong.

****

Ellen was having doubts. Serious doubts. She slid the low gauge needle into Dean's arm and adjusted the intravenous drip of normal saline. Lucas had his eyes closed and head pressed on the tan pleather chair while his precious blood was collected into a plastic bag hung beside him.

After Lucas announced he was going off on a treasure hunt for the Holy Grail hoping it would wake Calise, Ellen figured having Dean by his side might be an asset. And Dean's memories of their time in Russia were foggy but pushing through to the surface. Anyway, it would be a matter of time before he remembered the past. And seeing as Lucas wasn't going to exchange bodily fluids with him in any traditional manner, Ellen suggested a blood transfusion.

Even though Lucas insisted on waiting until Calise woke up, Ellen decided to lift the charm concealing Dean's memories. They needed all the informed allies they could get. Ellen convinced Dean to trust her, mentally preparing for hours of questions, answers, tears and pain. It might take time before he could sift fact from fiction and be reassured life would go on, just with a different take on good and evil.

What Ellen didn't know, is how he would feel about remembering he was the one who killed his demon wife back in Russia when she was on the verge of coming back to the good side.

But she had no choice. Lucas was leaving and he needed Dean. This was the only way.

"Got enough?" Lucas asked.

"That should do it." She covered the area with gauze before sliding the needle from his forearm. "Hold this tightly to stop the bleeding."

Capping off the tubing and replacing it for the infusion, she hung the muddy colored liquid next to the saline drip. "Sure you're ready for this big guy?"

"I was born ready, Ellen the Beautiful," Dean winked at her.

She laughed at his pet name for her in college. Ever the flirt, Dean had worn fraternity life well back in the day. Still buff, with butter-soft sandy blond hair that matched his sister's, Ellen wondered what his pet name would be for her after the transfusion.

Ellen missed Calise more than anything. Her one true friend. And she'd do anything to get her back. Even if that included making her best friend's brother a seer.

Seers could see the angels and demons walking the earth, and with Dean's fighting skills, Lucas would need him on this quest if the cup was still in existence. The only way for Dean to fight was to be able to see what was coming at him. Hands sweaty and with a nagging thought she was losing her grip on the rope of sanity, she opened the valve to let Lucas' blood comingle with Dean's. "Here we go, sunshine. I'm going to let the light in. Buckle up." She unlocked the luer lock of the saline drip and changed it over to Lucas' blood transfusion.

The dark liquid worked its way into the tubing,

snaking through quickly before hitting Dean's vein.

Boom!

Ellen watched as the whole room pulsed as if an invisible wave had passed through it. Dean moaned, threw back his head, and then the screaming started. She knew what he was seeing. The beauty and the horror. Grabbing his hand, she smoothed back his hair until he calmed down and could focus on her.

He blinked over and over, tears falling down his cheeks before he spoke. "Sweet Mary Mother of God, you are hot."

Ellen smiled, letting the heat of his words of adoration course through her veins like Lucas' blood was coursing through his. Dean would be okay. "What can I say? Another one bites the dust."

Chapter 6

Glastonbury, Somerset, England

Seamus Bron readjusted his backpack as he trekked along the stone fence in Glastonbury surrounding his childhood town. There was something to be said for being able to carry all of one's belongings on your back. He had no permanent home. No steady job.

Life as a drifter was mostly carefree and peaceful. He'd spent September and half of October picking apples and pears for North Perrott Fruit Farm in Crewkerne. He'd pitched a tent at night or slept under the stars. The thirty-eight kilometer hike brought him back to Glastonbury before sunset.

He climbed Wearyall hill carrying a staff, not unlike that of his forefathers. The wind whipped his shoulder length hair around his face and he paused to tie it back. The neat rows of homes resembled pupils in line for class. White home, brown roof. Orange home, brown roof. The colors seemed bent on a repeating pattern Seamus couldn't decipher.

Once atop the hill, Seamus knelt beside a dead tree and began to pray. Not just any dead tree, but the famed hawthorn tree that flowered only during spring and on Christmas. But vandals had cut all of the braches off the tree in 2010 and despite efforts to encourage it to take root again, it looked like the tree was really dead.

It was a sign. He was sure of it.

The story went that Joseph of Arimathea had landed in Glastonbury after Jesus was put to death. He'd thrust his staff into the ground and there a tree began to grow. A Holy Thorn tree. The Glastonbury Thorn, as it became known, flowered precisely twice a year and became a place of spiritual pilgrimage to believers.

But, the tree was still dead. Seamus felt its message deep within his own blood. The end of an era. The beginning of the end. He'd seen it everywhere. Felt it. The world was dying.

Rotting.

After finishing his prayer, he surveyed the countryside. Glastonbury Tor towered in the distance, trees giving way to a grassy expanse appearing to connect to the hazy blue sky like a pathway leading toward the heavens. The small town of Glastonbury nestled beneath. Seamus hoped The George and Pilgrim pub would hire him back for a few months to cook. His plan would get him through Christmas, but when tourism dropped, he'd have to move again. Maybe he'd go back South.

His stomach growled and he couldn't wait to order up a Henry VIII pie at the pub and have his favorite brew, Smithwick's. Hoisting his backpack up again, he gave the dead stump one last look.

Dead.

As was his family line. He'd end the line of his forefathers by never having children. But maybe that was for the best.

Seamus touched the dead branches. Pain emanated from the once living tree and he felt as though one of his own appendages had been chopped off. The town itself had died a little each day since the attack. Less joy in their step. Less pride in their town. Less pilgrims meant less income. Townsfolk were even packing up and moving to more profitable locales. He hadn't met a tourist or pilgrim on this hill in years.

So who were these ugly Americans making their way up the hill at this late hour?

His senses sharpened. More vandals?

"...my dad said, Glastonbury...don't know where else to start looking," one said.

Two men at least a decade Seamus' junior pounded up the hill. One looked like a typical asshole American, sandy blond hair, legs like trees, and a small beer-belly pouch poking out from his too tight Abercromie and Fitch long-sleeved shirt. The other looked like a small warrior. Italian? Hispanic? But speaking perfect English. He was shorter and looked like he'd kicked some serious ass in his life. His hair, like Seamus' was wavy, long, and dark.

Young Americans looking for what? A photograph of a dead tree?

"Hello, there. Can I help ya?" Seamus put on a friendly smile, knowing his own ragtag look sometimes prompted strangers to assume he was the threat.

"Yeah, we'd love that. I'm Dean and this is my brother-in-law, Lucas." The typical American extended his hand but Seamus kept his arms crossed over his chest. He didn't touch people. Especially Americans trudging around on his town's sacred ancestral ground. "Okay," the tow-headed man said, dropping his arm back to his side. "Do you live in Glastonbury by chance?"

No. But Seamus nodded anyway.

The one who introduced himself as Dean cleared his throat, fidgeting. Seamus knew whatever words came out of their mouths next, were lies. He could sense it. "We're making a…er, um…movie about what happened here. Can you tell us about this tree?"

"What do you want to know?"

The shorter man caught his eye. Lucas, was it? Not a good liar. Seamus felt rage and impatience radiating off from him like a bull in the ring. Clenched fists. Shallow breathing. The hint of a sneer.

So that was why he let the other one do all the talking.

Something about this situation felt wrong. Seamus had no instinct to run, but killing them just because they were lying to him wasn't the smartest idea either. So he twisted both his shoes into the earth, planting his feet firmly in his forefather's soil.

He'd have to get them to leave.

"Well, first off, who cut this tree down? This is the famous thorn tree planted by Joseph of Arimathea, correct?" Dean asked.

"Vandals. And yes, that is the legend." Seamus said.

"My, aren't we the talkative one?" The warrior growled before his companion jabbed an elbow in his ribs.

Face and the fighter. The talkative one was the face of the operation and the stocky fellow was the muscle. But why? If Seamus knew anything, he knew these men were *not* American movie makers. "I'm not sure I believe you two are here to make a movie," Seamus said.

Lucas edged away from Dean and began to circle Seamus. He spoke in a low, urgent voice. "I'm looking for someone. Someone who might come and visit this dead branch every day? Maybe you are the person I'm looking for?"

Who the hell were these guys?" "Oh…that guy," Seamus lied. "Sure, I know him. But why are you looking for him?"

"None of your business. But we can make the information you give us worth your while." The warrior pulled a tightly bound wad of Euros from his pocket.

Seamus relaxed. What threat were they to him? If they came to fight, he could defeat them with one hand tied behind his back. "I come here whenever I get the chance. It's the best view of the city. Used to be a pretty spiritual place. But there's no movie to make here. Just a dead tree and some old legends. Why don't we head into town and you can buy me a pint? I'll tell you about the guy I know," he paused. "If the price is right." Seamus started down the hill.

They followed.

He forced himself to amble back toward town, instead of turning around and beating them both senseless for wanting to make a movie and capitalize on his town's loss.

Rude.

They had questions. Now so did he.

The "somebody" these guys were looking for…*was* him. And if they knew he existed, there could be only one thing they wanted.

The cup.

Chapter 7

Paris, France—two days later

Dinner in Paris was more luxurious than perfunctory. Dining was an experience to be cherished rather than a necessity to be rushed. The British relished their teatime like the French languished over their evening meal. It was nearly nine o'clock before the angel Gabriel ended his brisk evening walk along the Seine and ducked into the same restaurant as his target.

Thick with smoke and rich with the smell of roast duck and red wine, he approached the *darkwalker* who dined alone. There was no laughing Frenchman cozying up to her who would keep the wine and conversation flowing in the wee hours of the night.

"May I join you?" Gabriel asked.

She'd seen him from the moment he entered the restaurant. He knew because her gaze had never left his face. She stared at him with no affection—devoid of emotion. Her statuesque demeanor neither betrayed pleasure or dismay at his arrival.

"Why?" she asked.

"I don't want to dine alone. Do you?" The rumble of the mingled voices, clinking of glasses and silverware reminded Gabriel that even when he was in a city's center surrounded by thousands of humans, he could be utterly alone. He ignored her lack of response and sat. He flipped the table's second wine glass over and poured himself a generous helping of the Cabernet already half consumed. He swirled the viscous liquid, a deep tawny color clinging to the sides of the glass before he inhaled the oak and currant of the vintage. "Excellent choice," he said after his first sip.

She raised an eyebrow.

"*Qu'aurez-vous, monsieur?*" the waiter asked with a bow.

"For starters, another bottle of this. Then we'll see where the night takes us."

"Very good."

"Audacious. Presumptuous. More arrogant than many of the Frenchmen I've met. You seem to be hell-bent on your own destruction. Why is that?" She leaned forward over the table, careful not to touch it with her elbows and tarnish her table manners.

"*Au contraire*, you are the *darkwalker*. You are the one 'hell-bent' on destruction." He calmly sipped his wine and enjoyed the wrinkle of lines forming at the corners of her eyes with her charming scowl.

"I'm the what?" she asked. "Jesus Christ, can't you just leave me alone?"

Gabriel laughed. "Nice guy, but I'm his buddy Gabe. Let's get that on the table right away. And no, I will not leave you alone until you are enlightened."

A commotion at the *maître d'* station caused Gabriel to shift his attention to the man waving wildly at him.

Sweet mother of God.

His ward was here.

****

Adrienne watched, more amused than she'd felt in

51

years as her uninvited dinner guest jumped up from the table spilling wine on the pristine, white tablecloth. "Seamus," Gabe's voice held a level of panic.

Adrienne decided to settle back to watch the show. Was he being busted by his gay lover? Games. Lies. That seemed to be all people were good for. But now the line was crossed. No more scummy men would invade her life. *Her life!*

The man who called himself Gabe, grabbed the shoulders of the other man who'd just flung himself inside the restaurant and looked about wildly. *Ah-ha! This was his lover.*

She second-guessed herself at once. This meticulously groomed man wouldn't hang out with the rugged traveler he now spoke to in hushed whispers.

Yet again, maybe this was the guy's plan all along. A ruse to make his boyfriend jealous? From the urgent conversation they were enjoying by the corner window, it seemed to have worked nicely.

Adrienne turned back to her table and sampled one of the *hors d'oeuvres* in front of her. *Ah...peace.* Extracting a carrot, she swirled it in the vinaigrette and took a small bite of the crunchy vegetable before her eyes returned to the quarreling lovers.

Her waiter returned with a questioning look. "I was the bait to make his lover jealous. Mission accomplished. Please dump his wine and remove his place setting," she explained in French.

"*Oui*, Mademoiselle." He cleared the place setting and made off with the empty wine glass after a futile attempt to blot the stain on the tablecloth. Adrienne wished she could turn her chair against the wall to further ignore the pair, whose heated discussion was now reaching an audible level.

Before she could savor another bite of her dinner, both men approached her table and each pulled out a chair for themselves with her in the middle. *The nerve!*

"Where'd my wine go?" Gabe snapped his fingers until the waiter approached. "If she told you I was leaving, the young lady was mistaken. Please bring two fresh wine glasses and that other bottle."

Adrienne had no words for their intrusion. Forcing shut her gaping jaw, she huffed at them both and shook her head. "How many times do I have to ask you—"

"We are so sorry for this impolite intrusion." Gabe's friend reached forward, offering his hand. After pushing aside his mop of disheveled hair, she got lost for a split second in his eyes. Eyes that seemed to house pain and a second emotion aimed directly at her...was it, pity? Likely pity for being drawn into their ridiculous lover's spat. "My name is Seamus Bron."

His jeans were too big and his corduroy jacket was too small, stretching over a broad chest and sturdy arms. He set a massive backpack on the floor.

Was Gabe sleeping with a traveling professor? Then again, she'd never met a professor with arms like a body builder. He grasped her hand with both of his. "Again, I'm terribly sorry, miss. I didn't realize Gabriel was bothering you. We'll be on our way and leave you in peace." Standing, he reached for Gabriel's suit coat and gave it a tug. Her false suitor looked like he might become unhinged at any moment.

She laughed, as if suddenly thrust into the middle of a Shakespearean comedy. "Well, your boyfriend hasn't given me a moment's peace in two days. And right now, I'm quite enjoying watching him be flustered. If your lover's feud has been resolved and you have time before the closing act of this play, I will invite *you* to stay through one glass of wine. Only if you continue to torment *him*." She winked.

"Uh...I can't promise..." he stumbled on his words and Adrienne couldn't help but watch his every move. "Wait, did you say boyfriend?"

"Sit down, Seamus. Did they follow you?" Gabriel asked.

After looking over both shoulders like he was a spy, Seamus slunk down in his chair. "They didn't *follow* me. I brought them along."

"Did one of them have dark long hair and the other cropped blond hair?" Adrienne asked in a conspiratorial whisper. Two men had just entered the restaurant in a not-too-subtle way and were pointing at their table. Enjoying the whole production, she gave them a quick wave and motioned for them to come over.

"You what?" Gabe nearly yelled. The look on his face was priceless. Adrienne wondered if she had time to pull out her camera.

The two men approached the table as the *maître d'* scrambled to haul over more chairs. Adrienne wanted to clap her hands with glee like a little girl who finally had real guests at her tea party. "Please, gentlemen, there's plenty of room. Where's the wine?" she ordered the now frazzled server. *Holy gay pride parade.* This kept getting better and better.

"They aren't the only ones you led right to me," Gabe said, gruffly.

Following where Gabe's finger was pointing, Adrienne peered around Seamus to a trio of men—all from her support group monthly meetings—closing in on their table. She knew those men *definitely* preferred the female persuasion. "I know them. These are my friends—"

All at once, Gabriel was on his feet. Seamus lurched for Adrienne and threw a protective arm over her shoulders. The first man, Adrienne remembered his name to be James, charged Gabe.

Adrienne didn't know who threw the first punch, but within seconds, the whole restaurant erupted in mayhem. Food was spilled. Tables were flying. The customers were swearing. Before she could figure out what to do, Seamus yanked her by the hand and pulled her deep into the restaurant, busted through the swinging kitchen doors, and out a back exit.

The night air stung her cheeks and the smell of garbage pierced her nostrils. Seamus pulled her down a ramp and around the next corner. They hugged the exterior of the brick building. She could still hear yells coming from the restaurant. "Hang on a second," she panted. "Why are we running?"

"Look, I don't believe in owing people favors," he interrupted her. "But I can't be seen. If they come back here, I need you to do something for me." He cradled her cheeks in his hands.

This man was definitely not Gabe's lover. On that, she'd been very wrong.

He gave off heat and intensity, the likes of which she'd never felt from any man. Right now, the heat from his hand touching her cheek coursed through her head and fell with gravity to the soles of her feet. His duplicity had fooled her. Hell, he probably fooled everyone. People brushed him off as nobody.

His elbow-patched suit coat said intellectual. His

backpack said traveler. But his eyes told the real story. A warrior. A fierce protector. Or why else try so hard to save one girl from a possible rogue punch in a restaurant brawl? Words long forgotten in today's world tugged at her subconscious.

Nobility.

Honor.

She'd never had this feeling before. She pressed her cheek into his hand, willing the sensation to continue to warm her on this cool, Parisian night. If he needed a favor, she'd give him one. If she did one good deed for one man in her life, she decided it would be for Seamus Bron.

"What do you need me to do?" she asked.

Before he asked for the favor, he paused. "Why would you call men like those friends? You have to know—deep down—they are not. I see their darkness surrounding you. But it wasn't always there." He removed his hand, appraising her with a quick head to toe once over. "A silver aura still tries to surround you. Why have you shut out the light?"

Anger mixed with pain and confusion. What kind of man speaks to a woman like this? With words that rang true. But the truth stung. His words were a mirror revealing her own hatred of who she'd become. Where was the innocent girl who loved tea parties and walks with her Father in the sunshine?

But the person she was today was her choice. Based on protecting herself from the pain of the world she lived in. That was what Daevas and his organization, the Novem-Stellae had taught her. For so long, she'd shoved down any decisions her heart had tried to make to stay safe. But not today. Something about this man made Adrienne willing to lay down her life if he asked her to. She wondered if the pain and loneliness coursing through her was palpable. He said he could see her darkness. What could that mean? How was it he read her like an open book, idly flipping her pages and finding the errors?

Her mind and upper sensibilities fought back. Sure, she'd gone astray from who she once was. It was called growing up. And for her, there was no coming back. The velvety words of a man in an alley in Paris weren't going to change that. "I have to go," she said, her mind winning out over her heart once again. Her walls of protection were thick. This man would not crack them and leave her in ruins.

Screams.

The crash of breaking glass.

Then two men from her meeting, the ones she's said were her "friends" busted out the back door of the restaurant and headed right for them.

Seamus wasted no time. He dove in and...kissed her!

A hungry desperate, you-aren't-kissing-me-for-my-benefit-but-for-the-greater-good-of-the-universe kind of kiss. She pushed on his chest in protest, which made Seamus pull her in tighter. She groaned when he ended the kiss and pulled away.

Surprisingly, the men had passed them by. Written them off as two lovers in the night?

Adrienne almost wished they'd come back. *What the hell?*

"Thanks, I owe you one." He gave her another kiss on the cheek before hurrying back inside the restaurant leaving her unsatisfied and feeling something she hadn't felt in a long while. Something she'd tried to deaden with meetings and solitude.

She felt *alive.*

And it hurt like mother-fucking hell.

Chapter 8

Milwaukee, Wisconsin

Shane brooded in his downtown shithole week-to-week rental, poring over maps. He hadn't been able to track down Ellen and tell her what happened with the demon. And it wasn't exactly something he could leave on her voicemail.

What the hell was that demon talking about with "true purpose" and "checking the relics?" Checking them for what? And on whose orders?

Must be a new faction on the move. Looking for something. And reporting to someone new.

But who?

Not Lucifer. Not Abaddon. If this was Nara's family's operation, Shane would have caught wind of it by now.

He needed an "in."

But that would lead right back into his old life.

Nara.

The drugs.

His daughter.

No, he couldn't go after his daughter yet. Not like this—he needed redemption. His daughter *had* to be raised by an angel if there was to be any hope for her. And the last time he checked, his get-into-heaven-free card wasn't stamped.

So even if he did find his daughter, then what? He was an unfit father and no angel would raise his demon daughter. At least he knew Nara had her squirreled away in the best schools under strict supervision. Giving her advantages only money could buy. Raising her with privileges he could never afford. What did he offer her anyway?

Love?

Love was underrated to a little girl who would want new dresses and a pony.

A flicker of hope wiggled into his head. If the relic the demons were looking for was so important, maybe it would help him on his path to redemption. Would Father reward him for stomping out this new faction? It was a long shot, but opportunities to reclaim his essence didn't exactly land on his doorstep. He'd have to take any chance he might have. Going about ascending the old-fashioned way would take too long. Shane needed a jump-start back into God's good graces.

A salvation shortcut.

He wondered how Lucas was holding up with Cali on her death bed.

Well that's a new emotion, empathy for my enemy.

Truth was Lucas was no longer his enemy. If Calise died, he'd have one more sin on his already heavy shoulders. Taking away the guy's one true love.

Five years of living with Nara and the look on Lucas' face in the middle of the road had hit him with a realization. He'd only desired to *possess* Calise, nothing more. No different from Nara's desire to possess him.

And possession could never be love. He knew the moment he fled the scene of his crime, he'd have to let Calise go. She was never his to begin with and could never be again.

Even after so many years of thinking *having* her was his right. His deluded mind told him no one else should touch what was *his*.

But after being Nara's possession, he was starting to see the error of his ways. He needed to redirect his obsession with Calise. Let it go. Shift sails and find his own road to redemption.

How could he save his daughter when he couldn't even save himself?

He returned his attention to the maps sprawled in front of him. Catholic churches and holy places of the continental United States. If demons were looking for something of high enough value they risked exposure, maybe that relic would also offer Shane the one thing he needed most.

He made another "X" on the map of Wisconsin, trying to connect the dots. How many real documented religious relics existed in Wisconsin? The Midwest? Across the country? And did all of those places have something in common?

He needed to narrow his focus:

There was Shrine of Holy Relics in Maria Stein, Ohio and Saint Anthony's Chapel in Pittsburg. But those were far away. He checked closer to home. Maybe La Crosse and Peshtigo Wisconsin. Michigan had a few, and some in Detroit and in the Upper Peninsula. Iowa, several in Illinois, Indiana, and Minnesota.

He had no idea where to begin. And alone, he had no chance.

But there was someone. He plucked out his cell phone and found the number. Back in his rock 'n' roll college days at UW-Madison, Shane had known lots of people. One guy in particular leapt to mind. He scrolled through his contact list and found the one frat guy he still talked to and hit call.

"Hey Brad, it's Shane. I know it's been a long time, but remember Rod? I need to find him…"

****

Ellen was losing it. Or had she already lost it? She shifted her position in the leather hospital chair next to Calise. "Cali, c'mon and wake up. I miss you. And Michael needs you. Lucas and Dean are off on a hunt for something that might save your life and I don't know how much longer I can sit around here and do nothing."

The IV dripped parenteral food into Calise's motionless body. Her heartbeat blipped with a regular rate and rhythm. The breathing machine kept a steady push and pull of air from her lungs and her oxygen saturation was normal.

Ellen squeezed the armrests with her fists. She was a professionally trained medical doctor not to mention an angel of the Lord—and she was helpless.

Though she was here to help the multitudes, Ellen's focus was single minded.

Help this one human.

Calise, more than any angel in heaven, was her best friend. If only she'd followed her instincts with…

Shane.

Once again, all the agony in Cali's life and hers were caused by that fallen angel. Her cell dinged. Speak of the devil. He'd sent a text. *"Found an 'in'. Got a job. Something's afoot and I'll keep you updated."*

St. Jude's church and the relic desecration. Ellen

couldn't put her finger on it, but something about it told her that whatever Shane was about to dabble in, she needed to go with him. She could feel it deep in her bones like when a crippled arthritic knew when the barometric pressure dropped.

"I'm coming with." She hit send.

"Can't. You walk in the light. You'll give me away."

Ellen went to pull back the heavy, black drape that separated Calise's bed from the ICU melee that lay beyond. Holding onto the fabric, an idea pushed at the corners of her mind.

A drape. A cloak! If she was cloaked, she could go with Shane. *"I'm coming with. I'll hide with the help of you-know-who. Meet me in the desert."*

Shane responded immediately with a firm *"NO! You will not involve them."*

"I'm going to ask for their help with or without your permission. You coming or not?" She smiled, waiting to see what kind of man he was. No one visited the *jinn* alone and came out unscathed. Close to a minute passed. Her heart sank. He talked a good game, but it looked like in the end, he would let her down. Like everyone always did. Then her phone beeped.

"I won't let you go to them alone. Where is the closest colony and when?"

Ellen said good-bye to Calise with a gentle kiss on the cheek and infused angelic light into her soul. "Hang on girl, between Lucas, Dean, Shane, and me, somebody will come back with help."

"Spring Green Preserve. Give me 3 hours," she responded.

"Not happy about this. But fine," Shane answered.

Ellen started making calls on her way out of the hospital. A two-week leave of absence for a family emergency. Cali's mother to come sit vigil. And a call to Lucas' Aunt in Costa Rica. Plus. She'd use her connections to make sure all angels in a fifty mile radius would watch the hospital and Michael.

Not like last time when Nara got past her guards and kidnapped Michael.

She needed to make a quick stop at home and get the essentials. One didn't simply walk up to the *jinn* and ask for their help. If they refused her, she and Shane would have to fight their way out. And odds were, they would not make it out alive.

Chapter 9

Shane was no fool. The *jinn,* sometimes known as genies, were unpredictable and dangerous. They had no reason to help them and no reason to hurt them. He collected the things he'd need to face the *jinn* including copies of holy books.

He flipped through some of the pages refreshing his knowledge of the *jinn*. As opposed to angels who have no free will in heaven and were created of light, *jinn* were created of smokeless fire and like humans, had free will.

Demonic possession was a falsity and propagated by the church to maintain a level of fear. The truth was, only *jinn* could possess humans. Sure, an angel was physically stronger than the *jinn.* Angels could defeat them by extracting their souls. But alone, he would only be able to take on so many before…

He shuddered at the thought.

Human possession.

He knew why there were so many books and movies made about it. Scary shit. Having some other entity inside you controlling your thoughts and actions. Word was, they could even jump inside angels and demons for a short stint. The *jinn* found possession entertaining. Spouting demonic names has always kept the truth of who they really were well hidden.

That's why Ellen is going to them. They were the

only beings who could truly hide among angels, demons, and humans.

Ellen needed their knowledge of cloaking. If she could hide her angelic light, she could mix into the demon world and help Shane get to the root of the artifact destroyer.

He memorized his destination on the map, grabbed all of his belongings, stuffed them in a duffel bag, and revved the engine on the foreign car he'd rented under a false name.

Milwaukee's downtown reeked of beer hops and ambrosia. Heading due west along the interstate, he finally made his way into the rural countryside of Wisconsin. Interstate Ninety-four passed through farmland and medium sized towns. He waved to his alma mater in Madison and after bypassing the city, he headed deeper into the homeland on Highway Fourteen.

He'd never been this way before. Small towns like Black Earth and Mazomanie west of Madison were dotted with ice-cream shops, diners, and cheese stores.

Shane needed to reach the preserve before Ellen. Maybe he could explain himself and make peace with the *jinn* before she showed up begging for them to hand over their cloaking knowledge to an obscure angel.

Once in Spring Green, he headed north and then east before parking on Angelo Lane with a snort. The *jinn* were often found in deserts. Who knew Wisconsin had a desert? A small sign read, "Spring Green Preserve: Wisconsin's Desert." The small expanse of land must be the place the invisible *jinn* of the area called home.

Picking his way along a narrow path in the rolling sand prairie, he agreed this piece of the Wisconsin

River Terrace actually was desert. He spotted prickly-pear cactus, false heather and three-awn grass among the small hills of sand. Closing his eyes and centering himself, he sent out a pulse of energy before *demonstrating* to his true demonic form.

He bit his lip allowing the wracking pain of the transformation to begin. His nails elongated and fingers extended with webs connecting his knuckles and arms. His teeth morphed into jagged points that would rip out his own tongue. His hair lay in piles around him and red horns pushed through his cranium into the shape of the letter "S."

Forcing this disgusting transformation was necessary. The *jinn* might show themselves to a demon who strolled into their territory.

Rustling issued from the bushes and sudden wind blew over the grass.

They know I'm here. "Come forth, *Jinn.* I know you can see me," Shane commanded.

A hiss and a crackle of branches. A bull snake with a diamond pattern and dark brown spots on his back slithered from the brush. The extra flesh where it breathed out of his mouth made the bull snake hiss sound more like a trilled letter "z" to mimic the sound of a rattlesnake. The animal curled into an s-shape and lifted his head to taste the air with his tongue.

"Evolutionary mimicry at its finest. But you and I both know who the viper is. You have no venom or rattle. Show yourself, *jinn colubrid.*"

The snake blurred, a black mist replaced the creature. The darkness spiraled upwards, condensing into the shape of an ancient man in white robes.

"Pop a pointy hat on you and everyone would call

you Merlin," Shane said before he could stop himself. He should be polite.

"What is it you want, demon?" the *jinn* asked.

Shane reverted to his human form and extended his hand. "I come in the company of an angel who needs your assistance."

"That angel?" The *jinn* pointed behind him.

He turned to see Ellen hiking in behind him.

She glowed a piercing white to the point of blinding them with her warmth and beauty. "I am your servant," she said, bowing onto one knee and lowered her head. "Forgive my intrusion into your world. I ask a small favor."

The old man spat on the ground and cringed at the gesture of reverence. "I work with no angels. And as I will not bow to you, do not bow to me."

Shane shot Ellen a 'be-careful" glare before she rose and grasped the old man's hand in greeting.

"We will not leave before I can speak with you in private," she said, her voice hard.

The old *jinn* sighed. "I'm afraid that's not possible," he said. "We are celebrating a wedding today." He turned to leave.

Ellen hurried after him, not letting him out of her sight. "Then we will celebrate with you."

Shane followed close behind.

"As you wish," the old man acquiesced, "as I will not forge ill will on this day of celebration."

The *jinn's* lives mimicked humans in every way. They lived in communities with local customs and even practiced traditional religions. Their magic made them seem more powerful than humans and their true appearance—faceless fire—was no less terrifying than his own demonic form. And like all beings, some were good, some were not, and others didn't give two shits about anything one way or another.

"What can we call you?" Shane asked.

"Effrit, as that is the name of my fractured tribe. What favor do you seek from us?"

Shane sensed an atmosphere of underlying anger from the benevolent-looking shape-shifter, but the anger wasn't directed at him and Ellen. "She would like to learn your cloaking skills. The angel is assisting me in a private matter."

"An angel working with a demon?" The *jinn's* face lit up. "Do you work for the cause?" He addressed the question to Shane.

Shane took a gamble. "I do."

"Your cause is our cause, sir," he bowed. "If you can find what the master seeks in the old churches, it will free my tribe. We want the ring found as much as the demons. In that case, we will help you as we have helped to cloak others. Your angel can work with our *sila*. It will not take long and you can be on your way as our wedding celebration is a private day."

Shane's working knowledge of the *jinn* was foggy before the visit, but in the last few hours, he'd brushed up on his history. King David's son, Solomon, was disturbed because a demon was tormenting a young boy and prayed for help. In response to his prayers, the archangel Michael presented him with a ring made of brass and iron, carved with the name of God, and set with four jewels. The seal on the ring, known as the Seal of Solomon allowed him to control both demons and *jinn*.

The old man had given them his name as Effrit.

Effrit jinn were highly intelligent and cunning. They lived in complex societies until the dark time when King Solomon enslaved them and while under his control, they worked tirelessly to build his temple.

Although not mentioned in the Bible, Shane knew the *jinn* were mentioned in the Koran, chapter 27, verse 17: "And there were gathered together unto Solomon his armies of the *jinn* and humankind, and of the birds, and they were set in battle order." After their enslavement, the *jinn* became fractured, living in these secret desert societies and always fearing the same thing. If the ring was found again, they would once again be enslaved. Demons working together with *jinn* could only be for one thing: reclaim Solomon's ring and destroy it.

That is why demons were desecrating churches looking for old relics. They hunted for Solomon's ring!

How fortunate they were to come across a tribe with a *sila,* who were rare and beautiful female *jinn*, the most adept at shape-shifting and very tolerant of humans.

Effrit stopped walking. One moment, they were surrounded by the vast sands of the desert, and in the next moment, the *jinn* village materialized around them. Shane was taken aback. Very human-looking *jinn* were hurrying everywhere dressed in their finest clothing. A gazebo was set up strewn with red roses infused with tiny white stephanotis. Lavish preparations had been taken for this ceremony. Chairs were set up and it was clear the festivities were close at hand.

Ellen drew in her breath. "This is so beautiful. We can come back after your ceremony. I thank you for your offer of help, but we cannot intrude on the wedding preparations."

"Nonsense. I'd prefer you finish your business and never return. No offense," he winked at Shane.

"None taken," Shane answered.

The *jinn* turned to Shane, narrowing his eyes. "But first, give me your hands, fallen one."

Shane let Effrit squeeze both of his hands.

The *jinn*'s eyes rolled back in his sockets and his form changed. His true form emerged, one of dark fire with hollow eyes. As fast as he'd shifted to his true form, it dissipated. "You will rise again. The girl that sleeps is your salvation. Unless you are diverted by the shroud."

"What shroud?" Shane asked.

But Effrit disappeared and reappeared next to Ellen who was already being led away by a stunning young woman...their *sila*. Even Shane couldn't tear his eyes away from her. She was magnificent. Dressed in a long, black dress with patterned gray sleeves and neckline, the *sila* was barefoot and wore bands of gold around her ankles and wrists. Her head was covered except her shimmering onyx eyes. The tail of a tiger—her other form—swished behind her. Ellen gave Shane a nod before following the *sila* into a secluded tent.

Something *felt* wrong. Shane couldn't put his finger on it, but his hyperactive senses had roared into full overdrive the second he saw Effrit's true form. Sure, he was in a *jinn* community where he trusted no one. Yes, Ellen had just gone willingly with a *sila* to cloak her angelic body and take on the visage of a demon. But it was something more than that.

The hairs on the back of his neck stood up and an unshakeable paranoia rose from the recesses of his being.

Effrit returned to Shane giving him a firm handshake. "I'm sorry I cannot postpone my daughter's nuptials any longer. If you and the angel would leave as soon as she reemerges from the *sila's* tent, it would be greatly appreciated."

Shane nodded and found a seat. So it wasn't just any *jinn* getting married today, but Effrit's own daughter. Perhaps that's why he was in a hospitable mood.

Violin and percussion music echoed from the woods. Effrit stood tall and proud when his daughter appeared. With spiked blonde hair and tangerine ruffle sleeves on an oyster-colored gown, she smiled and slipped her tiny hand through her father's arm.

All at once, the wind changed directions. Shane's heart began to thump and his hands balled into sweaty fists.

From the tent, Ellen let out a short cry. Shane ran for the tent and ripped through the opening. Ellen's demonic form halted Shane mid-step. Her hair was black and streaked with gray. Four horns protruded from each side of her head, black locks swirling around them. Her face was a greenish-gray and black lines extended down each cheeks. Her eyes glowed red. Three black leather straps held by o-rings barely concealed her chest, black leather boy shorts and black boots rounded out her demonic ensemble.

"Holy shit," Shane said. "Are you okay?"

She shook her head unable to hold the cloaked demonic form and reverting to herself. "Can't you feel it? They are coming!"

The *sila* backed away from them toward the exit of

the tent.

Shane and Ellen pulled back the curtain of the tent. The sky blackened with an impending invasion. Demons dotted the sky, swords in hand descending on the *jinn*.

But not just any demons.

A destroyer demon army.

Chapter 10

Paris, France

Seamus was gone and Adrienne was still reeling from his kiss.

Everything had happened so fast. She pieced together the last few days. Gabriel harassing her at her hotel then him showing up at the restaurant tonight. Intruding on her dinner.

Meeting Seamus.

The Americans looking for Gabriel and Seamus. And then her friends from the meetings looking for them all.

Something more was going on and she was going to find out what. She rushed back into the restaurant. Patrons huddled in corners complaining about the intrusion but still sipping their wine as the staff rushed to sweep up broken glass and right tables and chairs. She spotted her waiter, intending to ask him where everyone went, when Leon and Denis each grabbed an arm and led her outside.

"Get your hands off of me!" she said, elbowing them both in the ribs.

"*Aïe*, Adrienne!" Denis spat before releasing her once they were outside the restaurant.

"Leon…Denis? What the hell?" She shook off their hold and faced them square. These were her so-called friends from the Novem-Stellae. Why were they brawling with Gabriel, Seamus, and the Americans?

"Sorry," Denis said, "but you're coming with us. You have some explaining to do."

"Why?" she asked. "I haven't done anything wrong."

Denis lit a smoke and took a deep drag. "The leader will determine that."

"Yeah, right." Leon glared at her. "You saw with your own eyes, Denis. She's a spy."

Spy?

"I have no idea what you're talking about. I'm going home." She took a step forward and stretched out her arm to hail a cab. Uncouth behavior like this in public was not the Parisian norm. Seamus, Gabe, and the other two must be wrapped up in something pretty nasty.

A black sedan speeding up the road squealed to a stop. Leon jumped in front of her and grabbed her cheeks, squeezing them and forcing her to look him in the eye. "You can't be one of us and have dinner with an angel you bitch." His eyes flashed a blood red.

Denis came from behind. Then a black cloth was over her mouth. Adrienne struggled and kicked while they threw her in the sedan, then after a few breaths, everything went dark.

****

"I won't let them take her!" Seamus struggled, but Gabriel held him back. From across the street in a second floor window of a ratty, abandoned apartment, they'd watched Adrienne being dragged from the restaurant, drugged, manhandled, and thrown into the back of a black sedan "What are they doing with her?"

Gabriel held him firmly in place. "Why do you suddenly care Mr. I-Hate-Women? Look, she's a darkwalker Seamus. I was having some fun. I know you haven't kissed anyone in like…forever, but that's no reason to risk everything."

"You saw that?"

Gabriel waggled his eyebrows.

"I'm going after her." Seamus grimaced. Freaking angels, never a moment's peace. "Who knows what they'll do to her, because of you! Having 'some fun.'"

"Probably torture her, question her about why she was with me, rape her, kill her. You know…the usual."

"And that's okay with you? You're an angel. You're supposed to be better than this." Seamus cried. "Let me go." He struggled in vain against the angel's death grip.

"Shut it, Seamus. I'm sorry. I've become desensitized to human nastiness over the last couple of thousand years. Forget her. There's more at play here than you trying to protect one darkwalker. We have to stick to the plan. I told the two seers to meet us outside Paris at the secure location. I know *we* won't be followed, but I hope those Americans can manage to come alone."

Seamus couldn't accept this. Nothing had happened in his life for so long. And that's how he'd always liked it. Living from job to job. Town to town.

Gabriel thought he was so smart, but the angel didn't know anything about him. Seamus didn't hate women. He'd merely vowed on the day he watched his mother's throat ripped open by a demon that this would end.

No child of his would bear the curse. Safeguarding

long forgotten artifacts perpetually hunted by demons walking the earth.

To hell with the artifacts, let the angels hide them away. No family burden meant no family and that had always been fine with him.

So Seamus decided to be done with women.

But the honor code genetically built into his DNA was screaming at him for attention. His heart told him Adrienne could be saved. And more than that, that she was worth saving.

In the alley, he'd seen her true beauty. Ripped through her flimsy walls and glimpsed her potential to be an amazing woman. And her lips…

What he wouldn't give for another taste.

Maybe he could keep his vow *and* be rid of his family's burden. It never crossed his mind he could fall in love with someone but never have children. For the first time in a long time, he let a sliver of hope snake into his subconscious. What if he didn't have to wander the earth alone for the rest of his days? The glimmer of hope was almost too much for him and he pushed it down to deal with the task at hand.

Adrienne may be a darkwalker now. But only because she'd lost her way. And Seamus wouldn't rest until he saw her again. Helped her find her way back to the light.

But first he needed her to stay alive.

****

Adrienne blinked. Her head pounded and when she tried to lift her arms to feel for damage, she realized she was seated in a chair with her arms tied behind her back and her own scarf used as a gag.

Lights clicked on, blinding her. She was on the

stage in the meeting room where she'd attended weekly Novem-Stellae meetings for years. About a dozen members stared at her. People she knew and considered friends.

Denis and Leon appeared from behind followed by the leader of the group.

Daevas Lerwick—the only man she'd trusted and confided in since her parents' death—tapped the top of his microphone and cleared his throat. "Ladies and gentleman, it seems we have found a rat in our midst. A spy!"

Gasps sounded from the crowd and Adrienne rolled her eyes. This was complete nonsense. She tugged at the ropes binding her hands.

Perpetually clad in an Italian-made black suit, his slicked back peppery-gray hair and gentle smile had been a rope of sanity after her parents died. His words were those of a wise sage and she found clarity in an otherwise murky existence. They'd spent long hours conversing about the nature of human desires, the impermanence of everything, and the unproved hoopla of religion.

"Who among you would have suspected the lovely Adrienne of consorting with the enemy?" His voice boomed over the microphone.

The pitch of his voice made him sound like a game show host. Until now, she'd never heard the sinister ring to his cadence. How had she missed that? Had Daevas duped her?

In the aftermath of her parents' death, she'd taken to his words like a baby to mother's milk. His rules of living washed over and refreshed her like ice water in the desert. He made sense. Live for yourself. No one can help you and provide your happiness except yourself. Study the power of your inner strength. Once you are healed, then you can heal others.

It wasn't like Adrienne had been raised ultra-religious or anything, but when her parents were killed, praying to an unseen omnipotent Creator made her more angry than placated. Cold, hard facts on day-to-day emotional sustenance became her game plan.

Eat, sleep, and find personal happiness. Repeat until dead.

It had worked nicely for her.

Until a few hours ago, that is. Until the suppressed urge to only please herself and trust or please no other living human was zapped away with one kiss.

You're a damn fool. A kiss is just that. Don't fool yourself. He was selfishly using you to protect himself.

He'd even said so, she reminded herself. She'd never see his sorry ass again and now, she discovered she had consorted with all the wrong people.

On some guttural level, when Leon's eyes turned red and he said the word "angel" she thought for a moment all the childhood bible stories about angels and demons might be true. But that was impossible! Leon's eyes likely caught a flicker of a nearby stop light and when he said "angel," she must have misheard him.

Whoever Gabriel was, he must be an enemy to Daevas and the group. Her impromptu dinner date must have made her seem like she was consorting with the enemy. Once the ropes and gag were removed, she could explain all the confusion.

Either way, she was done with this group. It now felt viscerally wrong. And a piece of her knew Seamus was one of the good guys. In fact, the more she stared at the men on stage and the accusatory glares from the audience, the more she was beginning to think the line between good and evil might be more delineated than she cared to believe.

How had she ended up here?

And had Seamus judged her guilty by association?

This only raised more questions in her head. If Gabriel, Seamus, and the others were the good guys and Daevas' enemies, maybe there was more going on here than she was allowed to see.

But it was clear, the goal of this group was to protect and save yourself. Find happiness for yourself by any means necessary. And somehow, she'd screwed up and Daevas considered himself betrayed. She twisted at the ropes binding her wrists. Would they let her explain? Would Daevas show her mercy or would she pay for her mistake? Still barking out accusations to his followers, she sensed total loyalty was the only option around Daevas and retribution oozed from his pores when he felt wronged.

She flashed a glance at Leon, his right-hand man. He blinked and his eyes shone like a fiery plane crash. Blinked again, then he was back to normal. She would have liked to think she'd imagined it, but she knew better.

Fuck.

In a fraction of second, she went from hoping she could explain her way out of a mix-up to wondering what kind of evil organization she'd signed up for. And signed over her life savings to upon her death? Maybe because of an error in judgment, they were about to speed that process along.

"Yes, our own Adrienne was removed from a

secret meeting with our worst enemies!" Daevas ended his speech with a flourish. "Now you must discuss and decide her fate."

The small audience stood and converged, whispering to each other and pointing...making their loyalty clear.

Adrienne tried her best to make sounds of protest through the gag, but Daevas towered in front of her delivering a swift backhand to her cheek. The slap was so hard, her head rang like a church bell and tears completely blinded her vision.

So much for the search for personal happiness. Adrienne dug deep, finding her well of fortitude and defiance. She had joined an evil group. Satanic?

All she cared about right now was getting free. Otherwise, she knew before the night was over, she would be made an example of and tossed aside.

Or worse...

Chapter 11

Spring Green Preserve, Wisconsin

A demon army of destruction descended in droves. Shane couldn't process the "why" right now, as *jinn* and demons generally coexisted and often worked together. The abject horror on the faces of the *jinn* made Shane reach for the only other thing he cared about saving: Ellen.

The colony of *jinn* scattered in every direction as the army from hell focused only on their master's bidding. The first winged creatures swooped right past Shane, ignoring him completely, and yanked on the arm of a *jinn* lifting him into the air. Hovering midflight, the demon opened his mouth and sucked the soul from the *jinn* before breaking his neck and dropping the lifeless body back to earth.

Oh shit. Shane ducked back inside the tent with Ellen and the *sila* pushing them back inside against the emerging hell storm. Both their heads were tilted up, looking awestruck at the darkened sky filled with demonic assassins.

"Our only chance is to blend in. Cloak and Demonstrate," he ordered. Ellen squeezed her eyes shut for a moment to concentrate before releasing her demonic form. Shane, already changed, grabbed her hand to run.

"Wait," a voice said before they took for the skies. The *sila* emerged. "You will leave us to die?"

"Of course not," Shane answered. "We will fight."

"Then you'll need these." The *sila* placed a hand on each of their backs.

The flesh from Shane's back ripped apart and he felt himself growing a new appendage from his shoulder blades. He jerked away while Ellen cried out in pain. "What did you do?"

Ellen spun around. She'd sprouted a gorgeous pair of black, feathery wings. "Thank you," she said to the *sila* who crouched in the corner of the tent.

Shane reached around his own shoulders and found a pair of black wings he now had full muscular control over. "Let's go."

"Wait," Ellen shrieked. "What about them?" She pointed to the *jinn*, being plucked into the air one by one. "You said we'd stay and fight."

Every moment they wasted meant another *jinn* was dead. "I meant," he said, "let's go and fight!"

"I know we can't save all of them." Ellen was already airborne and heading into the fray. "But we have to try!"

He was about to head after her, but his eye caught a rustle in a small patch of trees ahead.

Effrit.

The older *jinn* had fallen to the ground in the melee and scrambled to get up. His upper half in human form, but his legs melded together in snake form, keeping him supine.

He was reaching forward and yelling out to his daughter who clung to a post under her wedding trellis. Dozens of the tribe had already been picked off, their motionless corpses blanketing the ground. An especially nasty female demon swooped toward Effrit's daughter.

Shane cupped his hands. "Ellen, protect the bride."

A demon in a black robe plunged toward Effrit. Shane concentrated on his new mode of transportation, extending out his own black wings and taking flight. He plowed headfirst into the demon, knocking it off course before it could grab Effrit. "Run!" he yelled to the *jinn* as he turned to face his opponent.

"Why do you stand with them?" The demon's voice was hollow and cold.

"Because I have free will in this life, you cocksucker." Shane dove into the demon and wrestled him in the air. The demon was strong, but Shane fought dirty, tearing his teeth into one of the creature's leathery wings, ripping it from his shoulder. Two more demons tried to join in the fight but Shane dove out of their path while he and the first demon plummeted to the ground. The few surviving *jinn* descended on the injured demons, their fiery forms covering then devouring them.

Shane scanned the skies for Ellen. She'd taken flight with Effrit's daughter and was now encircled by demons. They weren't attacking but seemed to be waiting for a signal.

"Release her," they boomed, all speaking at once. The young bride screamed and covered her ears. The sound of their voices must have pierced her ears like knives.

The girl began to struggle and the bride slipped from Ellen's grasp tumbling back toward earth. Shane reversed his direction and caught her in the air before the demons could change course.

The bride stared at him, suddenly doe-eyed and calm in his arms as he flew full-force away from the demons. "There is only one way to stop them."

"Oh yeah," Shane cried, zigzagging away from the demonic hoard. "What's that?"

"Let me in."

Oh, fuck no. Possession. "Isn't there another—"

Before he even gave her a chance to answer, the weight in his arms disappeared and she became a black mist pouring into him through his eyes, mouth, and nose.

Like he'd swallowed a viper, he began to cough and choke, trying to spit her out. Then his consciousness was shoved aside and he lost all control of his body. His wings stalled and he brushed into the treetops before regaining speed and ascending.

Kill them all.

He hadn't said the words. But his lips moved and he heard the sound of his own voice. It didn't sound like him. More like the alien voice people say is yours when you hear a recording of yourself and ask, "Is that how I really sound?"

He brandished the weapons he'd stowed on his person in case the *jinn* turned on them. He sliced open a demon mid-flight, guts spilling to the earth. The demon melted into black dust. More movements from his arms and wings that weren't his doing. *Die, demon filth.*

Get out! He yelled from the mental chair in the corner of his mind. An imposed time out from being Shane O'Grady.

And the pain! Excruciating. Like millions of razors slicing your brain while your body became one big middle-of-the-night leg cramp. And the tightness in his throat, a snake slithering deeper and deeper down, choking him.

Then super speed. His arms became weapons and the remaining demons were extinguished in less than the time it would take him to chew a piece of steak.

Together, they scanned the ground. Dead were scattered everywhere and his intruder's emotional rage, that had seconds before helped him wipe out almost a dozen demons, now shattered into an emotional plunge where he felt her gut-wrenching pain at the overwhelming loss of her family and tribe.

His wings stopping moving as she let his body fall. Into a cluster of red cedars, whose branches slammed into his every muscle and bone until he reconnected with the sandy earth and everything went black.

His eyes were open, but even the blinking was not completely controlled by him. Shane was a prisoner in his own body. The master puppeteer had grown strong inside of him, deciding his next move. Clawing for control of his every word.

The sky was empty.

The demons were gone.

Two sets of eyes blinked at the meandering clouds passing overhead. "Get ooooooooooouuuuuuu…."

Violent convulsions overtook him and he retched out a black tarry bile that coalesced into a small black dog.

Shane heaved a sigh of relief and got on his feet only to hear a rustling from inside a patch of prairie grass nearby. Crouching, he got ready to fight. He'd *never* let a *jinn* get close enough to do that again. But it wasn't one of the tribe pushing aside the tall grass who fell into his arms. It was Ellen, back in her regular body.

"Help," she gagged.

He placed her gently on the ground, cradling her head in his lap. The eyes staring back at him were not hers. "I order you to get out of her now!"

Afraid she would swallow her own tongue, he rolled her onto her stomach. With great effort, she pulled herself to her hands and knees. The skin on her back protruded and contracted. Something alien living inside her was pushing its way out. She coughed and gagged. The yellow head of a bullsnake appeared in her mouth.

Shane lunged for the snake's head. Effrit!

He hissed and poised to strike, but Shane grabbed its head and heaved the thick creature from Ellen's mouth while tears ran down her cheeks and she expelled the being.

Leaning backwards and pulling with all his weight, Shane fell backwards and released the snake, who slithered toward the dog where it weaved its body between the canine's legs.

Effrit and his daughter were the only two survivors.

Turning his attention back to Ellen, Shane crawled to her side and brushed the hair back from her face. Her chest was not rising and falling like it should.

She isn't breathing.

Without a thought, he lifted her chin and placed his mouth on hers.

****

When Shane's lips touched Ellen's, he felt something he'd never felt before, even with Calise. It took his breath away and blossomed like a ray of sunshine in his heart.

Hope.

The hope of a new beginning. The hope of joy and laughter and peace. A world of possibilities that shouldn't be his.

Because he didn't deserve happiness.

Heavenly angels were allowed to choose to live one life among humans. He was supposed to be here to maintain balance. Do good deeds. But what did he do? All the wrong shit. Fall in love with a human. A big no-no. Then in his quest to get her back, he lost himself and fell from grace. Seeking his first high over and over again...Calise's adoration had been his drug. And he'd chased it at all cost ever since.

He'd kidnapped a baby for the demon Abaddon, the ambassador of hell. Became a *transitor*—somewhere in between angel and demon—and then finally, after being on the verge of taking Calise by force, he succumbed to his inner devil and became the thing he hated most: a demon. His essence was ripped away and since that day, he'd walked the earth without the Father's light.

In his one human life as an angel, he'd royally screwed up.

And what for? One beautiful human.

Calise.

With the whole of creation, why had he cared about her?

Truth was he didn't care. He'd wanted control. Of Calise.

Since the moment he'd met her, he needed her to be his. He didn't really care if she loved him or not. He wanted her to be his possession. To be able to adjust the knob of her adoration toward him. It wasn't her *love* he'd been after all these years. Maybe he still didn't know what *that* was.

And now, due to his selfishness, she'd likely die.

Neither of them would find peace and happiness. Neither of them would be able to raise their child.

And with his lips pressed against Ellen, all of this flashed through his mind in a millisecond. He released his lip lock to suck in another breath.

This time, when their lips met, she moaned and he felt an arm wrap around his neck and fingers tangle in his hair.

With a primal hunger, what he'd begun as a life-saving breath turned into something else. .

He pushed her away and she arched her back. "More," she whispered.

Oh, shit. Memory loss? Was she still possessed? Unlikely, as the dog and snake were cuddled up together in the soft grass watching the whole thing.

"Are you forgetting who I am?" he asked, keeping his hands on her shoulders so she couldn't pull him closer.

"Shane." His name dripped off her tongue like a lover aching for release.

Feeling every hair on his body snap to attention and his blood rushing to the one place it shouldn't be, he jumped up and backed away. This was wrong on so many levels.

And yet, something about her made him long to close the distance between them and lose himself in another kiss. An image flashed in his mind: the men and Anna on the beach in Costa Rica. Anna was a seductress and a demon.

But surely Ellen wasn't! She was an angel.

He leaned in a little closer. Ellen's back arched and she almost growled his name. She grabbed at clumps of sand and let them fall through her fingers. Time slowed so Shane could see each grain individually fall to earth. Moments in time. The movement of the universe. He was but one grain of sand falling in an abyss.

Shane was lost in the moment and reached out to her to simply help her to her feet. As their fingers were about to touch, electricity coursed through his whole being, then the dog snarled and leapt between them, snapping at Ellen's hand.

"What the..." Shane lunged for the animal but came up empty, the black mist reformed into a person ten feet away.

"Don't touch her again," she hissed. "She's hurt."

Ellen was ripping at her shirt, her pants, trying to expose her stomach. Gash marks covered her left side, from her heart to her hips.

"El!" he wanted to rush to her side, but Effrit held him back.

"She was attacked by a descendant of Agrat bat Mahlat," Effrit said. "If I hadn't been possessing her, she would have died. Even with my strength, she was still injured. Her thirst for sex will remain unquenchable until the blood is out of her system." The *jinn* bride and Effrit leveled their gaze at Shane.

He searched through his memories. Agrat bat Mahlat was one of the four original succubi, female demons who seduce men to steal their energy and life force. Agrat bat Mahlat even seduced King David himself and gave birth to Asmodeus, the King of the Nine Hells and one of the seven princes of hell—the demon of lust. If Ellen had bat Mahalt's blood in her, he understood why she was acting this way.

Shane kept his distance from Ellen and followed Effrit and his daughter back to the site of her would-be wedding ceremony. The groom lay dead at the altar. Effrit's daughter fell to the ground in silence, crying and holding the husband she would never have.

"Why did they attack you?" Shane followed Effrit through the tribe's desecrated village, now a ghost town, heavy with death.

"It was my fault. A powerful demon came, seeking the cloak to further work for the cause. We helped of course. But I see now I've served my purpose. And it is clear demons and *jinn* have never been on the same side."

Shane could not hold his tongue any longer. "I lied. We do not work for this 'cause' you speak of. What is it?"

Effit mustered a half smile. "I thought as much. The demons seek to recover the Ring of Solomon that has long bound my people. Asmodeus seeks it as does the archangel Raphael. The hunt is on for who can recover the ring first. The holy men and line of seers have long protected these artifacts. The *jinn* of course, seek to see this ring destroyed so we may never be under anyone's control again. The demons seek it to appease and free Asmodeus from his curse. And the rumor is Raphael wants to control the demons so he can free someone he loves from hell itself."

It was all starting to make sense. The demon at St. Jude's. Agrat bat Mahlat's descendant fighting with a demon army to help free her son. And Raphael wanted his one love, Anna, freed from hell.

"I owe you my thanks," Effrit said. "The only reason my daughter and I are alive is because we hid in the two of you." She rushed back to her father's side, melting into his protective arms.

"This is unthinkable," his daughter said.

Just then, the *sila* appeared in the distance, her tiger form sleekly melding into her human one. Her hand covered her mouth and tears fell freely down her cheeks as she rushed to Effrit's side. "Are you the only two…?"

"Yes, my dear," he replied.

The *sila* took in the horrors around her. "Father! Sister!" She gave him a hug before rushing to her sister's side.

"We are alone," Effrit said to no one. "At least both of my daughters survived."

The girls joined arms with their Effrit. "The three of us must start again," the *sila* said. "As we have before."

Effrit smiled and pulled his two daughters close before addressing Shane. "Thank you both. We are in your debt so should the day ever come you need us, I can offer you the usual gift."

Three wishes from a genie. Great. How would he call in that favor? No lamp to rub. They were nomadic and nearly impossible to trace. But it never hurt to have someone out there who owes you. "But how?"

A slow smile crept across the *sila's* face. "Take this." She placed a talisman around his neck. "Thank you for not abandoning my people." And with that, the three of them changed to animal form and dissolved into what was left of their desert home.

The entire village along with the dead, melted

away and all Shane could see was the undisturbed desert as it once was. He turned his attention back to Ellen, who continued to writhe on the ground, her hands rubbing her own body with pleasure.

"How long will she be like this?" he asked no one.

"A while," Effrit's voice came from the snake sunning itself on a nearby rock.

"Can I wish it away?" Now that's an idea.

After a lengthy hiss, the snake moved his head left and then right. "Sssssorry," the snake said.

"And what am I supposed to do in the meantime?"

"Acquiesssssce her needssss or keep her trapped," Effrit answered before he slithered away.

****

"Is this really necessary?" Ellen's legs were tied and the ropes chafed her bound wrists. She refused to look at Shane, instead opting to stare out the window at the cornfields peppered with pastures of munching cows and horses. Fresh cut hay mingled with the smell of manure.

But she could only smell one thing…Shane. Her all-consuming thought was of him being on top of her, inside of her. She'd never felt this way before. Never so much as touched herself in the shower, and yet her mind was obsessive about one thing…sex. And no matter what she did, she could not push her desire down. Like a balloon in box, if she shoved it down one place, it just pushed through in a different part of her mind.

When he first tied her up, she hadn't objected. Thought it was kind of kinky actually. But he wasn't making good on her desires. If she could just touch him, she knew he wouldn't refuse her. The need for release inside her was boiling over. Her body trembled and she wanted it to stop.

And Shane could make it stop. "Are you sure you don't want to—?"

"Stop it, El. I said 'No'. This isn't you. I've told you already. When you saved Effrit's daughter, a succubus slashed you…well, let's say do you remember kissing me?"

Ellen slid as close to the car door as her constraints would allow. *Yes and no.*

Doing her best to squash the insatiable needy feeling between her legs, she turned emotion off and logic on. There were 8-12 pints of blood in her body. Millions of red blood cells being made and dying every second. But it would be several weeks for the entire blood supply to regenerate.

Weeks of feeling like she'd fuck anything close to her? *Shit.*

Stop swearing! She chastised the inner succubus who laughed at her.

She stole a quick glance at Shane. A memory flooded her brain. The first time she'd seen him. He'd helped a clumsy Calise to her feet at a frat party in college and then he went back to his girlfriend, the demon, Nara.

The words she said out loud to Calise, followed by the words she'd thought blasted back to the forefront of her mind. She'd said, "What's he doing with her?" but thought, "He should be with me."

At the time, she'd quickly abandoned the idea, instead doing what she was sent to do, assist humanity. Studying medicine. She was a doctor, for heaven's sake!

When Calise and Shane began dating, she knew it would end in disaster.

Humans dating angels always did.

She stole a sideways look at him. Even as a demon, he was hot. Strong hands gripped the steering wheel, sculpted forearms, massive biceps bound by his t-shirt. She wanted to run her fingers through his long, dark hair and take his cock in her hands and—

"Ellen!"

She snapped out her daze. "Sorry, what were you saying?"

"I was saying you have two options: I cover every ounce of your skin with clothing and you pull yourself together and help me…for *Calise*," he emphasized. "Or, I keep you in a devil's trap until your blood replaces the poison."

At the present moment, nothing in her blood felt like poison. It felt amazing. She felt alive and every cell of her being zinged with a humming energy she didn't know she had. If she could only share it…

She scooted closer to Shane's side of the vehicle, he recoiled. "I'm warning you, Miss Horndog. Back off!"

Like a naughty puppy, she hung her head and retreated. "I'll take the clothing. You're not leaving me behind and you never know, maybe I'll come in handy." She winked at him.

One thought kept coursing through her brain, *sex with Shane*.

If he slept with her once, he might be hers forever.

Chapter 12

Paris, France

Adrienne stiffened in her chair, pulling at the ropes binding her hands. She took a deep breath. *In with the good air, out with the bad. Remember who you are and that you are not guilty.*

Today was the complete opposite of the day she first met Daevas. He had approached her, not unlike Gabriel had earlier this week, in her hotel a few months after the worst tragedy in her life. Her family dying in a plane crash on their way to see her.

There was no dramatic highly televised event. No search parties. Just a call from the subsidiary airline and an offer of a settlement. The crash was kept quiet and had gone largely unnoticed by the local media in Podunk, USA.

There was nothing about it on Parisian television.

It wasn't until hours after they didn't arrive on their scheduled flight she even found out. They were on a puddle-jumper to get from rural Minnesota to the Twin Cities to make their LaGuardia connection before coming to Paris. There was a thunderstorm. It was dusk. The best the air crash investigators could tell her was there was some kind of engine trouble. Fourteen people died.

And at the time, she was flat broke. Too broke to

fly home for the funeral. No family or friends to help out. The settlement money and her inheritance hadn't come in for months.

But when it did, she began methodically pissing it away on boozing and staying holed up in her hotel room. The thought of returning to the states never even crossed her mind. Go home to what? No family. And the home she grew up in was sold at auction.

Daevas introduced himself to her in the courtyard as Gabriel had. But what he'd said made perfect sense. "The only person who can make you happy is you." He set down his coffee and dabbed at the corners of his mouth. "Now is the time," he'd said. "Don't you agree?"

She'd said nothing but felt the scowl melt from her countenance.

"Idealists say you cannot love another if you do not take care of and love yourself first. Don't you agree?" He extended his hand.

She shook it.

His words echoed in the back of her mind resonating some unspoken truth.

"What is it you want?" she asked, trying her best not to be rude.

"Peace and happiness, just like everyone else."

"And you can offer that to me?" She arched a brow in disbelief.

He smirked and straightened his tie. "Yes, of course I can."

She stood to leave. "Sir, I don't mean to be rude, but you can't bring my parents back from the grave. My search for peace and happiness ended the day they died."

"If you let others dictate your own happiness, well, then yes of course, walk away and be miserable for the rest of your inconsequential life. But if you believe— even the tiniest bit—that your parents would want you to move on without them and find happiness, sit down and let's talk." He patted the seat of the chair she'd vacated.

Adrienne sighed. Her parents would have wanted her to move on. Be happy. God knows they'd left her with enough money to buy happiness, but it still wasn't enough. *Five minutes*. She'd give the guy five minutes and if he was some salesman asshole, she was out of there.

Looking at Daevas now, as she sat tied to a chair at what was beginning to look like her own execution, she knew he'd never lied to her. He believed with absolute conviction every word out of his mouth was the undiluted solid truth. Maybe it was. She went through the seven precepts of the Novem-Stellae movement in her head:

1. It is said: "Care for others." This is a lie. The truth is you cannot care for others if you do not care for yourself first. Put no one's needs before your own or you will never be able to love and care for another.

2. It is said: "Abstain from pleasure in abundance." This is a lie. The truth of human nature is to seek out and relish pleasure. Have no other priorities except doing what pleases you. Seek out what is owed to you and take it. There are no hidden treasures, only those you can gain in the here and now.

3. It is said: "All men are created equal." This is a lie. Not everyone is created equal. If you follow these precepts, you will see yourself as the higher being you

really are.

4. It is said: "Do unto others as you would have them do unto you." This is lie. Treat others as they treat you so they can learn to treat people better. Respect should be earned, not given.

5. It is said: "Do not kill." This is lie. We kill every day to eat and sustain our life. It is a part of nature to die or to be sacrificed for the greater good.

6. It is said: "Do not covet what is not yours." This is a lie. Everything can be made yours by hard work and dedication. Seize the day!

7. You are the most important thing in your life. And you need to take care of yourself first in order to be a better person in the world, and for the world!

For the first time, she looked on the 7 precepts with a fresh mind and saw them as the beautiful corruption they were. Daevas explained them as the true precepts of earthly happiness.

But looking around the room of selfish bastards right now she realized, too late, she'd been wrong. Dead wrong.

Now, when she needed help the most, there was no one who'd have her back. No one who cared about her at all.

****

"I said, 'We leave her.'" Gabriel repeated. "She will be our destruction. We must go now."

Seamus had never questioned Gabriel. Heck, he rarely talked to the angel. Gabriel didn't know Seamus' agenda and Gabriel never seemed to have one. No matter what the angel said, Seamus would not leave this poor innocent woman to the wolves. "It's your fault they drugged her and took her away. We need to fix this." Something about the black cloud cloaking Adrienne made him clammy. If Gabriel wouldn't help her, fine.

He would.

Even if it came to nothing. Even if she didn't appreciate it. Sometimes one person showing kindness in an unkind world made all the difference. "You know, you're the worst angel ever. And for most of my life, you're the only person I've been stuck talking to."

Gabriel opened his mouth and covered it with his hand in mock surprise. "Your life of solitude has been your choice. And really? You're calling me out, Mr. I'd-rather-die-than-carry-on-the-family-name. You're the one who's lived like a vagabond doing Lord knows what. I've been here waiting for some action for two thousand years. I had more excitement floating on clouds in the heavenly realm."

"You float on clouds up there? What, like a fat cherub with a bow and arrow?"

Gabriel shook his head. "Figure of speech and some of those cherubs are a damn riot. Not like hanging out with you. You've barely said "boo" to me in decades and now all of a sudden I'm supposed to swoop in and save one darkwalker. Why? Because a girl finally looked at you without laughing?"

His words stung. Seamus took a swing at him. Gabriel ducked out of the way. Seamus rushed him to tackle him to the ground, but it was about as easy as pushing a cement wall out of your way. "I really don't like you," he panted, shoving him harder, "and if my heavenly reward is hanging out with jerky angels like you," he moved him about a centimeter, "count me out."

"Go ahead and punch me. I like you all feisty. Now that I see your nuts have finally dropped, I'm with you, my ward." They both relented, backing away from each other. "Are you sure you want to save this girl? Because we'll have to kill everyone in there. We can't be followed. Clear?"

"Crystal." Seamus stretched out his hand and they shook.

Gabriel brushed off his suit and headed for the stairs. "I'm liking you better by the minute. I suppose it'll be you who waltzes in as the hero and I clean up behind you, leaving my usual path of human destruction." Gabriel rubbed his hands together and took the dusty steps two at a time. "Fine by me. It's about time I get to do *something.*"

Seamus balked. Maybe he hadn't entirely thought this through. And yet something inside him, at his core, was waking up like a bear in spring. Yawning and stretching and consumed with an insatiable hunger. Was someone else already there? Saving Adrienne? A deep part inside of him wanted to be her hero and to hell with the consequences.

"Let's move," Gabriel said once they were outside again, breathing the cool, night air. "I can find them."

They tracked the goons to a rectangular red, brick building in the 18th district where the windows were boarded up and there was one front door and bay window street side and one back door to the alley. Darkwalker central was disguised with a sign reading, "Novum-Stellae Life and Wellness Center: members only."

They walked by, peeking through the crack of space in the front window. Three men hovered over

Adrienne who was bound in a chair on a stage. A few people were gathered in a crowd conversing with a man in a black suit. Gabriel interlaced his fingers and pushed them away from his body cracking his knuckles then gave Seamus a quick nod. "You first, Superman."

All at once, the crowd began to disburse, exiting through the front door mumbling words like "guilty" and "liar". Seamus stooped to tie his shoe and slipped a rock in the door jamb, preventing it from locking. He ducked behind the back row of folding chairs and surveyed the room, which smelled of recently extinguished candles and moldy cheese. Adrienne remained on the stage, guarded by the same two blokes who'd abducted her.

The room was larger than he would have thought from the outside, with floor to ceiling columns forming an aisle between the rows of folding chairs leading toward the stage. The pristine white walls were studded with pictures of various members, all with the same smug expression and dead eyes staring at him with obvious disgust. Purple and gold curtains were draped near the back probably leading deeper into the building. This is where the man in the black suit had disappeared moments earlier. Seamus slipped forward keeping behind the columns, and working his way across the inland tan and green marble floor toward the stage, crouching in-between the folding chairs.

His thumping heart and sweaty hands did not lend him any advantage. He took a deep breath, willing his heart rate to slow and his breathing to steady. If he could take down the guards and untie Adrienne, maybe they could get out quick. One of the men on stage looked his way but failed to see him. The bloke had glowing red eyes.

Demons. Thanks to being of direct lineage to Joseph of Arimathea, Seamus was a seer. Even as a little boy, he could see the angels and demons walking among humans.

Looking back to the entrance, he saw Gabriel leaning behind one of the columns looking at his nails without a care in the world. Some protector and angelic backup!

The angel flashed his million-dollar smile and gave Seamus an enthusiastic thumbs up.

Once Seamus was about five rows from the front, one of the men on stage advanced on Adrienne. The man's eyes turned red and Seamus knew he was going to *demonstrate*, killing Adrienne in his true form. Not wanting to let that happen, Seamus pushed one of the chairs in front of him. It squeaked across the floor in audible protest, gaining the demon's attention.

"Hey, who are you?" a demon said, stepping forward.

Seamus held his ground, watching surprise turn to hope in Adrienne's face. He smiled. "I'm looking to become a new member," he hedged.

"No you're not. I remember him from the restaurant," another said. The demonic duo sprang into action, jumping off the stage and lurching forward to grab him. Seamus shimmied backwards through the aisle looking over his shoulder for Gabriel. "Little help here!" but the angel was nowhere to be seen.

The demons overturned rows of chairs each coming at Seamus from a different direction.

Seamus froze. *Let them catch me. It gets me closer to Adrienne.* He pretended to bolt, but allowed the beefy guy to snatch him and wrap his arms around his chest. The demon carried him onstage like a sack of potatoes.

There was a glint of joy on Adrienne's face. "Thanks for coming."

"Sure, no problem." They plopped him in another folding chair on stage and one of the other two goons went to fetch more rope.

"Friend of yours Adrienne? You know the rule: nobody's your friend. If someone is nice to you, it's because they have hurt you or are about to hurt you!"

"What kind of shitty rule—"

Before Seamus could get out another word, the guy in front of him punched him square in the face. The bells of his childhood chapel rang in his head as extreme pain vibrated through his skull. Licking at the blood running from his nose, he laughed. "That all you got, sugar?" Then blew him a kiss.

"You punch like a girl Denis," the demon holding his arms in place said.

"I do not." Denis wound up again and Seamus braced for another hit but the goon's fist stopped in midair.

Gabriel.

"No, he's right. You do." Gabriel crushed the goon's fist before spinning him around and slamming the ridge of his hand into his throat, crushing his windpipe.

As soon as he saw Gabriel step in, Seamus moved his left leg back and moved his right leg forward and stood with a jolt, seizing the goon's left arm. With a twist and spin motion, he threw him over the chair so he landed on top of his dead buddy.

Gabriel laughed. "Nice one," he said, before stomping on the demon's head for good measure. "Get a move on, Seamus. We got lucky when everyone left. Let's hope that holds."

Seamus set to work freeing Adrienne's wrists. Her mouth hung open. She said nothing. Shock. Once her hands were loose, he yanked her up and dragged her toward the door. She tugged at him and he spun around to find the angel egging on two newly emerged demons.

"What about…?" she stuttered.

"Gabriel? He can take care of himself. We need to go. Now."

Seamus wasted no time watching what came next. The demons wouldn't stand a chance.

Adrienne would have questions.

And Seamus didn't have answers to give.

Aren't we off to a great start?

****

Seamus pulled Adrienne outside the meeting facility and around a couple of corners a safe distance away from their captors for her to feel like they had some breathing room.

"Wait a minute," she huffed, sinking onto a park bench across from the Musée d'Art Brut and Art Singulier. "Those guys are…are they…did he *kill* them?" she asked. Paris had always been her safe playground, and now everywhere she looked, she saw enemies and danger. Her illusion of the city was shattered.

"Sorry, yeah. Pretty sure he did. You might want to leave Paris, go somewhere safe."

That's it? She gave Seamus a long look. He'd said it as nonchalantly as someone who needed to relocate to find a new job.

Who is this guy? Can I trust him?

Her past life experiences told her everyone wanted something from her…usually sex or money. Was Seamus like everyone else? He couldn't be. He'd risked his life and limb for her safety, asking nothing in return. For the first time, she felt a deep sense of peace just sitting next to him.

"So you rescued me so I could run away and hide? There will be a police investigation. They're probably on their way to my hotel right now."

Please don't let Seamus be pretending to be a "good guy" and then stab me in the back.

"There won't be an investigation. Somehow, you got yourself wrapped up in a secret organization, run by—"

He stopped but she wasn't going to let him get away with not answering.

"Run by who? Say it. I saw their eyes."

After today, she wasn't sure she could handle any more falsehoods. Seamus remained quiet. Maybe he was right to do so. She almost couldn't bear the truth. Of how far she'd strayed. How far she'd fallen. When someone else held up a mirror to your soul, it was more than uncomfortable. She knew in her heart she'd let Daevas lead her astray from the path of righteousness.

"You already know, Adrienne," he said, holding her hands in his. The warmth of his touch traveled up her arms and sent a wave of flurries through her body. She leaned in. The hunger in his eyes told her he wanted to kiss her. Like he had in the alley.

But he released her hands and tucked a stray lock of hair behind her ear. "I'd love to say, 'Come with me' but my path is far too dangerous for someone I want to be safe. And happy." His words were melting the walls she'd spent years building. And it scared her to death. "Please get out of Paris. Don't stick around. It won't be the cops at your door in a few hours, if you know what I mean."

The pain on his face told her his whole life had been spent avoiding this evil. She wanted to take him somewhere safe and hold him. Tell him everything would be okay. She wanted to take care of him.

From behind, she sensed a hulking form approach. Adrienne jumped and Seamus wrapped his protective arms around her. It was only Gabriel.

She broke free from Seamus and stood to face him. "What did you do? Why did you kill them?"

He patted her on the head like a puppy who'd learned to shake.

Patronizing dick.

"Just doing my job, milady. You know, sending demons back to hell. By the way, you are most welcome," he said, keeping her at arm's length.

"Who are you?"

"Did you miss Sunday school as a child or something?" He frowned. "Surely you've heard of me."

Gabriel. The bible. The annunciation. It couldn't be. "Wait, you're saying you're *the* angel Gabriel?"

"The one and only." He bowed. "Now, I'd love to stay and chat, but we saved you against my better judgment. Now run along, play nice with others, and stay away from darkwalkers."

"Where is she supposed to go, Gabe?" Seamus barked. "We've turned her world upside down and now I'm telling her to run. I know what I said before, but maybe she needs to stay with us for a while."

Gabriel crossed his arms and shook his head. "You could have been killed back there. And you know I can't let that happen. Especially over a woman. She clouds your reasoning and your purpose. She has to go."

They bickered like brothers. So it *was* Seamus who came after her. Gabriel would have let Daevas' men kill her. "I won't be a burden," she tried to say, but they weren't listening. The thought of leaving Seamus made a cavern in her heart, the pain of their possible separation making her anxious. She needed him as much as she hoped he needed her. "After that heavenly rescue, you really think you can get rid of me that easily?"

Gabriel blushed at her praise. A pulsating glow emanated from him giving soft light to the dark street corner. She covered her eyes. "Ouch. Turn that off. You smell like a warm baguette and the light hurts my eyes."

Seamus chuckled. "Turn down the charm, Romeo."

Gabriel huffed and stomped away. "Say your good-byes. We seriously have to get moving, Shay. And you know she can't come with us. I'll give you five minutes." With that, he disappeared around a corner, leaving them alone.

"Angels and demons are real?"

Seamus nodded, bowing his head. "I'm sorry. But your perfect little world isn't really perfect, if you know what I mean."

Adrienne concentrated on breathing. That was real, wasn't it? "Your choice in friends is abysmal, even if he is what, or who he says he is. But I do want to thank you for coming after me. Why did you?"

"Honor, loyalty and everyone else before myself," Seamus said, "My mantra."

"That kind of thinking will get you killed," Adrienne scoffed.

Seamus fidgeted with a pocket on his coat. "Funny. That's the kind of thinking that's allowed me to survive."

She needed more. "So it had nothing to do with me, per se. You would have saved anyone?" she asked, fishing for the answer she so desperately wanted to hear.

"I'll tell you the truth, people hurt people. That's why I pretty much avoid human contact."

"I won't hurt you, Seamus." His name rolled off her tongue like she'd said it a thousand times. She remembered the word Gabriel had called her. "What did he mean, calling me a darkwalker?"

Seamus' demeanor and expression was unreadable. "A darkwalker. A movement gaining strength in this century of selfishness. It's the people that can drive around a person who was hit by a car because they have to get to work. It's the people stepping over the bum in the street because he might have a disease. It's the people who live only for themselves in a shell of an existence."

Is that what I am? Whoa. Am I really that bad? And yet how many times had she seen people do those exact things and thought nothing of it. "And what of it?"

"The world is dying, Adrienne. Evil is winning. And those who fight are becoming fewer and fewer. The universe is about balance and lightwalkers are in the minority. But I see beauty in you. Not in your clothes or your hair or your pocketbook. I see the lightwalker inside of you, struggling to be let back out." He pulled out a knife from his pocket. "I only know of one way to help protect you in this world. To give you the sight...I saw my Father do this once." He opened the blade and dragged it along his palm. "Give me your hand."

Squeamish, she shook her head.

"Trust me. If you've ever allowed yourself to trust anyone, trust me."

She gave him her hand. The blade didn't hurt immediately, but after she saw the blood, the sting came on strong.

"Hold my hand," he instructed.

As soon as their palms touched, she saw visions in her head—Denis and Leon as the monsters they were. Red eyed demons. All her walks in Paris flashed through her mind in a second. One angel to thirty demons. One human with a trail of light among hundreds of humans dragging along their own darkness.

She was among them.

Tears fell down her cheeks. "Oh my God." The visions played backwards until she was a little girl. When she was little, running around in her back yard, playing with her friend on the swing set. Her parents sitting on the grass nearby, surrounded by a subtle white light.

She had been a lightwalker as a child, until...

Seamus held her close, allowing the portal to open. Trust for him and only him seeped into her soul. "I might not be able to take you with me right now. But who says I can't tell you where we are going." He whispered a location in her ear. "Find me. If all goes well, I vow to never leave your side again. How does that sound?"

He placed his other hand on the back of her neck and pulled her to him. When their lips touched, she felt electricity like she'd never known. Jolts of life zapped into her. Her stomach did mini back handsprings.

Her old self. Her joys and loves.

This kiss made their first kiss seem like a peck on the cheek. Seamus held her to him in desperation and they slid closer.

She didn't want it to end, but like all good things...

"Good-bye," he said loud enough for the nosy angel to hear. "I hope our paths will cross again." He winked. "My preference being anon."

Anon—Shakespearean for "soon."

He kissed the top of her head and whispered, "Keep your eyes open and be careful, but don't stare at them." He stepped into the road and hailed her a cab.

"Okay," she said, before he closed the door for her. She watched him walk away. Alone in the back of a cab with a bleeding hand, her heart began to sing.

Now is the time all right, Daevas. The time to turn my life around.

The Paris streets passed her by as she opened the window and gulped in the night air. Nighttime in the City of Light had always given her comfort, even joy. The Seine, the rich history of the ancient buildings, and the scents of perfume, cheese, and late night cafés.

But tonight, she saw a different Paris. Streets littered with dog feces left by irresponsible owners. A dirty river polluted by industry and humans...who didn't care. People stumbling home from bars, bums sleeping in alleys, and lovers whispering lies in the moonlight. All because they didn't care about anyone except themselves.

The truth was so clear now. So simple. How had she missed it?

And then there was Seamus. A hero. Not a movie star kind of hero. But a guy who asked her for nothing and came to her rescue because it was the right thing to do. A lost trait in today's world: selfless instead of selfish. A man worth pledging your loyalty to, knowing he would never let you down. Someone to cherish because they'd cherish you right back.

After sifting through all her belongings in the hotel, she opted for a small suitcase with clothes and money. She settled up with the desk clerk and turned in her key, wondering what the housekeepers would do with her useless trinkets. She caught a cab to the train station and paid her fare for the TGV which whizzed out of Paris at a determined clip.

She made her way through the cars, looking for Seamus. If this was the direction they were heading, this should be the train he'd be on. Finally, after sliding open the train's last jiggling door, there he was, along with, the shimmering angel Gabriel and the two Americans that caused all the commotion at the restaurant.

Seamus rose and greeted her with a hug. "I'm glad you made it."

"Wouldn't miss it for the world."

Gabriel huffed and rolled his eyes. "What the hell, Shay? You literally just said good-bye to her and told her where to find us?"

"Sure did. You can't exactly throw her off the train

now, can you?" They took a pair of seats a few rows ahead of the others.

"Look," she turned to them, "you need me. I'm your resident expert on Novem-Stellae and France. I know I can help you. I've read more on Mont St. Michel than anyone. I could probably walk around there blindfolded!"

"You told her where we're going?" Gabriel didn't hide his astonishment.

"Look," she continued, "if it hadn't been for you motley bunch of yahoos, my world wouldn't have imploded and I wouldn't be running away from Paris." *And I'd still be living in my bubble of bullshit and self-delusions going to meetings run by a human who works with demons! Maybe I should be thanking them.*

"I don't think we've officially met," one of the Americans said, rising and kissing her hand. "I'm Dean Rowe."

She inclined her head.

"Now can you recap how to you came to be with this 'motley bunch'?"

"Well, let me see," Adrienne started, "I was having a nice quiet dinner alone—"

"With me," Gabriel rose his hand.

"When you showed up to ruin my evening. And then you," she said, pointed to Seamus, "stormed in followed by these brash Americans—"

"Wait, *you're* American," Gabriel clarified.

"I gave up my citizenship years ago. I consider myself French," she said, a piece of her heart tugging to get back on American soil.

Dean cleared his throat and pretended to straighten a non-existent tie. "I'd like to protest being called brash. Americans get a bad rap. I'd say we're more 'rude' and 'uncultured.' But I definitely protest the word 'brash.'"

A part of Adrienne's bantering brain kicked in. If these four boys thought they were so funny, she'd hunker down and give them a run for their money on sarcasm and wit. "Fine, rude is assumed when we discuss Americans. And uncivilized is certainly a given. That was actually an add-on with the word 'brash.' But I'll retract it if it offends your delicate sensibilities." She refocused on Dean. "So when the *Americans* created a ruckus and decided to grace us with a fist fight in a Parisian restaurant, I was whisked outside where Seamus here, promptly decided a heavy make-out session would somehow shield me from danger," she teased.

Gabriel sniffed. "Never thought you had it in you, Shay."

"But I *was* trying to protect you. And it worked, didn't it?" Seamus had a childlike innocence to his voice that made a piece of her cold heart warm a little.

She squeezed his knee. "Oh sure, it worked great until I was abducted by people I thought were my friends but are really a part of an evil secret society out for…what are they out for?"

"World dominion?" Dean offered.

"Shifting the moral compass," Seamus said.

Gabriel shook his head. "Try creating hell on earth, idiots."

Adrienne scooted out and lifted her bag to place it in the overhead compartment. Seamus rose to assist her, stowing it away with a smile. "I've got it," he said.

"Well, this has been nothing but educational and

informative, and I'm so looking forward to visiting the last place in this country I've been wanting to see, but then I'll see about finding a new home, thank-you-very-much."

"What do you mean?" Seamus held her wrist and a change came over his polite and innocent demeanor. The flicker of some greater knowledge than he'd already imparted about life and the universe was right there, staring at her for one second and then…it disappeared.

She'd hoped he'd respond like that. Because the only place she felt at home, was by his side. But how do you tell someone that? Someone you just met.

****

Seamus could do nothing but beg in an urgent whisper. "Do not erase her memory, Gabriel. She knows nothing of who or what we truly are. She needs the little bit of the knowledge she gained today to be safe. Why were you having dinner with her to begin with? Who are you to decide who is worth saving?"

She slept with the most adorable snorts and puffs of breath, bouncing gently up and down with the click-clack of the train. Dean was crunching on a snack from his bag and Lucas held his ever quiet, hyper-vigilant lookout.

Dean held up his hand. "Let me get this straight. The mighty angel Gabriel who told Mary she'd been impregnated by the Holy Spirit and dictated the Koran to Mohammed now saves hot darkwalkers for kicks? How the mighty have fallen, huh?"

"Shut up, Seer," Gabriel sniffed.

"I've asked you for nothing." Seamus ignored the American though he completely agreed with him.

"Literally nothing. My whole bloody life. Can you do this one thing for me?" Seamus needed the angel's word. If Gabriel erased Adrienne's memories, she'd still have his blood coursing through her veins and yet have no memory of him. *Of them.*

"Fine," Gabriel said. "For now. But if she becomes a liability to our cause, she *will* be eliminated. Understood?"

"Eliminated?" Dean piped up. "What are we playing, a game or something? I'm here to help my sister. That's it."

Seamus opened his mouth to speak, but closed it again. Seamus knew where the cup was as well as Gabriel. But no one said Gabriel would even let him near it, let alone lend it to these two. The seer, Lucas barely spoke. Always faraway. And yet the story of his wife and her coma hit Seamus hard. Would the cup even work to save her?

It's not like Lucas was allowed to check out the cup with a divine library card or anything.

"Enough babble from all of you. Speak no more until we reach our destination. There are prying ears everywhere," Gabriel chided.

Truth be told, Seamus placed more stock in the words of these Americans than in the mighty angel Gabriel who always had his own agenda. Like the time he'd told him they were in charge of relocating Jesus' burial cloth from the House of Savoy to the Holy See. Seamus was able to examine the woven herringbone twill cloth with dried blood in the image of the holy face of Jesus. Too late, Seamus realized they'd tricked the Holy See, keeping the real shroud and passing a forgery to the Vatican. No matter how many times he asked about it, Gabriel would never comment about the exchange. Only saying cryptic things like, "It had to be done."

Dean moaned in frustration. Not talking would affect this guy the most. The American sure liked the sound of his own voice.

Gabriel rolled his eyes. "Do I need to tie your tongues? Because I'll do it! It's not safe to talk until we reach the cathedral."

The door slid open and let in the rankest smell Seamus' nostrils had ever encountered. Three Parisian demons. The pungent odor of moldy cheese and rotten wine vomit filled the cabin.

The demons stopped in the aisle beside Seamus. "Gabe, what's up? It has seriously been way too long, my brother from our estranged Father. How is Pop?"

Seamus watched Lucas pretend to be involved in reading a map while Dean—who would be a terrible undercover agent—glared at the demons like a bar roughian looking for his next fight. His white-knuckled fists gripped the arm of his seat.

Gabriel cracked his neck and stood up. "You want to have a go with me, Vassago?"

"Hell yeah," said the one with shaggy blond hair and pointy nose. "Who are the humans?"

Before his words were out, Seamus was on his feet, twisting the arm of the demon, and shoving a dagger in his back. The demon disappeared with pop and a flash.

Dean jumped over the back of his chair and had the second demon on the ground pummeling him. The demon created an illusion of his body turning to jagged spikes, which Seamus dissolved so Dean wouldn't get hurt. As soon as Dean's blade pierced the fiend's skin, he dissolved in a black fog.

Adrienne screamed. The third demon had grabbed her by the hair and was dragging her toward the exit. Seamus reached for his blade realizing he'd already lost it sending the first demon home.

"Hey," he heard Lucas say.

Being a seer did have its perks. Everything happened in slow motion and he could see actions long before they occurred. Lucas threw a knife and Seamus spun knowing exactly which direction the demon would move.

The knife whizzed by Seamus.

The demon had a perplexed look on his face when he went to pull out the knife lodged between his ribs. His words were garbled from the blood spilling from his mouth. Then in a flash of black mist, he was gone. Seamus rushed forward grasping Adrienne's outstretched hand before she toppled out the open door. "I got ya," he said pulling her close.

She clung to him, wide-eyed, her whole body trembling. "This was a mistake. I shouldn't have come."

"Shh," he whispered in her hair, pulling her into a seat next to him.

"Damn, I lost another knife," Lucas said.

"Bravo!" Gabriel clapped his hands in what Seamus read as outright glee. "I haven't had this much fun in centuries. You two can stay!"

Lucas pulled his sleeve back down to cover his throwing knives. "We don't want to stay. We came for one thing and we're not leaving without it."

There was a creaking of brakes and a subtle forward pull, the train was stopping.

"This is where I must leave you. I will meet you at our destination," Gabriel said. Then he vanished.

Chapter 13

Novum-Stellae Headquarters, Paris

Agitation pinched at the demon, Nara. "Tell me everything you know about this Adrienne Perdu," she demanded.

Daevas knew better than to show any demon disrespect, much less the daughter of the Ambassador of Hell.

"Not much. She was a perfect candidate for the organization. Distraught from losing her parents, strikingly wealthy and fiercely private. We bled most of her wealth and the rest she's signed off to us in her will. She was a regular at the weekly meetings. How could she have betrayed us? Been in the company of *them*?" he asked.

"That's exactly the type of information I need you douchebags to find out," the pitch of her voice rose. "Yesterday!"

"May I inquire as to how your father is?" Daevas should have kept his mouth shut. She backhanded him across the face.

"He's bloody-well perfect. Think of us as one and the same. My orders are on his authority."

"Yes, of course. Anything you wish. Please just tell me what to do."

Once she'd given her instructions to Daevas, she

left the room to call her father in private. "Put the phone to his ear," she instructed the caretaker.

"Daddy, I've found Gabriel. He will lead us to the cup."

Heavy breathing and a gurgling sound came from the phone. "Forget...about...me," he labored. "Stay the course. Find the Ring of Solomon."

Nara's family had led the darkwalker movement for decades and just when it was exploding with new members, enough to secure their family's power seat, Lucas Rojas showed up.

It was five years ago when Nara had finally reconnected with the angel she had always hoped would stand by her side. And when Shane O'Grady came back into her life, she took one look at his angelic face and decided on her life's goal...to make him fall.

And fall he did, but not on her terms. She found he still pined for his human college fling, Calise Rowe who happened to be dating the seer she was hunting.

Shane's abject jealously overtook him and he fell from grace while on the verge of raping his beloved Calise.

Bastard. Even though he left Calise to die. Even though Shane fathered *their* child. It had been a lie. She'd never won him over from Calise. She knew that now and it only made her want him dead even more.

Nara would not be duped by him again. And Shane would never get to see their daughter, Melki again. Not over her dead body. Not after that stunt. Jumping out of the car to see if that bitch was still breathing! After he'd vowed to kill her.

No matter.

It had worked out fine. Or it would. Lucas' Aunt

had weakened her father, Abaddon, the Ambassador of Hell and leader of the Darkwalkers, to the point where he was bedridden and needed around the clock care. For five years she'd searched for a cure. And now it was within her grasp. She had a plan. If Lucas was after the Cup to save Calise, she'd let him find it. But not to save Calise.

She needed it to save her father.

To bring him back to his full power.

And then kill them all. Herself.

And now Daevas had one of his own on the inside with the ragtag group of seers and the angel Gabriel...some darkwalker named Adrienne. Why her father was so damn concerned with the lost ring confounded her. "Why the ring? Why are you always talking about the ring? I have people looking. There's nothing. I'm closer to getting the Cup."

"Keep...looking, for the ring," Abaddon forced out the words. "Before the others find it." The phone line went dead.

The others. Abaddon was worried Asmodeus would find it first. The demon had been tricked and trapped by the archangel Gabriel in the days of Solomon. But there was another player in the mix as well. A wild card.

The archangel Raphael was also hell bent on finding the ring and no one knew what team he was playing for these days. His true love, the demon Anna, was back in hell. And word was, Raphael was turning over every stone to find the ring to control the demons and have her released.

But then what?

The ring offered the owner power over both

demons and *jinn*. It also allowed the wearer to control the weather and the ability to talk to animals. In the wrong hands…

She laughed.

She *was* the wrong hands.

With a snap of her fingers, two minions lumbered into her room. "Redouble the efforts to use our sources to locate the ring. And make sure we do not lose sight of Lucas Rojas."

"Yes, Ma'am," they bowed and backed out of the room.

Five year old Melki padded in a few minutes later with her nanny. Her daughter was the only sight that brought any warmth to her cold heart. The little demoness pulled her hand free from the nanny and hopped into her mom's lap. Nara stroked her long black hair.

"Can you play with me?" the child asked.

"Mommy's busy, dear. I'm sure—"

Melki cut her off. "Daddy would play with me. When is he coming home?"

Rage surged through Nara. The girl's memory needed altering again. When would this child learn? She rocked her back and forth and entered her mind erasing the girl's memories of Shane until she snored lightly and went limp in her lap.

"Take her," she instructed the nanny. "And keep her busy. What the hell do I pay you for?"

The nanny bowed, apologizing profusely and carried the little girl out of the room. Nara should send her away to a private school, but some part of her couldn't do it. When she was eighteen and came into her full power, she'd understand. She'd pick Nara over

Shane. But children were fickle, foolishly thinking they could love two parents who hated each other.

It was childish not to choose sides. And for her daughter's sake Nara hoped Melki grew up quickly and stood beside her family, forsaking her loser father.

However, right now, she needed to concentrate on two things: stealing the cup from Lucas when he finally attained it so she could heal her father, and obtaining the Ring of Solomon to secure her family's stronghold over demons, *jinn*, and humans alike.

Chapter 14

TGV Train, France

Adrienne's thoughts betrayed her after a demon almost threw her out of a moving train. She wished she'd never laid eyes on this bunch of jackass men. Maybe Seamus was using her? Maybe he was another damn liar. Like all other men: just out to get his dick wet. She had been perfectly fine surrounded with nothingness and she wasn't about to entertain silly girlish ideas of love at this point in her life.

Since her parents' death, she'd let hate seep inside of her.

Hate was alive, a flowing entity. Jealousy and lust. Wanting those she hated destroyed and miserable. And who cared? Her thoughts weren't guns. She couldn't pierce skin with her words. Fuck people. Fuck happy fake people. Fuck everything. Seamus couldn't save her. *Show her the light.* They'd called her a "darkwalker." If she walked in the dark, fine. She wanted to stay there. The dark was safe and cool and never abandoned her for something better or died in a senseless plane crash. The dark was loyal to her and would never disappear in the night. And so she gathered the darkness around her and moved forward into each new day.

Fuck living breathing anything. She wished the

world and her misery would end and she could retreat into the darkness forever.

The knot in her stomach was a spot of permanent encampment and she welcomed the pain. It reminded her to trust no one, rely on no one, and show herself to no one. Love was not real. People never did the right thing unless it was the right thing for themselves.

Anger when it finally consumed a person, just sat there. Dormant. Waiting. Seething. In every small daily activity, it waited. Anger was patient. Adrienne's anger was beyond patient.

"Adrienne," someone said, loosening the knot in her stomach.

Her name was repeated over and over again.

"Snap out of it!"

The voice was soothing and familiar, like a life rope descending to her in the cold abyss. But she did not reach out her hand to grab the rope.

Her cheek was caressed. People were yelling at her. She lay motionless. Lifeless. It was pure peace. No pain. No agony. No love. No…Seamus.

It was the lips on hers that brought her out of it. Soft, tender. Not needy but so very insistent. She puckered her own lips and let one word escape, "Seamus."

"That a girl, c'mon back to us."

When she blinked, she found Seamus staring at her, desperation saturating his features. Where had she been? Dark thoughts. In a dark, lifeless place. No feeling. No emotion. It was so…easy.

"Listen to me. That demon holding you, it did something to you. I need you to come back to us. To me. Come away from the darkness."

His voice was steady. It would have been so simple to fall into nothingness. Let her soul go willingly down the path of least resistance. To feel only the pleasures she could well afford. But her skin prickled and the sensation reminded her of life. Living. Even with all the pain and suffering, there was beauty everywhere. And maybe even love.

She sucked in air and sat up. Seamus was by her side. "What happened to me?" She looked down at her arm, the dark fog rising from her skin visible. "What is this?"

"Shake it off," Dean said. "Push it away. Be stronger than *it*."

Closing her eyes, she willed the darkness to leave her and begged to be allowed back in the light. When she reopened them, the darkness had faded like the morning fog. Nothing more rose from her skin. Not darkness. But also, no light.

"Come with me," Seamus led her far away from the others, unwrapped a sandwich, and handed it to her. "Eat this."

"You saved my life. Look, back there, when the demon's touched me…" She couldn't put her feelings into words and didn't want to.

"Listen, let's focus on something else. Tell me what you know about the sunken cathedral. Because we're here."

For Adrienne, the sunken cathedral was supposed to be the first stop on many exciting sightseeing ventures when her parents landed in Paris. But that trip, the one Adrienne's mother was most excited about, never happened.

And now here she was. Without them.

The demon's touch brought negative emotions to the surface, like her anger that her parents were long dead and she was now about to visit Mont-Saint-Michel without her mother by her side. When they got off the TGV train in Rennes, they arranged for a driver to take them the 60 kilometers to their destination. Once in the car, Adrienne pushed down her negativity, instead giving them all the history of Mont-Saint-Michel she had in her mental database.

A tidal island in the Normandy region of France, Mont-Saint-Michel appeared in pictures to be more a place of fantasy than reality. A rock looming over a desert of sand and water that was twice daily surrounded by tides. The story went that the archangel Michael appeared to St. Aubert, a bishop of Avranches in a dream and asked him to build a church on the top of the rock called Mont Tombe.

Thirty permanent residents ran the hotel, restaurants, and souvenir shops lining the stone streets hugging the winding road leading to the monastery where seven Benedictine monks lived. Two million visitors per year came to take in the view of the expanse of sand and sea sitting under the watchful eye of the gilded statue of St. Michel perched atop the spire of the abbey church. Legend held the tides came in with the speed of a galloping horse. When the tides receded, they left behind quick sand with a fragile dry crust.

The car bumped along the narrow causeway leading to the monastery past grazing herds of the world's only saltwater plant-eating sheep. The driver opened the car door as vehicles could travel no further. Adrienne let her mouth gape. The cathedral sat at the top of the island like a castle. The city was built around it like stepping stones rising upwards. And how it glowed! Even in the sunlight. Majestic and serene.

She reached for Seamus' hand as they kept pace with the tiny city's other tourists, making their way up the rampart's stone stairs to the first overlook. Adrienne rested her elbows on the cold rocks and took in the vast expanse of nothing. The tide was low, so the fortress was surrounded by vacant shoreline.

Adrienne's tears began to fall. She allowed the memories to trickle in, like the tiny rivers threatening to rush the cathedral at high tide. She remembered the last conversation she had with her mother:

"Mom, I've seen so many old churches since I've been here. It's a day trip all the way to Normandy. Besides, it's probably just another dirty old church."

Adrienne's mother frowned over Skype. These live video chats with her parents in the states kept Adrienne grounded. She hated being so far away from the people she loved the most. "Can you please grant your mother this one wish?"

Adrienne laughed. "I will go, of course. But I have so many other beautiful things to show you instead. Why that Mont-Saint-Whatever place?"

"It was named after my favorite angel—Michael— the leader of the army against Satan's forces. Scripture even suggest that Jesus *is* the archangel Michael. So who knows? Besides, it gets surrounded by water twice daily as the tides come in and out, and the sheep are a delicacy, and the monks there are—"

"Yes, yes, fine. I'll book the trip. Now finish packing and have a safe flight. I'll be at the airport waiting for you!"

"Good-bye, Adrienne. We love you, sweetie."

Good-bye Adrienne. We love you, sweetie.

The last words her mom ever spoke to her. Why hadn't she asked to talk to her dad? She should have told him how much she loved him. How lucky she was to have parents who trusted her, and understood her need to travel, and…

She'd never see her mom's smile again.

Never have her dad's arm wrapped around her shoulder.

Never get to laugh and share food and culture in a country she'd grown to love.

And over what? A malfunctioning plane.

Afterward, she'd wanted to slap everyone who told her God had a "master plan." *Horseshit.* She didn't believe in a master plan anymore. She wasn't even sure she believed in God anymore. But hanging out with angels and demons puts things in perspective fast.

With Daevas and the Novem-Stellae, she'd chosen to believe in herself. Realize life was short. With no hope of a happily-ever-after in this life or the next. Her plan? Run out of money or get old and die alone in a nursing home.

Yee-mother-fucking-ha.

Yet, here she was. In awe of a structure built centuries ago based on faith and standing next to a man who had more faith in her than she'd ever had in herself.

She continued telling them about Mont-Saint-Michel and how badly her mother had wanted to come here. The story went that the archangel Michael poked a hole in the skull of a bishop who wasn't listening to him. Is that what she needed done, so she would open her mind and heart once again?

"I'm so sorry about your parents," Seamus squeezed her hand.

They followed the tourist-laden path stopping at a patisserie where she ordered a *pain au chocolat* and a *tarte aux fraises*. Her diet was ruined anyway. She might as well splurge. Seamus and the Americans must have been famished based on the amount of food they ordered.

After they all ate, Adrienne took the lead as they made their way through the thin, winding corridors toward the fortress-like cathedral. Rounding each corner, she found herself straining to see the golden spire at the top of the cathedral. The streets were much like any other French town with small buildings so close together they almost share a wall. But here they climbed up, circling the rocky island as the streets led higher and higher. As it was late in the season, there were less tourists exploring the small gift shops, hotels, and restaurants than she expected.

She felt safer than she had in years. Was it Seamus by her side?

Certainly, it wasn't the protection coming from some parent-killing God.

Seamus made her feel like she could still be a part of something great. But it was an elusive and fleeting feeling. Something she could scrape with her nails, but not find a handhold to grab onto.

When they reached the abbey, Seamus and the Americans went inside to look around while Adrienne stayed outside to soak up the midday sun. The abbey had an open courtyard with upside down U-shaped supports. She paused at another overlook.

"You okay?" he asked.

She nodded. "I'll be right in. Give me a minute."

Seamus gave her hand a squeeze before heading into the church with Dean and Lucas.

Engulfed and then released by the rhythmic tides, this rock fortress had turreted walls defending the small city. The church sat at the pinnacle in full regalia, a crown for the surrounding barren landscape, its bell towers reaching to the clouds.

Something dark fluttered on the horizon and she shielded her face with her hand. The tourists here seemed to be looking every other direction. It couldn't be a crow. It was too big for a crow. Giant black wings and…legs?

Squinting to get a better look, the thing glared at her with ruby eyes, squatted to ground on the greenish-gray mud flat, then rocketed into the air and out of sight.

She looked around. *Did anyone else see that?*

She should she tell someone! Seamus, or one of the monks. Since she and Seamus shook hands and exchanged blood on that park bench, her whole world view was upside down. She hadn't even told him about the train. About how the demon's eyes burned red, his skin felt like tanned leather and with every other blink, she glimpsed his hideous visage. Now was she really seeing demons flying around Mont-Saint-Michel?

Rushing inside the church, she was met with rows and rows of benches for the righteous. Her head swam and she took a seat staring forward instead of at the wooden ceilings. The entire place was empty except for a group of men whispering in pews near the front.

Seamus' familiar voice brought her back into focus. She caught the intensity in his voice as he and the others spoke to a bald monk in a brown robe with a roped belt who maintained a serene, yet unconcerned face.

Sliding in the pew behind them, she tapped Seamus on the shoulder. "Sorry to interrupt, but we've got company. I saw someone outside."

The monk made a rolling motion with his hand indicating she could speak.

"Well, maybe I saw it wrong, but…" The go-ahead-and-tell-us look on Seamus' face gave her confidence. He had something she'd conveniently forgotten existed…compassion. "I saw something with black wings and red eyes land in the sand then fly up into the air. But first, he looked at me. And it wasn't a bird if you know what I mean."

The monk held up his two index fingers at shoulder height and ran them along an invisible line to his hips.

Adrienne looked to Seamus and the Americans.

"It was humanoid?" Seamus interpreted.

She nodded.

"They know we're here," Lucas said. "We haven't much time."

****

Seamus didn't like having to drag her by the wrist behind the monks, but she was stubborn! There was no way he was going to let her stay out in the open…in harm's way. He needed to know she was safe.

"You can't keep leading me around like an animal," she started again. "Look, I can help! And I'm an independent woman who doesn't need to have doors held for her, doesn't need a man who can cook for her…"

Seamus laughed a little on the inside as she

continued to tick off unnecessary male attributes because he was a pro at every one.

"…don't need a man to be protector. I can protect myself you know. I don't need—Wait, a second. Where are we going anyway?"

The private quarters of the Benedictine monks was a simple affair. They ate in a generous kitchen heated with the only wood burners in the cathedral, slept in plain rooms on simple cots with one chair, and a window. Their particular sect's vow of silence was proving inconvenient, so Seamus had latched onto the monk that could do American Sign Language as well as monastic signing and tried to convince him the importance of breaking their vow, if the need arose.

Gabriel and Dean were already in the kitchen, sharing a simple meal around a wooden table while Lucas sat off to the side, sharpening a knife.

The Americans rose when Adrienne entered. "Sit down gentleman. Adrienne believes chivalry to be an unnecessary evil and long since dead. We wouldn't want to give her the wrong idea, would we?"

He felt an elbow jab him in the ribs before Lucas and Dean sat back down with a chuckle.

Gabriel had remained seated, in deep repose staring out a small window. "Tell us, darkwalker. Who followed you? And who do you really work for?"

Wrestling out of Seamus' grip, she huffed. "Stop calling me that! And no one followed me. I don't work for anyone."

"So you have no loyalty to either side then. Is that what you are saying?" Gabriel said.

"Enough," Seamus snapped. One of the monks held up his first three fingers and let his index finger touch his mouth twice. Then tapped his right hand over his left wrist.

"The tide is coming in tonight?" Seamus asked.

The monk nodded.

"Maybe that will work in our favor. Is there any way to bless the water as it rushes in? Plus, at the close of the business today, we should try to clear the island and close the roads. What do we have, two, maybe three hours?" Seamus turned again to the monk, who nodded in reply.

"Is anyone going to tell me what's going on around here?" Adrienne asked.

"No," they all replied in unison. Seamus bolted the door and stood there with his arms crossed in case she wanted to make a break for it.

"For now, let's say, whoever kidnapped you before sent in reinforcements," Lucas offered.

"Can you stop sharpening knives for one bloody second? It's like nails on a chalkboard," Seamus said.

"You'll thank me later. We all need sharp minds and weapons if we hope to get through this alive…" Lucas replaced one knife back into its sheath to start another. "If we help you ward off this attack, can we finally discuss the exchange of the item in question? My time is short. I will fight, *if* I know I am leaving with what I came for."

"I'm sure arrangements can be made." Seamus knew the cup was here. And he would make sure Lucas and Dean left with it in their possession. With or without Gabriel's "permission."

"Yes, yes of course." Gabriel put his feet up and laced his fingers behind his neck.

How did I get stuck with this angel? Seamus

wondered. Their rocky relationship had consisted of the two of them harping on each over the same thing over the years: Gabriel: "Have a child. Or the line of Joseph of Arimathea dies," and Seamus: "I am a vagabond and like it. I don't care. Leave me alone."

Oddly enough, Seamus was feeling a shift occur within him. Adrienne, her expression now softened, stood by his side. Deep in his soul, he felt a connection and warmth for her like nothing he'd felt ever before in his life. She was a reason to fight and live. She'd given him hope.

Even Gabriel seemed less and less concerned with Seamus' safety, maybe finally hoping the gig was up and he could hitch a one-way ticket back upstairs and stop babysitting his family line.

It's not like moving every few months was the lot in life Seamus wanted. It was thrust upon him to survive the demons chasing the artifacts he'd inherited. Then again, he didn't choose his lot in life. But no one wants to be born with an angel breathing over their shoulder who pushes biblical responsibilities. What good had come of protecting these artifacts for two millennia anyway? The world had grown more evil and selfish with or without Seamus' help. Maybe he should give Lucas all the artifacts if he was such a great seer and fighter of demons. Leave him and his lineage out of it.

And then he and Adrienne could...

Seamus had to table that thought for now. He redirected his attention to Lucas and Dean. "So what are we up against?"

Lucas shrugged. "It depends. Fighting a few demons whose goal is to bring Adrienne back and question her is one thing—"

"More demons?" she asked.

Dean snorted. "I'm finding out there's no end to them, sister. Want to help? Fight legions of Satan's minions and then Gabe here can erase your memory. Then you can go back to your prissy former existence in ignorant bliss? Sound fun?"

The look of horror on Adrienne's face made Seamus wrap a protective arm around her shoulder. "You won't be fighting any demons."

Dean stood up and checked the aim of his newly modified shotgun out the window. "I'm kidding. Don't get your panties in a bunch. You'd get us all killed. All Lucas and I want is to get what we came for and boogie board back to the states."

"Wait a minute, so you buffoons are saying…" Adrienne started.

"Shhhhhh," Gabriel held a finger to his lips and Adrienne's eyes went vacant. She sat down like an obedient child on the floor and crossed her legs. Her mouth stayed clamped shut.

"Is this necessary?" Seamus said, sitting next to her and holding her hand.

"She can hear and process what we're saying, but I'm not going to listen to her whine and ask a million questions. And to think I was trying to save her! She's really quite annoying."

"Damn man, that's harsh," Dean said.

"You try trailing along behind his bloodline for centuries and tell me how *not* to become apathetic about the fate of humanity. I was sent to do one job. That's it. I've done it. And honestly, at this rate with the forty-year old virgin here," his thumb aimed at Seamus, "my gig should be up soon. So…yeah. Yippee-ki-yea."

Dean mouth was agape.

"I'm not a virgin, Gabe."

"Pretty sure you are."

"Am not."

"Are too."

Lucas got up. "I'm in a room of imbeciles! Both of you need to shut up. I want my wife to live! To do that, we need the cup and to get out of here. I will work with you if you two will work with me. Agreed?"

Sullen, they both nodded.

"Now," Lucas continued, "the tide comes in tonight. Gabriel, can you and the monks bless the water when it rushes in, make it holy water?"

"I see where you're going," Gabriel had a twinkle in his eye, even though Lucas was only reiterating ideas Seamus had already suggested.

"Dean and I will bar the road and then wait in the courtyard. Seamus, you and Adrienne make sure everyone gets off this island. Pull fire alarms, get those hotels to kick everyone off for tonight. The less human casualties the better. Then you two…hide."

"Hide? That's what I'm supposed to do?" Seamus huffed.

"It's what you do best," Gabriel said with smirk.

Chapter 15

Eastbound on Highway 14 outside of Spring Green, Wisconsin

"Put these on," Shane tossed Ellen a department store bag after his stop at the mall. "And don't forget the gloves." What the hell was he going to do with her?

He hoped she could contain herself, but succubus blood was not going to be an easy thing to resist. For anyone. And not only for the person affected. For anyone near them. And he was no angel...anymore.

Even being near Ellen, he felt it. He felt *her*. Like she pulsed a wave of mind-numbing electrical stimulation that went right to his...

"How does this look?"

Her long arms, even covered in the long, black, satin gloves begged to be touched, especially now that she was back to her human form. He wanted to reach out and entwine his fingers through hers but even that innocent gesture would be dangerous.

"You're still oozing sex through every pore of the fabric." He stared at the road.

Fingers dressed in ebony made their way up his thigh toward... "Stop it!" He slapped her away.

She slinked back to her side of the car. "Shane, you're going to have to shackle me or something. I literally can't help it."

"So, it has nothing to do with my great body or my stellar personality then?" he tried to joke. He'd always seen her as off-limits. As Calise's best friend and an angel to boot. It was only her tainted succubus blood talking. She'd never want anything to do with a loser like him.

"No, I would have sex with anything breathing at this point. It's not you, I swear!"

There is my answer. But there was no escaping her pulsing essence that filled the space between them and hit him square in his manhood. "Gee, thanks. Good to know."

"Sorry Shane. I didn't mean it like that," he glanced over long enough to see her blush. "It's not like you're not...well, you know."

He laughed at her backpedaling. "No worries, fruitcake. But I can't bring you in public like this. So what do you want to do?"

She gave him a sly smile.

He huffed and shook his head. He needed her by his side. Badly. So he'd have to take one for the team.

****

Ellen eyed the hotel room with distaste. It was the cheapest hotel in Madison but for their needs, it would suffice. The unholy succubus blood was more in control than she was. She had no choice but to let it course through her veins controlling her every sense and emotion hoping one day it would ease and she'd be herself—and hopefully still an angel—again.

Shane approached her from behind while she poured him a drink. They'd stopped for a bottle of Patron and Triple Sec per his request. Ellen lined the glass with complimentary coffee sugar and added some of the lime juice she'd added to their shopping cart.

The voice inside her head told her having Shane thrust deep inside her would ease the pain. Her skin felt like millions of needles were pricking at her. She ached for release. She told herself she'd erase his memory after they were done. He'd never remember. A necessity.

But why? the voice said, *He might want to remember.*

After handing him the drink and letting him take it down in one swallow, she peeled off her gloves, spread her fingers, and ran a hand from the base of his neck up his head and through his hair. It felt heavenly.

I shouldn't.

He's fallen. He almost killed my best friend.

But for this moment in time, none of that mattered. All was forgotten except this. The here and now of *them.*

Deep down, she'd always wanted this. Wanted him. But he had been off limits. First as Calise's lover. Then, as her worst enemy.

The lust of her blood took over and Ellen could do nothing but let it unfold.

She guided his shaky hands down the front of her shirt and into her unbuttoned pants. He slid one finger inside her and she moaned and threw back her head. He seemed resistant but his glassy eyes told another story. He was hers and couldn't resist her.

The power alone was more intoxicating than any drug.

He was weak to her spell and she enjoyed the domination.

"Ellen...I can't stop..." Shane's voice was like the

buttercream frosting on a birthday cake. Sticking your finger in to have the first taste. Shane was the first lick and Ellen only wanted more. An insatiable desire to be carnally satisfied coursed through her blood. His body would placate her desires for now, but he'd need to rinse and repeat, because before they'd even started, she was already hungry for more.

"I'm sorry about Calise…," he murmured, withdrawing his hand from her pants. But he wasn't stopping. With two free hands, he slid off her jeans and helped her step out of them.

"Shh." She lifted his face to hers and placed a gentle finger over her lips. "We both love her. But tonight, we need each other."

The heat of his touch seared her shoulders.

"I've been a bad girl, Shane. Even before today, I've thought about you. You're the only angel I've ever wanted."

Shut up! She admonished herself for letting that slip.

"I've always wanted you, too, El."

She let his words sing around their airspace and penetrate her hollow heart. She was going to erase this memory anyway. And even though she knew she should walk away from him right now, she didn't have the will or the strength.

****

He picked up her sublime naked form and carried her to the bed, drizzling kisses down her neck without touching her lips, like that was too sacred. Her heavenly glow saturated the room and warmed his corporeal body. A low moan escaped his lips and he sank onto the bed pressing his mouth on hers and tasting her sweetness. The scent of jasmine and her ambrosia flavor gave him an instant erection. She arched her hips and he met her body with force.

Some sane part of his brain told him to stop. That this was wrong and no good would come from it. But that part of his mind became a quiet echo against the overriding deluge of the roaring waterfall of lust.

"Don't stop, it's fine. I promise you won't remember."

Her voice melted him like music from a fine German classical guitar made of spruce and Brazilian rosewood. "Maybe I don't want to forget, El."

The succubus surfaced, begging for attention. Ellen's eyes changed to red-black diamonds. A growl escaped her lips and she rolled her head back. "Enter me," a voice other than Ellen's commanded him.

He was a slave to the demon's desire and obeyed.

"No," she pushed him off. "In your true form, I see him ripping at your skin trying to come out and play."

Oh hell, no. She did not just ask that. He might kill her if his demon form took over. He stood and took a step toward the dresser. "El, I can't…"

She licked her lips and gave him a naughty smile. "Will this help?" She eased into the demon form the *jinn* had taught her to use as a cloak.

Shane couldn't hold back his beast any longer.

He roared in defeat as his demon form took hold and he mounted her, ripping at her hair and pushing his enormity inside her. Screaming in delight, he continued to ravage her through the night, ripping at her with his claws and allowing his load to spill inside her over and over again.

****

Sleeping with Shane had seemed like a good idea…until the next morning. Ellen erased his memory in the angelic tongue while he snoozed next to her. She limped her battered and beaten body to the shower and took stock of herself in the mirror while the water was heating up. He'd been a monster in bed, literally.

The succubus blood inside her smiled back at the mirror, barely satisfied and already hungry for more.

While the succubus sang, Ellen cried, the tears of her actions washing down the drain along with her secret hopes of Shane ever having real feelings for her. That wasn't at all what she'd wanted with him. She'd donned a demonic image and drove him to this. She couldn't bear to be with him as herself, to look at him through her own eyes.

She reminded herself this was a spell. A trick.

It wasn't *her* Shane wanted. It was the succubus in her blood.

It would never be *her*.

She stepped out of the shower mouthing a silent prayer he'd never remember last night and somehow she would forget it, too.

****

Shane was punching digits in his phone and checking his messages. "I have a lead. The next artifact to be hit is at Holy Hill. That's less than two hours from here. Ready?"

"Who is your contact?" she asked, grabbing fresh clothes so she could dress in the bathroom, in privacy.

"Remember that slimy demon I threw out of the frat house back in the day?"

"Sure," she yelled through the closed door, remembering the night all too well.

"He works for Nara's family and doesn't yet know I've left her. He's a double agent. Working for Nara's family and some other faction out in Vegas which bids out his services. I've known for a while but didn't do anything about it until now. I promised to let him live if he rats out the Vegas faction. Turns out, they are the ones behind all these artifact thefts. I just can't figure out why. Or at least, why now. We need to get moving."

Ellen nodded, gathering her things and following him to the car. She already missed the crazy sex demon who'd called her "El." As far as Shane knew, she was keeping this succubus thing on a short leash and they'd caught a quick nap for a few hours at this shady hotel after the attack in Spring Green.

That couldn't be further from the truth.

After covering up the last of her exposed skin, she slid into the car next to Shane. "Ready?" he asked with a wink.

Her hair was pulled back into a ponytail so he couldn't see the bare patches where he'd clawed out chunks of her hair. Makeup hid the bruises on her face and sunglasses rounded out her disguise. "I'm always ready." She put a hand over her mouth warning her inner succubus to shut up for two freaking seconds.

Shane shot her a sideways glance and shifted the car into drive. "Simmer down, there missy. I know I inspire all kinds of fantasies and such, but let's stick to the plan. Can you promise me that? Just stick to the plan."

Ellen nodded, turning an invisible key to her mouth and tossed it out the window.

He pulled onto Interstate 94 and headed east

toward Lake Michigan. "If we can both go in cloaked and not give ourselves away, maybe we can find what these demons are really looking for. And why."

"Can we get a bite to eat first? I'm starving." Ellen didn't try to muffle the growling of her stomach. A fast food sign stood at attention in the distance and she pointed in that direction.

Shane sighed and hurried them through the drive-through. Less than two hours later, they rounded the steep bend and made their way up to Holy Hill. Ellen had been here many times, including when the Shrine was elevated to the status of Basilica in 2006. She loved the story of this particular landmark.

Around 1850, a recluse named Francois Soubrie made his way to the top of Holy Hill after reading about it in a 200-year-old French manuscript telling of a sacred hill west of Lake Michigan. Soubrie had murdered his fiancée in a jealous rage and left France for a Canadian monastery where he found the manuscript. He decided to pray for forgiveness on the sacred hill but was struck by paralysis in Chicago. When he finally reached Holy Hill, he had to drag himself up the hill where after a night of prayer, he was healed. He built the first chapel on that spot and never left.

The neo-Romanesque church was built in 1926 as a National Shrine of Mary on 435 hilly acres in Hubertus, Wisconsin. For miles in every direction, the church was a landmark, its spires reaching to the heavens and dominating the area with a peaceful, spiritual presence. Many authenticated and documented healings had occurred there since Soubrie.

Turning left onto Holy Hill road, Shane flinched

and began to hyperventilate.

Ellen grabbed the wheel and steered them off to the side of the pavement. "Consecrated?" She asked, but she really didn't need to. The succubus blood inside her recoiled. "If you can't get in, then how will they?"

In front of them, a man rounded a corner, trotting down the hill carrying a backpack over his shoulder.

"Damn it." Shane squinted at the man as he passed. "A darkwalker."

Ellen had seen their numbers grow from hundreds into thousands over the last few decades. Led by their selfish desires and known to the angels by their black misty trail, she wondered if they knew they served Lucifer himself.

There was only one reason she could think of why one would be here.

"Let's follow him." Shane eased out of the vehicle, Ellen right behind him.

She stepped off the pavement onto the side of the road and her tennis shoes crunched in the gravel.

The darkwalker looked over his shoulder and picked up his pace.

"Hey, wait up. We're your ride," Shane yelled through cupped hands. "Slow down, man."

The darkwalker broke into a run.

Ellen created an illusion of a branch in his path. Not seeing it, he tripped to the ground giving them time to catch up.

The darkwalker backed up on his hands and knees eyeing the duo as they sauntered up to him.

"What's the rush? Didn't they tell you you'd have an escort on the way back?" Ellen offered the man her hand, blinking once and concentrating the way the *sila* had taught her so her eyes glowed red and he'd think he was in the company of friends.

"N-No." He brushed off his dusty jeans and readjusted his backpack. "I'm supposed to rendezvous at the bottom of the hill."

Shane clapped him on the back like they were old friends. "Seriously, they need to work on the chain of command around here, don't you think?"

The darkwalker let his shoulders sag and relaxed into an easy stride between them back to the car. "I guess so. It's not like that was the easiest job back there. So the more help the better until I get my money and can pass this thing off." He gestured to his backpack.

Ellen hoped Shane had a plan because hers was to push this guy to the ground, grab the backpack and run.

"No worries, Rod gave us your money and told us to make the exchange here."

The darkwalker seemed to breathe a sigh of relief. "You know Rod?"

Ellen's anger rose hearing the name. Of course they knew Rod! The same demon that had almost raped Calise at the fraternity. She gathered her angelic essence and buried it deep, as the *jinn* had taught her so as not to give herself away. Her inner succubus leapt for joy thinking it was time to play.

There leaning against Shane's car was Rod in the flesh, creepy as ever. Food and drool pooling in the corners of his unkempt beard and long, yellow fingernails rounded out the grossness of the small demon. Ellen shivered and Shane gave her a curt nod. She caught his meaning. Ellen could draw Rod in, distract him, and get him to talk.

Shane would get the backpack.

"Shane O'Grady in the flesh. And Ellen, too?" Rod laughed. "My how the mighty have fallen. Give me the bag, darkwalker." Rod tossed the man a small bag Ellen could only assume was his blood money for whatever relic he'd lifted from Holy Hill.

They needed Rod alive. Taking him down now was like busting the guy who sold drugs to your kids. Ten more were willing to take his place. You had to infiltrate, work your way up the chain of command and set your hook for the big fish.

Ellen had a guess as to the demonic sect behind this game in Vegas. And if her hunch was right, they were in deep trouble. Peeling off a glove, she extended her arm to Rod before the darkwalker could hand off his loot. Rod tensed at her touch and she felt the heat of desire coursing through him.

Perfect.

"Am I free to go?" The darkwalker asked, looking around with a nervous twitch. "I was told I'd be promoted for this."

Rod never took his eyes off Ellen. "Drop the bag and scram. You'll get more than what's coming to you. That I can guarantee."

The guy dropped the bag as instructed and took off in a sprint down the hill.

"Never thought I'd see you two righteous mother-fuckers again. And my, what glorious fate has fallen upon you, beautiful?" A forked tongue extended from his mouth and began to lap at Ellen's exposed skin.

She suppressed down her revulsion even as the succubus in her blood rejoiced at the touch. Time had not been kind to him. He was nearly bald with crooked, yellow teeth and skin flaking off his pockmarked face.

The backpack was in Shane's possession in a flash. Rod never even noticed.

"Let's get out of here. Sit in the back seat with him, El. But hold it together, will you?" The look on Shane's face told her he didn't trust her at all.

Her inner angel shot him a look. He'd called her "El"? Was he jealous of the attention being garnished on her by this filth? "Give me five minutes alone with him first," she hissed, her need for the man—any man—overriding her reasonable self.

Shut up! She tried to quiet the succubus inside her. What a bitch! But with the cloak in place so she would appear to be a demon, the real Ellen was no longer in charge. The succubus had full reign.

Shane jumped in the driver's seat and revved the engine. "Let's go."

She knew she should get in the car, but her core throbbed demanding release. Not a want. A necessity. One that Rod could fill. Her mind was a teeter-totter of emotion, but the succubus was winning, overriding any control Ellen thought she had. She turned to the weak-minded demon and whispered in his ear. "Tell me who you work for and then I can join your little game too."

His eyes grew wide. "Yes! You *should* join us! Asmodeus wishes to free all the demons. Darkwalkers are our minions and soon the *jinn* will be under our control. You would be an asset to our cause."

"Wouldn't I though?" She winked at him.

"Inside the car, El. Now!" Shane's commanding tone turned her stomach.

No one told her what to do. Besides, she wasn't done with the demon yet. She could extract even more information.

After she had her way with him.

Her entire body tingled with coarse desire. *Demonstrating*, she snarled at Shane and yanked Rod by the arm, dragging him into the nearby woods.

Shane's footsteps were heavy in pursuit, making her run faster, dragging Rod behind her like a ragdoll. She leapt over logs and skimmed down mossy hills.

But Shane caught them, shaking her shoulders. "Stop already."

Fully *demonstrated*, she had eight inches on Rod and with a roar, snatched him up by the ankles, swinging him back and forth like a pendulum. "He's mine first. I will not be denied."

Smiling, Shane took a step back and crossed his arms. "I hope you got some info out of him before you killed him."

Looking down at the still body, she realized she might have been a tad aggressive. Good thing angels weren't damned for killing demons because she'd accidentally snapped Rod's neck. "Shit." She dropped his limp body and covered him with damp leaves before turning her attention back to Shane. "I guess you'll have to do then."

Before he had a second to object, she pounced on him.

Chapter 16

Mont-Saint-Michel, France

"Does anyone know anything about music?" Gabriel asked.

"I insist you release Adrienne. I'll be personally responsible for her," Seamus would not allow the angel to go any further with her under his power.

"Fine." Gabriel waved his hand and Adrienne slumped forward, gulping in air.

"You do that to her again, it'll be over my dead body." Rubbing the small of her back, Seamus reached down to help her up and pulled her close to him against the far wall. She remained mute, giving a simple nod to him when asked if she was okay. He was sure being under Gabe's control was not on her to-do list again anytime soon. But the harsh punishment had rendered her compliant for the moment. "It'll be okay. I promise."

She squeezed his shoulder.

"Touchy, touchy. Now, back to the task at hand, do any of you know anything about music?" Gabriel asked a second time.

"I do, I do! Pick me!" Dean raised his hand like they were in elementary school.

Everyone stared at him and the angel pointed to him like he was calling on a pupil in the classroom.

"You're Dean, right? The seer's lover's brother or something?" Gabriel asked.

Lucas cleared his throat. "Calise is my wife and the mother of my child," he corrected. "She's the reason we're here, if you remember anything we discussed on the train."

Seamus knew this guy meant business. It was beautiful to see a man single-minded in purpose for his true love. A pang of something foreign passed through him and he pulled Adrienne closer.

"Fine. Whatever. I'm sure you two lovebirds get along swimmingly," Gabriel never did have patience. "So then—"

"She is my soulmate." Lucas enunciated each word. "I'll kill every bloody demon who comes near us on this island, but I will not go home without that cup."

Gabriel clapped him on the shoulder. "You are a relentless prick. I kind of like that. Now, all of you, come with me." He led them to the hall where the monks were praying. "You hear this chant?'

They nodded.

"What you are hearing is your typical concert pitch. Concert pitch is A440 which equals 440 hertz. However, back before the Nazis tried brainwashing the masses with this shit, every instrument was tuned to A432. Universal pitch is A432, which is the frequency at which the universe vibrates."

Dean raised his hand again, waving it wildly. "Like the OM of people meditating?"

"Like the OM of Tibetan Buddhist monks. Also what ancient Egyptian instruments, medical tuning forks, and Stradivarius violins are tuned to. But we are in a very special spot. I brought you here, because these monks are capable of chanting in A432. If I can help them remember, I can have them switch their frequency to universal pitch. The sound would disable any demons who heard it which might give you three a fighting chance. This place will become a safe haven, and we can openly discuss what you came here for," he pointed to Lucas.

Even Seamus was impressed. "Can people hear the difference with the naked ear?"

"Yes, A432 sounds more pleasing to your ear and promotes peace and oneness with the universe. Human ears have been irritated by the switch to A440 essentially causing the fall of most civilized art and culture on this planet." Gabriel shrugged his shoulders. "I still can't believe your path was so easily lost. I used to have hope for humanity, but no more."

"Your friend is quite the uplifting one," Adrienne whispered in Seamus' ear.

"I'm an angel, darkwalker. I can hear you. Oh and good luck to you and your selfish ears when they change to A432. It will hurt you, too." Gabriel gave the flourish of a bow. "I'll be kicking it with the monks, my posse for a bit. Try to stay alive. Seamus, I'd say look for me to protect you, but honestly, I've changed my tune on this whole 'I'm your protector' thing. The sooner you croak, the sooner I get my one way ticket home 'Mr. End of my Line.'"

And with that, he was gone.

"For the most part, Raphael is way nicer," Lucas said.

Seamus sighed. "Two millennia takes its toll on a guy, I guess."

"What is everyone talking about?" Adrienne said.

Dean wrapped his arm around her and started down the hallway. Seamus hurried to keep up. "Basically sweetie, here it is. God is real, blah blah blah. Angels and demons walk the earth. Your boyfriend Seamus has spent his every waking moment slaying demons and by my estimation, he's quite good at it. Those two," he gestured to Lucas and Seamus, "are the descendants of the Jews who buried Jesus and took stuff from the tomb. Gabe is the angel Gabriel who has protected Seamus' lineage for a few millennium. But truth be told, you're safe with us. We're all hot, sexy demon slayers and world protectors. So chalk it up to having a great day and what will be a fun night killing Lucifer's minions. "

Inserting an arm to separate them, Seamus pushed Dean aside. "Too much information too fast, American. No one can absorb that much at once."

Adrienne paused and turned to address them all. "I believe you. I'm not sure I would have picked you three to be heroes, but what the hell is a hero anyway? I haven't had anything true or real to fight for since my parents died but I think today might be a good time to start."

****

Lucas was not a fan of having Adrienne in the mix, but at this point, anyone who wasn't against them was an asset.

He and Dean separated from Seamus and Adrienne to plan a strategy for the evening. Seamus had confided in them the monks did indeed protect the Cup of Life so a few demons weren't about to stand in his way. One way or another, he was leaving here with that cup. And he would save Calise's life.

"How do we know if we make it through tonight they'll even give us the cup?" Dean asked, carefully dipping the tip of each bullet in the liquid mixture Lucas had stowed in his pouch.

"We don't," he answered honestly. "But at this point, we don't have much choice, do we? I texted your mother and she said the hospital is putting more pressure on her to pull the plug. Cali isn't getting any better. We're running out of time."

Dean nodded. Mr. Ever-Joking was somber. "I got the same info. I hope we aren't on a wild goose chase. You know I'd do anything to save my sister," he stopped loading his magazine. "And I'd do anything for you."

Lucas paused. Dean was talking about Russia and what had happened there with Dean's wife. When Nara had kidnapped Calise and Michael, Lucas went to find them. Dean had come along, thinking they were hunting for his sister. But when he opened the door to the prison where they were keeping Calise, he never expected to see his own wife as Liza was holding a gun on his sister.

Liza had left Dean. He hadn't known why. At that point, he didn't care. He did what he thought was right and fired his weapon, killing his wife and saving his sister. What he didn't know, was that Liza was a demon looking for salvation right before he killed her. She wasn't going to kill Calise, she was going to help her. On her deathbed, Lucas had offered her one of the precious relics he had, a thorn from the crown the Romans made for Jesus. The embedded blood in the relic offered Liza a chance for redemption and with her last breath, she was saved.

Dean cleared his throat. "About Russia, look, I knew Liza was a bitch, but a demon? When she up and bailed on me and Max, I still hoped she'd come back. Figured I could do better. But the truth is, when it smacked me in the face and I saw her with a gun pointed at my sister, I never hesitated before I shot her dead. Deep down, I knew she was evil. And Lucas, when you gave her the chance at salvation, you saved both of us." He took a deep breath. "So you're my brother and whether you like it or not, you're my best friend."

Lucas was moved. After having been a loner his whole life—hiding from everything and everyone—having a family meant more to him than he ever thought possible. His whole life he'd avoided people because he thought he poisoned anything he touched.

Then he'd met Cali.

She was his everything. The only thing that got him out of bed in the morning and kept his heart beating every day. He would die a thousand deaths and chase her through a thousand lifetimes just so he'd never have to be apart from her again.

She'd given him everything. Love. A son. A family.

Lucas leaned forward to give Dean an awkward man-hug, his eyes wet with emotion.

Dean gave a deep cough and picked up his gun in a fake manly-sort of way. "Uh, we're friends, Bro, not kissing cousins. Tell me again why you prefer Sig Sauer over a Glock."

Lucas laughed, rubbing a palm over his cheeks. "I like the way a Sig feels in my hand. It's more comfortable for me, so I'm a more accurate shot with it." As usual, the well of Dean's emotional bare-all was short-lived and they went back to their comfortable banter about weapons and fighting.

Every bullet was dipped in the myrrh and aloe which had touched Jesus' body in the burial tomb, making them lethal to demons. Every extra mag was loaded, each knife was carefully stowed on their person, and they made a walk through the small fortress of a city soon to be under siege if what the darkwalker said was true.

"Are we even sure Adrienne saw a demon? And why would seeing one demon herald an attack?" Dean asked, peering inside the restaurant, La Ferme, which was serving the last of the day's patrons.

Lucas shrugged. "Better to be proactive than reactive. If there is no attack, fine. We get the cup and leave. But if there is, we need to be ready."

The stone walkways leading around the outskirts of the city showed nothing unusual, except the sun setting over the flat marshes, and the native sheep scurrying off in anticipation of high tide. Shops closed and the owners headed for their vehicles in the small parking lot next to the one road leading away from the castle.

Saint Michael watched from his golden perch atop the monastery. Every so often they saw Seamus and Adrienne talking with tourists in hushed whispers, as if they were learning the town gossip. Then they'd see those same tourists rushing for their cars.

"Still about five cars here and the sun has set. What do you think?" Dean stood at an overlook of the parking lot.

"I think we need divine intervention," Lucas murmured.

No sooner were the words out of his mouth, than his guardian angel appeared leaning against a storefront window. This time Asmoday wore a white-cotton dress, which hugged her to mid-thigh. Long lace-up white boots and lacey gloves completed her outfit. "Ask and you shall receive," she said in her buttery voice.

Dean wasted no time walking up to her and lifting her hand to his lips. "Did it hurt when you fell from heaven?"

She recoiled, pulling her hand away from him. "What are you talking about?"

Lucas chuckled. "Dean, this is Asmoday. *My* guardian angel. Go find your own and quit trying to hit on her."

Asmoday moved closer to Lucas, putting a protective arm through his. "I had to break protocol. I should only appear to you when you are alone." She gave a gentle nod to Dean. "Seer, it would be my pleasure to summon your guardian angel if you like. *He* is a rotund cherub fond of his Cupid's quiver and I'm sure he would love nothing more than to make his presence known to you and start popping up all the time."

"Of course I get an old, fat guy and you get *her*." Dean rolled his eyes and stomped away. "Thanks for nothing, God!" he said, before jingling the change in his pocket and ducking into a store.

"I don't like him," Asmoday said, in a plain, matter-of-fact voice.

Lucas shrugged. "You get used to him." He led her over to the lookout. "I'm close to having the other descendent give me the cup. Supposedly it has been protected by the local monks, but we suspect the

159

darkwalker with us was followed here by demons."

"The girl *was* followed and a small army is on its way. I can't fight for you I'm afraid, but I do have an idea that will get the innocents off the island. Make this fight quick, Lucas. You must kill the leader. Without him, the others will retreat. I'm afraid the one who needs the cup doesn't have much time." Her face held genuine concern and Lucas knew his guardian angel didn't want him to lose Calise any more than he wanted to lose her. Maybe his angel's emotions were tied to his with united purpose. "Come with me. There is someone you need to meet."

Lucas followed her through an alley and down a set of stone steps that led to a bolted door. She knocked on the door with two short taps followed by three long knocks.

A young monk opened the door dressed in the usual brown tunic belted with rope. His shaved head and sharp eyes indicated a recent recruit. "Who are you?"

Asmoday bowed and deferred to Lucas. "You do not know us, sir. But my friend requires an audience with the Friar Nicolas. Tell him a seer wishes to remind him, history *can* repeat itself."

The door shut with a thud and footsteps scurried away from the opening. Lucas wondered what he was supposed to say to this Friar and how it would help.

"I must leave you here," Asmoday said. "These are not just *any* sect of monks. Their Friar has trained them to fight and Friar Nicolas was there the last time evil forces waged battle upon this holy site. Tell him you are aware of the conflict he fought on a moonless night in nineteen sixty-seven. I pray then, he will help you."

The door opened once again and this time Lucas was ushered inside. A glance over his shoulder proved Asmoday had once again vanished. Lucas followed the young monk deeper and deeper into the ground beneath the abbey. Cool rocks held sconces with flickering candles lining the walls and illuminating their descent. Rooms with wooden doors dotted the hallway. The young monk led Lucas inside one of the small rooms.

There lay an old man, taking the deep, measured breaths of one near death. He pushed himself to a sitting position on his elbows with the help of the monk. He assessed Lucas with squinty eyes from a wrinkled face. But his body was not what Lucas looked at. The man was a true lightwalker, bathing the room in a warm, cream-colored radiance.

Lightwalkers were more rare than darkwalkers. It was easy to make selfish decisions time and again. But the righteous way was crooked, jagged, and arduous. Few could follow it and those who did were not the great heroes of history, but were unnamed and died alone. This was one of those great men.

Lucas dropped to one knee next to the man. "Sir, I do not mean to disturb, but your abbey will be under attack tonight. I understand you have lived through this before."

"Speak to me of what you know after you tell me of whose family you belong," the old man said. Lucas understood his request.

Lucas removed a chain from around his neck, the necklace that housed a piece of the actual crucifix and would summon angels in disaster. "I am of the house of Nicodemus. My family has protected sacred artifacts and slain demons for more than two-thousand years."

The man reached out and took the necklace, turning it over in his arthritic hands. Squeezing his palm shut, he closed his eyes and mouthed a short prayer. "What do you want with me, son?" he asked, handing the artifact back.

Lucas placed the necklace back over his head. "Tonight will be the same as the moonless night in 1967. There are only a handful of us to fight. Humbly, sir, I'm asking for your help."

A spark appeared in the man's eyes and the warm of his aura filled the room. "The last time we were under siege, I was the only survivor. Since then, I have spent all my good days training these holy men to fight Satan and his demons. Tonight you say? But why?"

Lucas didn't quite know how much to tell him. He didn't want to kill him with fear or make him want to get out of bed and try to fight. Did the man need more proof than the necklace? "I came with the descendent of Joseph of Arimathea for the cup but we were followed. I've seen too much death and dying in my short life. My wife is going to die if I cannot have private conference with those I arrived with and leave here with the sacred cup. Please, help us." Lucas removed a thorn from a hidden pocket in his shirt. He pressed it into the lightwalker's hand.

The old man began to shake. He looked at what Lucas placed in his hand. "*Mon Dieu!*" Fresh wounds appeared around his head and blood began to flow from the wounds. The scent of flowers filled the room.

Shit, Lucas knew better. A true believer with a remnant of the Crown of Thorns. He'd induced the stigmata, the body marks corresponding to the crucifixion wounds of Jesus. He was displaying one of

162

the five Holy Wounds, the others being the wrists and feet from nails or in the side, from a lance.

The Friar's eyes rolled back in his head and his back arched. He pressed his hands together in prayer. "He is experiencing the ecstasy," the other monk said, slipping a thin, white, round object in his mouth. "The Body of Christ."

Receiving Communion seemed to rejuvenate the Friar.

Lucas stood and backed away as young monk tended to the Friar.

"Thank you," the Friar said, as tears of blood rolled down his cheeks, and soaked his pillow.

"Leave him to me," the young monk said, ushering Lucas to the door. "I heard everything and I believe you. We are ready to fight and will stand by your side."

He was shut out of the room with the old man still clutching the thorn. Lucas had no idea if what he had done would help or hinder their cause.

He ran through the stone pathway, heaved open the door, and made his way back to the streets. Dean was eating a sandwich and drinking a bottle of water. "I can't fight on an empty stomach. I got you a sandwich too."

"I think you should have Ellen check you for a tapeworm when we get home. Right now, we need to find the others." Lucas ignored the food and Dean tossed the rest of his in the trash. Lucas led them to the main cathedral where the bell hung. The same monk who'd greeted them earlier in the day knelt by the altar with five others standing in a row, heads bowed in their evening prayers.

"I saw Father Nicolas," Lucas said, interrupting

them.

"We heard," one of them said.

"Are there still people on the island?" Dean asked. "And why are you talking?"

The last monk in line came over to them. "We have decided to break our vow of silence for the next twenty-four hours. The island will be evacuated within the hour except for us. The tide coming in has been blessed, and we are honored to stand beside you to fight the beasts." He reached inside a hidden pocket in his robe to reveal a sword. A seventh monk rushed into the chapel. Lucas recognized him as the one from the basement.

"How is the Friar?" Lucas asked wondering how information was disseminated so quickly around this place.

"Honored to have met you and under observation by our medics. You forgot this." The young monk handed Lucas his thorn. "I, too, am ready to fight by your side, son of Joseph."

Dean clapped the young monk on the back. "Hurry up with the prayers then. There'll be plenty of time for that later."

Seamus and Adrienne rushed through the wooden chapel door as the young monk knelt for his turn at prayer. "The island has been emptied and we are out of time. They're here," Seamus said.

The monks led the way to the abbey garden. The sight outside stopped them all in their tracks. Demons swooped through the air by the dozens.

All the monks followed the flight pattern of the beasts, as did Dean and Seamus.

"I need a weapon," Adrienne said.

"Go find Gabriel," Seamus said, pushing her back

inside.

Adrienne planted her feet and put out her hand. "I'm not leaving you. If I lose you Seamus, I've lost myself. Now give me a gun."

Lucas had watched them go from bantering to inseparable. Cali was just as stubborn. But he knew as Seamus did, this was not where she belonged. So he stepped in. "I will take care of him, Adrienne. He wants you safe and will protect himself better if he's not watching out for you. Please trust me. I have his back."

Seamus stepped in front of her. "When we make it through this, I give you my word you will have the cup. But you will do something for me."

Lucas believed Seamus was a man of his word. "Name it."

"Take all my artifacts. Release my family from this curse. I am taking Adrienne away from this life. We are going to disappear."

Lucas clasped Seamus' hand. He understood what the man wanted. A moment's peace. A life of looking over your shoulder was a life of unrest. He would know. Adrienne and Seamus were soulmates. Lucas could tell, only because he'd found the same beauty in his own world. A selfish love where being out of your soulmate's life for even a moment caused physical pain. If Calise died, so would Lucas.

So if he could offer one gift to people who finally found each other and deserved a shot at happiness, he'd do what he could.

Happiness—Lucas knew—was a choice. And for Seamus and Adrienne, right now that meant being in each other's arms right now and forever. "Agreed. Now let's go."

Seamus turned and pulled Adrienne to him for a tender kiss.

"Don't be a hero," she said, above a whisper.

"I never am," Seamus replied.

Chapter 17

Holy Hill Road, Hubertus, Wisconsin

"Aren't we the hot mess?" Ellen smoothed out her now tattered clothes. "Oh shit, I forgot to—" A hand held her wrist firmly in place.

"Uh, no one is erasing *that* from my memory, ever." Shane buttoned his pants and blew her a kiss.

Ellen was steaming. What an asshole. Taking advantage of the succubus blood and *enjoying* it? "I'll make sure to find you a succubus of your very own when this is over. You do realize you fucked *her*, and not me, right?" The vile language issuing from her mouth surprised even her.

He laughed. "Look around you, El. Rod is dead. From you. I'm walking on sunshine. From you. And you know who the demon in charge is. Again, all thanks to you. Quit crediting succubus blood which could never be as sexy as you are."

Turning his back to her, his boots crunched on the leaf-strewn forest floor. She felt her cheeks warm as she hurried to keep up. "Are we leaving the body here?"

"Why, did you want to bury it or something? It's probably gone already and if not, the animals are hungry too, you know. Must you be so selfish?"

Shane O'Grady was a piece of work. And the succubus blood screamed his praises. She was getting weaker and the demon was getting stronger. Ellen was clinging for life hanging off the edge of a cliff and the succubus was stomping on her fingers. She prayed the memories she'd erased would not return to him. And now she needed to act fast to clean up her latest indiscretion.

He laid the mop of his hair on the headrest back in her car, which was still parked on the side of the road. Slipping in the passenger seat, she pulled the door closed with a thud.

Better safe than sorry.

She began to speak the incantation in the angelic tongue…

"El, don't!" he said. Then his eyes went vacant.

He gave his head a quick shake as he came to. "So where to now?"

"Sin city, baby," she said, while her blood-borne succubus did the happy dance. "The lair of Asmodeus, the demon behind all this."

****

Dazzling lights twinkled out of the abyss. From nothingness to glitter and razzle-dazzle. That's what it was like flying into Las Vegas at night. The desert surrounding the city was barren and starved of water. But Vegas made no apologies for bleeding the Colorado River dry and diverting what the city and its inhabitants and visitors needed to thrive.

Shane reached across the empty seat between them and poked Ellen in the ribs with a pencil to rouse her from her cute-ass slumber. "Have you been here before?"

After rubbing her eyes and stretching the little she could in coach, she peered around him and out the tiny oval window. "Wow."

The city invoked something in everyone. It was like a sparkly diamond, an oasis of pleasure, or the clanging jangle of good luck. Shane had been here a few times trying to follow his righteous path and save the sinners, but in this city that path was blocked with slot machines, strippers, and twenty-four hour booze.

Evil seeped up from every nook and cranny and lurked around each corner in this town. Shane had tried to focus on the destitute. But no matter who he offered to help, everyone was looking for the same thing: an easy fix. A chance at the big time. One more slot pull away from a fortune. Or a call girl away from deadening one's personal demons until the money ran out.

And it did. It always did.

Money and luck always ran out.

The shimmering city gave humans the promise of something an angel couldn't offer: *immediate* hope. Long term, save-your-soul-after-you're-dead kind of hope was a thousand years in the future to someone whose luck could change with each quarter in a slot machine. For these humans, there was no thinking past the here and now.

"Do you really think Asmodeus will fall for this?" Shane jangled the fake relic. They'd conjured a replicate of what the darkwalker had taken from Holy Hill after examining it and then leaving the darkwalker's backpack on the road. An anonymous call to the church office sent an old priest scurrying down the hill to collect what had been stolen.

"Missing something?" She waved out the window. "Keep the original somewhere else next time." The priest gave her a look of who-the-hell-are-you two and then examined the contents of the backpack.

"How did you get this?" the priest had said.

But by the time he'd reexamined the contents of the paper bag, Shane already had the car in gear and they zoomed away.

****

"All we need to do is get in the door," Ellen said, grabbing the seat as the plane prepared to make a bumpy landing. "But I can't go into Asmodeus's lair like this." Her tattered clothes said street hooker instead of rich, club girl and had commanded quite the look from the airline attendants. "I need a shower and new clothes."

The succubus blood pushed at her insides begging for more unrelenting pleasure. She wondered when the blood's effect would diminish. It had already seemed like an eternity. Even if time cleansed her blood, would she ever really be back to normal?

But what is normal anyway? Maybe hurling down a path of her own undoing was the path she was supposed to be on. Could all her urges toward Shane really be chalked up to the succubus blood alone?

The plane banked to the left and her shoulder would have pressed into Shane's if their seats were adjacent. He might not remember being with her, but she would sure as hell never forget.

His strong arms. His lustful desire played out again and again inside her. *Great, I'm wet just thinking about being with him.*

She cleared her throat, trying to suppress her insatiable desire. "Can we please check in to a room so I can shower and get ready before we go see

Asmodeus?"

"We can, but I'd have to steal money to pay the bill. I'm totally fine with that, but whatever you want," Shane shrugged his shoulders in passive disregard.

Ellen had told the hospital she was on a personal leave until further notice because of Calise. She never spent money. Really, never. She lived at the hospital. Had all her checks direct deposited, went to medical school on a scholarship and lived alone and simply in a modest apartment. She pulled out her phone and checked the balance in her account. She had over two-hundred and fifty thousand dollars in checking. *Live it up you bore!* This wasn't even her inner succubus talking. "I'll pay. My treat for having to deal with me."

The plane bounced on the tarmac and began its taxi to the terminal.

"It beats being alone," Shane shrugged.

So that was it. She was only marginally better company than no company. Unbuckling her seatbelt, she stood in the cramped space, eager to bolt from Shane who had no memories of their raunchy sex. Which had been earthshattering for her even if she was basically an in-body observer.

When people began to move, Shane held her fast by on her covered arm. "That came out wrong and I obviously upset you. That's not what I meant at all."

"No, I'm boring. I get it. As soon as we figure out what's going on I can get word to Raphael, you'll never have to see me again."

"Wait!" he said.

Ellen pushed past other passengers in an uncharacteristic rush. "Meet me in the lobby of the Mirage in two hours or I'm going without you," she called over her shoulder.

She breathed deeply after exiting the stuffy cabin, only to exit into even stuffier, more sweltering air that was the stifling Vegas desert heat. Hailing the first cab she saw, she asked to be taken to the Mirage.

The only reason she even knew the name of a hotel on the strip was because Calise and Dean had surprised their parents with a twenty-fifth anniversary present of a trip for the four of them to Las Vegas. Ellen had laughed thinking of Cali's mother sauntering around strip clubs and casinos.

Cali and Dean had planned a clean week of seeing the magicians Siegfried and Roy, watching an impersonator show at the Imperial Palace, and watching the Blue Man Group in the Luxor. Cali had said her mom loved riding the gondolas in the Paris hotel and shopping in Caesar's palace. They'd even done a day trip out to Hoover Dam for a hard hat tour and horseback riding in the desert.

The whole thing made Vegas sound tame. While Dean and his dad hit the poker tables here and there, Cali said she and her mom sipped drinks by the magnificent pool of the Mirage, replete with waterfalls and unrelenting sunshine.

When Ellen's cab pulled up to the Mirage, she saw a barrage of people gathered around a large structure outside the hotel. It was a volcano and the old girl sounded ready to explode. Ellen stood with the other vacationers and watched the volcano rumble and fire spew forth before simulating a real explosion. She clapped along with everyone else. Her inner succubus ruined the moment by reminding her every time a man—any man—came within five feet of her that her own pressure was once again building and begging for release.

Shushing her inner whore, Ellen walked up to the reception desk. A dark-haired boy in a crisp white shirt stood in front of a 20,000-gallon tropical reef aquarium highlighting angelfish and tang. "I'd like to check in please."

The boy behind the counter looked no more than twenty-one. "Name the reservation is under?"

"I don't have a reservation. I'll take any room you have available," Ellen gave the human a gentle smile. Surely, the best way to get good service here was still to be polite.

The boy actually took his hands off the computer and gave her a look of pure pity. "This is Vegas, miss. Everyone needs a reservation."

Her blood boiled. She had no idea about any of the other hotels. Although she knew it was a bad idea, she peeled off a glove and reached over the counter and touched his arm. The boy flinched then his expression melted. "Please, any room. I'll take anything."

His fingers returned to the keyboard but his gaze never left her face. "I did just have a cancellation on a non-smoking King with a whirlpool for three-hundred nine dollars a night. For an extra hundred, I'll walk you to your room myself, beautiful," he said with a wink.

The succubus roared her pleasure and Ellen fought against the demon, forcing the emotions to abate.

"Thank you, Gregory," Ellen said, reading his nametag. "But that won't be necessary."

Hopes dashed, he returned to the job at hand. "Do you have a credit card and photo ID for check-in?"

After the awkward transaction, he slid the key over

the counter and she proceeded per his instructions to the elevator bank that would lead to her floor. A ding-ding-ding of bells assaulted her on the path he'd told her to follow.

The center path to the elevators forced her straight through the middle of the casino. Every make and model of human being sat side-by-side pouring bills into rectangular machines with flashing lights and enticing sounds promising to win them a jackpot. Blackjack and crap tables had crowds packed around them.

Women in furs stood next to the street person. Men with slick-backed hair in three-piece suits sat next to guys in unbuttoned Hawaiian shirts with flip flops and unmatched shorts.

This was a hovel of the rich and poor, young and old, sensible and ridiculous. And all anyone hoped for here was money. Ellen wanted to go from person to person and inform them about heaven and not being able to take cash with you and that a clean soul was the best thing to transport, but...

She pressed fourteen on the elevator noticing the obvious deletion of unlucky floor thirteen. Exiting the elevator, she followed the signs to the right and slid her card key into the door lock. The green light opened the door to a palm-tree decorated room with a delectable looking shower and whirlpool tub next to the bed.

She filled the tub, clicked on the TV, stripped off all her clothes and threw them in the waste basket.

To gain access to Asmodeus' club, she'd have to look hot. That necessitated a bath. Pouring in a tiny, complimentary bottle of pink bubble bath and making sure the hotel phone would reach, she climbed in the tub, and both she and her inner succubus breathed a sigh of contentment.

For the moment.

She hit zero on the hotel phone. Ellen was almost relieved to let the succubus take over. Right now, having what was left of her blood zipping around her veins might not be a bad thing. "Concierge. Bring me up a lobster tail and a bottle of champagne and send someone to run out and get me a new outfit. I'll give you my size. The cost is irrelevant and if you have everything I need delivered to my room in under an hour, there's an extra grand in it for you."

Chapter 18

Mont-Saint-Michel, France

Night had fallen and the temperature dropped leaving a deep chill in the air. The crescent moon illuminated the demon army dotting the sky like stars. Every winged creature carried an unwinged hellspawn, waiting for some unspoken order to attack.

With Adrienne whisked to safety, Lucas addressed Seamus. "Ever taken on this many before?"

"Once," Seamus answered without emotion.

"How'd that work out?" Dean asked, shouldering his shotgun.

Seamus cleared his throat. "Look, I have had lots of experience with different styles of fighting, but you know what never fails? A swift kick to the groin and finger jab into each eye. Then run like hell."

Dean laughed. "Funny. That might work if half of them weren't in the sky and we could see a damn thing!"

"A handful of monks trained in Savate—an old, French martial art—and the three of us aren't exactly the match of the century," Lucas said. "But Dean, don't use your eyes. You are a seer. Use all your senses. Feel them."

A group of the trained monks moved as one out into the middle of the grassy area. They stood back to back, staring skyward with mouths agape. Some made the sign of the cross.

In the blink of an eye, a minion demon dove down from the night sky like a comet, his tail flicking and cloven hooves clawing the air. He snatched up a monk and sliced off his head mid-air.

"Holy shit," Seamus said. "I thought you said they could fight."

All the ground troops dropped on them at once, red eyes blazing.

"So let's go." Wasting no time, Dean charged forward feigning a straight on attack, then at the last minute sidestepping the enemy. He rammed the blade in his left hand through a minion's head from one ear to the other. At the same time, he leveled his sawed off double barrel shotgun at one of the winged beasts. He'd cut down the handle to make it more like a pistol grip. Dean discharged a barrel of hot buckshot sending a winged demon back to hell.

He turned back to Lucas and Seamus. "Holy crap, I didn't expect it to work so well!" Lucas wanted to laugh, but didn't have time as he had problems of his own. He extracted two throwing knives whipping them at his advancing attackers and landing them both straight between their eyes. Through the puff of smoke left in their wake came two more.

A winged beast snatched another fighting monk from behind, hurling his body into the air before ripping him in two then dropping the limp halves back to the ground.

Lucas moved forward, no time to think about how badly they were outnumbered.

"Split up!" Lucas called, charging left with three

monks on his heels. They went head to head with the ground minions. Seamus and Dean went right, staying close to the two monks.

Lucas was surrounded. Three winged beasts swooped in trying to snatch them up, but Lucas and the monks managed to foil their attempts. The monks were ramming their heels, knees, elbows, and fists into any attacker in their way. Lucas drew his Wakizashi swords and began slashing demons, spilling their intestines, and severing heads from bodies. The scene was reminiscent of a Middle Age killing field. He knew he needed to gash open a pathway like a maggot eating its way through flesh to find the demon leader.

Wiping the crimson life-forced infused fluid off his face, Lucas cast a quick glance at Seamus and Dean to see if they were taking advantage of the blood soaked opening he was creating.

A winged demon snapped the neck of one monk and tore the jugular out of another with his teeth. They were dying out here in the open, like a rabbit in an open field caught in the eyes of a raptor. Casualties amid clouds of black dust continued to litter the field.

"Move under the pillars," Seamus yelled.

Lucas pulled back so they would be protected by the roof and support columns surrounding the grassy courtyard.

They regrouped. "Let's harpoon that mother fucker and pull him down to us," Lucas pointed to the black-horned demon he'd identified as the leader. "If we can take him down, we might stand a chance."

The hoard moved in like the fog off a stormy sea. Teeth gnashing, crimson eyes piercing, horns scraping the columns like chunks of ice across the hull of a ship.

Bewildered at their impending doom, they readied themselves for the onslaught that could be their demise.

The scene exploded into a mass of violence. Lucas slashed and ducked at everything he could then heard screaming pain coming from Dean who was slammed into a column then slid to the ground as the demon horde seemed to swallow him whole.

In that fraction of a moment, he found himself being strangled by the grip of demon hands slowly piercing his flesh. As his vision tunneled, he thought this was the end.

Then he heard a gut-wrenching bellow for help, one word, "Gabriel!" Seamus screamed just as he was literally going to be devoured alive.

The door to the courtyard tore from its hinges letting out the white light of the angel Gabriel. Time froze. With the enchanted voices of singing monks all the demons miraculously fell to the ground incapacitated, holding their ears in blistering pain and whining like a dogs bombarded by ultrasonic frequencies.

"Sorry it took so long," Gabriel said, striding into the courtyard like the avenging angel he always should have been. "It's more difficult than I expected to teach people to sing in tune with the universe."

"What's happening?" A hellspawn screamed, trying to claw at Seamus from the ground.

"Don't do that." With a flick of Gabriel's wrist, the demons near Seamus flew across the courtyard like dandelion seeds in a gale force wind. "Back to Lucy you go." Gabriel snapped his fingers and a sound boomed through the sanctuary. The monks' song continued to resonate even more than before, singing the Light of the Universe's praises in the pitch of the cosmos.

Lucas took a chain wrapped around the waist of one of the fallen monks and slid the blade of his Wakizashi sword through one of the links where it stuck. He hurled the sword at the demon leader cowering low in the sky, his ears covered like the rest. The sword lodged through his thigh where the bone gripped the blade like a boa constrictor holding its prey.

Lucas gave the chain a forceful pull, bringing the demon to earth. As soon as he was in reach, Seamus grabbed the demon's free leg and grappled him to the ground. With a powerful hacking motion, Seamus severed his head from his body. Blood splatter from the demon's whole body dissipated and lifted in a thick black, wretched fog.

****

Lucas knelt beside Dean watching the steady rise and fall of his chest and found a pulse.

"Is he alive?" Seamus asked.

"Yes."

The wide-eyed monks continued the chant in universal pitch following every move Gabriel made.

Gabriel began to glow with a piercing white light, transforming into a radiant angel, a heaven-sent savior.

"Thank you God's servants." Gabriel said. Immediately the chanting ceased. "Your voices prevailed over evil and we are once again bathed in God's holy light. You," he addressed the monks, "tend to your kin. Those who gave their lives today will require a saint's burial. Others will need healing through care, medicine, and prayers."

The remaining monks bowed profusely to Lucas

and Seamus. Their gesture said, "It was an honor to fight beside you both."

Lucas had no words. They had all volunteered to commit their lives today and none of them would be the same. Each of them now shone as brightly as the old Friar.

New lightwalkers.

"May the Lord bless you and keep you." Gabriel dismissed the now silent monks, who bowed their heads and walked out humbly, gratified after battling the powers of darkness.

When the last of the monks left, Gabriel turned to Seamus and Lucas. "Was that too much? The whole bathed in light and booming voice usually goes over pretty well."

Seamus lifted his foot out of some sticky-black tar-like substance. "Are all angels as self-righteous as you?"

"Only the awesome ones," Gabe answered. "At least demons are easy to clean-up after," he said, kicking the remains of the last demon into blessed water where it sizzled and disappeared into nothingness.

Lucas heard snippets of the rest of their conversation as he made his way to the infirmary with a still unconscious Dean.

After several minutes, his brother-in-law stirred. "Did we win?"

Lucas nodded. "Barely."

"Rat bastards," Dean said, opening an eye and groaning.

Lucas and Seamus helped him into a deep tub filled with the warmed influx tide of Holy Water which now surrounded the sunken cathedral. The wounds on Dean's back and legs healed as soon as they hit the water. "Human-born demons can't fly," Seamus said. "Never fun to fight the ones who cross over from hell. Next time we'll need wings ourselves to take out any more of them."

Dean laughed and allowed himself to sink deeper into the healing water. "Next time? Thinking about next time already, are you?"

****

Seamus didn't know how hungry he was until he took the first bite.

The monks served them a late meal in silence before pulling the door shut on their main dining hall to give them privacy. Seamus sat with one arm wrapped around Adrienne, who spooned soup into her mouth and ate quietly with her head down. She rested her head on his shoulder between bites.

Seamus wanted to give Lucas the cup and get them on their way. Gabriel would probably accompany them to the United States. Then, just maybe, he'd have a moment's peace and be able to sort out his feelings for Adrienne.

She'd been oddly silent since he'd retrieved her from the safety of the monks' lower rooms and she rushed into his arms. He wanted to talk with her alone. To tell her everything. But Lucas and Dean were adamant they get the cup and leave immediately.

Whatever injury Dean had sustained on the battlefield was minimal, as he was back to being full of piss and vinegar in less than an hour, recounting the battle like a football player after scoring the game-winning touchdown. *Americans.*

Lucas sat at one end of the table and Gabriel at the other. Lucas wore a haggard look of consternation and Gabriel, with the excitement over, wore his usual bored expression staring off at nothing in particular.

Seamus enjoyed the retelling of the epic battle with Dean's added regalia. He hoped Adrienne wasn't impressed because this was not the person she'd be spending her life with. He'd never wanted to be a warrior. It was thrust upon him. He wanted peace and her to love him for everything but this part of who he was.

"...And when you took out the leader, Seamus. That was awesome! You have no fear, man!"

Seamus blushed, worrying about the look of awe that briefly swept across Adrienne's face. "You weren't so bad yourself. And why weren't you out there sooner my dear guardian angel?"

Gabriel ticked off on his fingers. "One, I'm not your guardian angel. That's someone else. I guard the artifacts. And two, the time to fight is not now. They were here on their own business. They were after you," he pointed to Adrienne. "Now why don't you tell us why?"

Adrienne coughed on the last of her soup. "I have no idea."

Gabriel was no stranger to the stare down. "Tell us, darkwalker. Tell us more about your organization and its objectives. There is some piece of information you must have whether you know it or not. And whatever it is, they don't want you to share it....now think."

Lucas straightened up in his chair and even Seamus was hoping after all they'd been through, she'd shed some light on the inner workings of the darkwalkers.

"I've told you before. Daevas approached me when I was in a dark and vulnerable place. My family had just died and I was alone. Their precepts appealed to me. Live your life the way you want. No consequences. No responsibility. My parents died in a senseless accident and I either wanted to make sense of it or move on with my life. If you haven't ever been stuck in the pit of depression, I'd doubt you'd know what I'm talking about."

At that she stood, tears pooling in her eyes. "I'm no help to you. People have died in the last two days because of me. And for what? I don't belong here with you," she looked at Seamus, "or anyone. Thanks, I guess, for the undeniable proof of heaven and hell."

She left the room and Seamus stood to follow her.

"Sit," Gabriel commanded. "She is assimilating truths most humans are told in the form of fairy tales. Although she says one thing, she is in denial. Let her be for now, Seamus."

He sat, knowing how shitty the truth can be. Ignorance really was bliss and maybe now Adrienne would never have bliss in her life again, because of him.

Lucas cleared his throat. "Can we please get to the reason why we came here so Dean and I can leave?"

Gabriel nodded and gestured for Lucas to continue.

"I implore you both. As I said, my wife and soulmate lies in a coma from a car accident. She was hit by a car driven by a demon. We have a son and I would give my own life and soul if it meant saving hers. You have something that can wake her and as the other living seer from the line descended from the tomb, I humbly ask to borrow the cup, bring it to the States with me, and let Calise drink from it. I believe this will wake her from the coma. Please," he begged. "I've done all you've asked and she's running out of time. I need the cup."

Seamus couldn't help but be moved. Here, he'd sat on these artifacts his whole life, lived on the road under the demon radar, often putting himself in danger for no good reason except to feed his adrenaline. Now an honorable man needed his help. He knew the right answer.

"Yes," Seamus said. "Provided you have protection taking the artifact to and from the States. And if you grant my favor in return. Take the rest of my family's artifacts so Adrienne and I can start a new life."

"What?" Gabriel blurted.

"I thank you, Seamus, and we will remain in your debt," Lucas said. "So if I can get the cup and whatever other items you'd like me to have, I'll get going…"

Gabriel cleared his throat. "I love the touchy-feely sentiments all being passed around here, but there's kind of a big problem."

Seamus was confused. Although Gabriel was technically *his* guardian while the line of Joseph of Arimathea protected the artifacts, Seamus had never really done much with the family heirlooms since he and Gabriel brought them here. His ancestors had even planted fake cups all over Europe and started all kinds of rumors just to keep it hidden. "What problem? We will give him the cup. I gave him my word." He directed the words to Gabriel.

"Helping them is noble. But the problem is we don't have the artifacts…exactly…here." Gabriel grimaced bracing for Seamus' reaction.

"What in the hell are you talking about? Of course we have them. I brought them here with you!" A flurry of memories played through Seamus' mind. Could Gabriel have tricked even him?

Gabriel heaved a substantial sigh. "Let me go back to the beginning. And Seamus, you deserve the truth…"

Chapter 19

Las Vegas, Nevada

Damn heels. Ellen wobbled off the elevator trying to get her bearings in the stilettos and the hotel. When she'd checked into the place, no one had turned to look at her. Now, all eyes were on her. *I must have food in my teeth or something.*

She tugged at the back of her skintight black leather dress. Maybe she hadn't pulled it all the way down and her underwear was sticking out or she was dragging toilet paper behind her. She smoothed her hand over her gelled back hair. Her inner succubus roared for the limelight.

Ellen knew she'd have to let her out to play eventually because this was seriously not her personality. The idea of getting answers from the big cheese of demons was going to necessitate her straight-laced self to go and take a hike and let this waning vixen inside her bloodstream put on one last hard core show.

A man in a suit about twenty-years her senior, left his drink at the slot machine and sidled up to her. "How much?"

"Uh…" Before she could answer, another arm pulled her in the opposite direction.

"You ready to go, darling?"

The voice sounded familiar, but the man attached to it couldn't be the same.

Shane had cleaned up.

Nicely.

An impeccable suit, tailored to show off his every attribute, replaced his usual garb of ripped jeans and t-shirts. Ellen blinked a few times to make sure it was him.

"Back off dillweed, she's not for sale." His eyes flashed red for a splinter of a second and the man scurried back to his lonely machine.

Slipping her arm through his, she followed his lead through the casino and out the front door into the hot, evening air. A limo was waiting with a valet who opened the door for her. She hadn't meant to look like a hooker, but when the outfits were delivered, the choices were slutty or sluttier. The succubus led her hand to this outfit and Ellen succumbed to the blood scorching in her veins until she was dressed, hair and make-up complete.

A succubus wasn't a demon seductress for no reason. Ellen—demure and plain—now oozed sex. And a small piece of her, loved it. She'd almost miss this blood when it was gone. And right now, the blood was going to help them get some answers.

Shane uncorked the bottle of champagne cooling in the back of the limo and poured her some.

Taking the slim glass and allowing the golden bubbles to slide down her throat, she permitted herself to really look at the cleaned-up Shane. Whoever he robbed to get this look was worth it.

Polished shoes. Tailored black pants that tugged tight between his legs. A hint of lavender in his silk shirt and patterned tie. An unbuttoned black suit coat showed off his massive upper arms. He was clean shaven, his hair slicked back, and his strong hands holding the delicate flute with an authority that made her want to jump across the seat and take him.

Confusion overtook her. She'd chalked all these emotions up to the succubus rearing its wanton head. But now Ellen was starting to wonder if "it' had merely opened a door to a piece of her that was already there. In her mind, she'd kept telling herself she'd "let the succubus take over," but now she was starting to think the succubus left the breadcrumbs and she was the one following the path.

Being this close to Shane, heat seared her inner thighs and her insides sang a siren's song calling her sailor home. *Again.* This was the succubus.

Want help with Asmodeus? Her inner demon seemed to tell her. *Fine. Give me Shane one more time.*

One last time. No more. He's better than this, Ellen shot back at her now alter ego. "I'm not going to make it. Shane. Can you help?" She finished her beverage and crawled toward him.

"Ellen, don't." His eyes raked over her body and she saw him stiffen. "Please…"

Her succubus howled and thrust its way to the front shoving any remnants of Ellen out of the way then stomping her into a hole where she was trapped. She unzipped his pants and released the tense flesh, taking it in her hands.

As soon as her fingers touched him, Shane moaned and his body burned with lust. "You know I can't possibly resist you. Fuck El, I want you so bad."

She opened her mouth and flicked her tongue

around the tip. He looked delicious and she needed to taste him. Slowly, she slid her mouth around him, relishing every hill and valley. Her mouth was full of Shane. His body shook beneath hers. Liking his reaction, she moved her head up and down, licking and loving every inch of him.

He shook harder and before she was ready to let it end, he erupted in her mouth.

She smiled and looked up at him. "My turn," she said.

****

Of course, Asmodeus's domain wasn't on the Las Vegas strip. It was way the hell out in the *real* desert. Shane held out his hand to help Ellen from the limo. "Do not erase that memory. Please."

Ellen licked her upper lip. "Later."

Shane wasn't fooling himself. This was not Ellen. It may have been her body, but the thing inside her was not. The lust he felt was fake and the reactions his body was having to hers was scripted by the succubus.

After they got the answers they needed, he'd be on his way. With less succubus blood coursing through her veins, Ellen would be back to her old self soon and back to her day job as an angel and a savior. He hoped Calise was still alive.

Something about the artifact thefts was connected to Calise. He could feel it. Some deep part of him knew if he solved this puzzle, it would somehow help Calise get back to Lucas.

With dirt for a parking lot and cacti as security, a neon purple bathed building with huge columns loomed in front of them. Dozens of people lined up waiting to get in. After a short wait, the bouncer, a no-nonsense demon, opened the double doors to admit them.

They were assaulted by pounding rave music, and glitter and dazzle as far as the eye could see. Shane kept a tight grip on Ellen's hand. The bar took up one full wall, the top shelf labels lit up and reflected in the mirror behind the bar. Red velvet ropes led to private tables tucked in corners of the massive two-story structure. Women dressed in skimpy sparkly thongs draped the four corners in dance cages. Not to leave the women wanting, men who were oiled and buff carried drinks around on a tray held on a belt right above their erections.

"Classy," he had to yell into Ellen's ear so she could hear him over the din.

She pointed to a private room with full-length glass windows suspended next to the second story dance floor where a few men sat surrounded by their own private party. One of the men pointed to one of the women on the dance floor. A crony tapped the girl on the shoulder and she was escorted across a suspension bridge to the VIPs.

The club sported demons and humans only. Shane felt Ellen's body ripple next to him. Her hand became cold and her demeanor changed. Her eyes changed to ruby red. She gave him a smile saying, "Let's do this."

Shane wondered if their plan might work. Ellen was cloaked and with the succubus blood, she might be able to even pull off the whole seductress act and help him gain access to Asmodeus.

He led her up the stairs and onto the dance floor. The only way this would work was for her to get noticed. "Dance," he said, trying not to make it sound like a command.

Her eyes danced before her body did and Ellen transformed into the most desirable creature not only in the bar, but in the whole universe.

Women and men alike stared at her while she moved her hips and let her arms pulse in time with music. Shane realized he might have been next to her, but he was not her partner.

She was lost in the music. In the night. In the moment.

The trance music was now owned by Ellen and she seemed to control its every thump and grind. Blue-green strobe lights flashed to pink-purple. And spotlights whizzed around the club. Shane was mesmerized with Ellen. When women came to her, she melded her body with theirs, intertwining limbs and bodies in a rhythm Shane couldn't tear his eyes from.

Ellen licked the neck of the girl closest to her.

Uh-oh.

The girl went into hysteria from the touch, pushing to get closer to Ellen. Shane moved closer realizing everyone she touched—demon or human—would hurl themselves at her looking for their own satisfaction.

Ellen reached out a hand to keep Shane at a distance. She faced the girl squarely and tipped her chin up so she could brush her lips against hers. But she didn't. Ellen wrapped one arm around the girl and whispered something in her ear before giving her a small push. The girl stumbled away shivering in a private ecstasy and found the bar where she slumped onto a stool.

Shane looked in every direction. Ellen's actions hadn't gone unnoticed as she resumed her own private show, then on to the next song. She moved like water, a liquid dance where her limbs flowed and connected to the world around her, sucking everything nearby toward her like a supercharged vacuum. A crowd gathered, men and women. Demons and humans.

Like reaching out to touch the fabric of a god, they began to paw at her.

Shane looked on in amazement at her control. If anyone got close enough to touch her, she snatched them up and linked them with another person. She transferred the attachment they felt for her to the next person. Within seconds, there were six duos not able to keep their hands off each other while she maintained her own private circle in which she continued dancing.

An evil smile curved up at the corners of her mouth and Shane felt his need for her surface again. No one would touch her. She was his.

His mind reeled. *Mine.*

Why wasn't she dancing with him? A possessive anger flooded his senses. Did he want to protect Ellen or have the succubus satisfy him again?

A man in a black suit with sunglasses tapped Ellen on the shoulder. Shane pushed through the masses of people and watched her follow the crony over the suspension bridge to the VIP area. He followed her.

Staring back at them was a trio of badass looking demons.

In the center, sat Asmodeus.

Chapter 20

Mont-Saint-Michel, France

"I'll tell it to you as I remember it," Gabriel said to the group:

Sent to guard the Son's body, the archangel Gabriel was proud to stand with his brother, Raphael at the tomb.

The two humans had proven their worth asking for the Son's body so it could be buried in a proper fashion. But what the angels couldn't foresee, was the magnitude of arsenals they'd leave the tomb with. Gabriel and Raphael were sent to keep the tomb safe from scavenging by demons looking to tear his body to shreds.

While the men worked in the tomb, the angels remained hidden, until they could keep quiet no longer. Gabriel had volunteered to protect the tomb. After all, he'd been the one chosen to tell Mary of her Immaculate Conception, he felt the need to see this through to its conclusion.

He would be remembered as the only angel on earth to bear witness to both the birth and death of humankind's Savior.

Gabriel watched the younger and wealthier of the two men with fascination. Joseph of Arimathea—Jesus' Uncle—in asking for one small favor, had ostracized himself from the Jewish elders. Watching a man with actual honor and virtue swelled Gabriel with emotion. Most often he saw men as selfish and taking his words and twisting them for their own benefit or entirely misconstruing the message he'd given them.

Joseph's belted podere was made of a rich, brown fabric, which flowed with his careful movements around the body. Although this was meant to be his own tomb, Joseph made no mistake he would not need this tomb for himself now. Joseph appeared to be a man who was truly honored to be of service to God.

Nicodemus had already caught the eye of the angel Raphael and so Gabriel went back to observing Joseph. The younger and spryer of the two, Joseph worked tirelessly arranging and rearranging the body, his eyes wet with unshed tears for his nephew.

"Joseph, this is your tomb, is it not?" Nicodemus spoke Aramaic in a quiet and reverent voice. He went about anointing the body.

"Yes," Joseph answered, "but in my proclaiming him the Messiah, I am dead already to my people. I'll be imprisoned or killed soon, and there will be no proper burial for me. No matter. I only hope my meager tomb is fit for the King of the Jews."

The spoken words swelled Gabriel's heart. This man should be protected, and Gabriel would gladly volunteer for the task. In those few words, Gabriel realized if he and Raphael secured the tomb with a large stone, they could instead see these two noble men to safety.

Joseph rested both his hands on the slab, his whole body quivering from exertion, grief, and fear. Lit solely by the two candles the men carried in, the cool, dark tomb was plain, unadorned.

"It is fit for him, friend," Nicodemus said. "When I came in the night to meet Jesus, I, too believed he is who he says he is. Did I bring enough myrrh and aloe?"

Joseph nodded. "This is worth a fortune, friend. It will surely be enough. Why did this happen? I still feel as if this is a dream. They crucified him between two common thieves!" He paced the small space, wringing his hands. "Where are his so called disciples, now? Peter denied him outright today, and they all ran and hid like thieves."

"Perhaps, we should have done the same? Our lives are forfeit now," Nicodemus replied.

"I would never abandon my nephew. Never. Let us remove the wood and thorns from his body." He gently extracted a blood-covered thorn and several pieces of the cross whose splinters were stuck in his nephew's hands. Raphael leaned forward out of the shadows and watched the two men intently. Gabriel knew what he was thinking. If they left the tomb with any items containing the Son's blood, they would be powerful weapons in the war against Lucifer.

The men made a small pile of the shards of wood they removed. They had freed six bloody thorns from Jesus' head. Nicodemus prepared the body with a combination of myrrh and aloe. "Give me that vial, and I will collect the extra myrrh that drops from the body. Right now, I feel as though everything that comes in contact with his body is precious, like gold."

Joseph held the vial and collected some of the extra myrrh and aloe that had touched the body. "Here." Joseph handed Nicodemus the vial. "Keep this." Joseph collected a few splinters and three of the six thorns they had gingerly removed from the Son's head. He opened his cloak and put them in a cup.

Nicodemus flashed him a look as he continued his work. "Is that the cup he drank from on the cross?"

Joseph nodded.

"What will you do with those things?"

Joseph shrugged. "Show my children. And my children's children if I live that long. This cup, the wood, and these thorns touched my Lord the day he died."

The angels could stay hidden no longer. Gabriel and Raphael appeared from the shadows.

"It is much more important than that, gentlemen."

Both men recoiled and spread their arms to hide the body they were preparing behind them. Nicodemus found the courage to speak. "Stay back. Who are you?"

"We are here to help you. First, let me give you the sight." Raphael waved his hand in front of them providing them with the ability to see the white glow of the angels' eyes and their golden auras.

"What…What are you?" Joseph stammered.

"I am Raphael and this is Gabriel. We are angels of the Lord. We are here to protect you upon your exit from this tomb. Joseph, you are now holding the most powerful weapons against evil, mankind has ever known. Nicodemus, I suggest you take some of the pieces of the cross and three thorns as well, along with that vial of myrrh and aloe Joseph collected."

Raphael moved closer to the terrified men. "Hurry, they have already found you." A low, droning growl rose from outside the tomb. The men did as they were told and hurried to finish their work. They covered their Lord in cloth and collected their belongings.

Raphael led Nicodemus while Gabriel took Joseph out of the tomb.

Gabriel turned back and took one last look. The body was gone. Sitting there, looking quite peaceful was another of his brothers, the archangel Michael, who gave him a questioning look.

Had Father sent him to collect the body?

There was no time to find out.

The terrified men clung to the angels realizing hundreds of demons encircled them. The large rock slid by itself and sealed the tomb from the demons. "Are you ready, brother?" Raphael grabbed Nicodemus.

"Yes, God be with you," Gabriel said, holding fast to Joseph. The demons moved in to attack, but the angels with their respective humans, vanished.

Gabriel relocated them to Joseph's home.

"Thank you. You are the angel Gabriel?"

"Yes, the same who announced to your sister, Mary the impending birth of the Savior."

Joseph's eyes widened. "Of course, she did confide in me the story. I have several who must join us if we are to run. Where shall we go?"

"Britannia," Gabriel answered. He had a plan. "Soon enough, I will come for you." A sharp banging came from outside the front door. "Let them arrest you. Drink from the cup. It will sustain you."

When the time was right, Gabriel came for him after making the necessary preparations.

They traveled by boat, many other believers traveling with them as far as France—the two Bethany sisters, Mary and Martha, Lazarus (who Jesus had raised from the dead), Eutropius, Salome, Cleon, Saturnius, Mary Magdalene, Maximin, Martial, and

Trophimus.

By the next account, history was recorded accurately in the ninth century by Rabanus Maurus in the "Life of Mary Magdalene":

Leaving the shores of Asia and favoured by an east wind, they went round about, down the Tyrrhenian Sea, between Europe and Africa, leaving the city of Rome and all the land to the right. Then happily turning their course to the right, they came near to the city of Marseilles, in the Viennoise province of the Gauls, where the river Rhône is received by the sea. There, having called upon God, the great King of all the world, they parted; each company going to the province where the Holy Spirit directed them; presently preaching everywhere.

****

Gabriel took a deep breath, resting his head in his hands for a moment before forcing himself to meet Seamus' gaze. "Joseph and I went to Glastonbury. That is where he planted the thorn tree that grew there until recently. Over the centuries, I protected the artifacts and the line of Joseph. But the cup was never safe with us. It was too powerful and attracted too much attention. Joseph of Arimathea passed it to his brother-in-law, Bron. Hence it became Galahad's destiny to find the cup as Galahad's maternal grandfather was a descendant of Bron."

Seamus could not believe the words he was hearing. Of course he knew the legends. But growing up and reading the Arthurian legends, he took them for just that, legends. He thought his family had made up the tales to keep the real cup safe. "So Lancelot's son born through Elaine *did* find what he was seeking?"

"Indeed he did. As it was meant to be, Seamus." Gabriel's expression turned sad. "Galahad was a noble man of virtue and knew that the cup, in the wrong hands, would cause great evil. He gave it to his great aunt, who was an abbess in a nunnery. It was taken to America in the fifth century and is safely hidden among the most holy there. I'm sorry Lucas. The cup is not here. It never was. And I will not disclose its location and put the relic in jeopardy for the benefit of one human."

Seamus hung his head. "So all this time? A waste!" He slammed his hands down on the wooden dining bench. "Tell me where the cup is, Gabriel. It is promised to Nicodemus' heir."

He felt a hand on his shoulder. Lucas. "Thank you, Seamus. But if anyone understands the frustrations of being a part of this lineage, it is me. You may have lived a quiet existence up to this point, but I beg you from the bottom of my heart, come with me to the United States. Whoever is in possession of this cup will only hand it over to you. I need you."

Seamus floundered. He could not go to America. "No, I should go back home and…"

And what? Seamus had nothing and no one to go home to. Unless Adrienne…

"I will go with you, Seamus. Let's help them." Adrienne strode into the room with a renewed strength. "With or without this angel's help." She narrowed her eyes at the angel.

"It's pretty in the States, I swear." Dean gave him a punch in the shoulder. "And you'll have me to hang out with, what more could you ask for?"

"But Adrienne…" Seamus had envisioned this

playing out differently. If only he could give the Americans the cup and other artifacts and he and Adrienne could carve out a peaceful life...together. "I promised I would never put you in harm's way again after today."

"And I promised I'd never leave you." She kissed his cheek and headed for the door. "I'll go pack."

"She can totally come. What the heck?" Dean said after she was gone.

"Remember the words of Edmund Burke," Lucas said. "'All that is necessary for the triumph of evil is that good men do nothing.'"

Cups rattled and glasses spilled. Gabriel was shaking violently hanging onto the table for support. "Stop this. At once. There is no saving your wife," he pointed at Lucas. "Be grateful you found love once in this life. No one can use that cup. You cannot protect it. It *will* fall into the wrong hands. I'm sorry, I cannot allow this." Gabriel stood and backed up against a wall. "I just want to go home!" he cried. "Can't any of you understand? I can't take it anymore down here."

Lucas threw up his hands. "Wait!"

But with a flash of light, Gabriel vanished.

"Damnit!" Lucas yelled. "Why do angels always run when you need them? This is like looking for a needle in a haystack. Where would we even begin looking? Abbeys? Monasteries like this one?" He gathered his things. "I am asking you to come with me, Seamus. But I need to leave immediately. If Calise dies because of this delay..." his voice trailed off.

"Lucas, of course I'm coming with you. I gave you my word," Seamus said, hurrying after him. "And you're right, you know I need to be there. Whoever has the cup, won't give it to you."

"I guess we're off to the see the wizard then," Dean chimed in.

"With or without Gabriel's help, I guess." Seamus did a three-sixty scanning the room for the vanished angel.

Lucas sighed. "My guess is he's bound and determined to stop us."

"I'll get us transportation off this rock and secure the next flight home," Dean said.

Lucas placed both his hands on Seamus' shoulders. "Are you sure you want to do this?"

"Gabriel is supposed to protect me right? What can he protect me from if I never do anything dangerous?" Seamus laughed at his own joke. "But I need to talk to Adrienne first."

"Make it snappy. We'll be waiting."

****

"What are you thinking?" she probed.

"Why are you doing this?" After years living inside his own head, Seamus wasn't exactly one to bother with small talk. Yet, for some reason, her voice tugged at him from the depths of his soul. He wanted to confide in her. Tell her everything. Being alone had been his life. He reveled in hours of painting and logic games which bled into days of abstract thought. Being the sun in his own universe was all he knew. But all he'd really been looking for was his moon.

"Don't you want me to come?"

He lifted her suitcase off the bed and sat on the firm mattress. "It's not that. You really want to know what I'm thinking?"

In a few hours, the island would be waking up.

Tourists would bustle about, shops would be swept, and the doors would be open to another day as usual. Even after everything that had happened here last night.

People. People worked, played, lied, and cheated.

"I think humans are selfish bastards. Only out for themselves. And the beauty and simplicity of life around them is completely ignored while they trudge forward on their 'me-me-me' paths of self-destruction. They repopulate the earth with more brainless darkwalker drones, then die, having accomplished nothing." He should leave now. Certainly a deep well of hatred in him was brimming if not overflowing. And saying all this to a darkwalker. Even if her shadow had begun to fade.

Silence, for the first time in his life, became deafening awaiting her response. Any response.

"I'll just leave," he stood.

A tug at his shirt.

"Seamus, wait."

His name, coming from her lips, wilted his overwhelming desire to flee. If he left, he may never hear her speak his name again. He sat down, braced for the worst.

"It's just...I've never met anyone like you. I dove into the world's selfish nothingness, to busy my brain. I am selfish, Seamus. *I'm* one of the people you hate."

"I don't hate you, Adrienne. I just need to make sure..."

She placed a finger on his lips. "Let me finish. After my parents died and I got the inheritance, I gave up. I am a victim of my own demise. And I gave in to the worst thing ever: the path of least resistance. I was surrounded with empty people and I pushed out of my mind the fact I was utterly alone and nothing like them. I figured life was too short to make a difference and if I could spend my days making myself happy, then that's what I would do."

"We are all our own worst enemy. I know from my own experience. Excuses. Lies we tell ourselves. I'm done running away. But are you?"

Adrienne said nothing.

Shut up, his mind screamed. *You're scaring her!* Seamus knew people hated holding up a mirror to themselves for their own actions. Looking ahead and placing your feet where you want to go is easy. Staying put, and fighting yourself was much harder. That was why he'd retreated from society. No one had shown him any worth on this miserable planet. Who was he protecting the damn artifacts for?

Selfish bastards who understood nothing of grace?

Let them rot in hell.

And if he joined them, so be it.

The only peace he'd found in this life was now inches away from him and he was scared to death she'd run away too. But if she was coming along, he needed to be sure this was for real.

That we are for real.

Fingers intertwined with his. A heat traveled from his fingertips, up his arm, spread out through his chest and hit the top of his head and the tips of his toes. *Was Adrienne the one? Would she be worth it?*

"The only place I want to run is into your arms. Teach me, Seamus. I want to learn. I want to be a better person."

Seamus squeezed her hand and looked her square in the eye. "I have one requirement then."

"Name it."

"If you go down this road with me, you have to be *all in*. Can you do this?"

"I'm all in. Where do we start?"

Seamus sighed. Words were just that. And she spoke them so quickly. He wanted so badly to trust her, but how could he? Everyone he'd ever trusted in his life had let him down. His subconscious screamed at him that she, too, would fail him. His heart and his head were in disagreement on this one. His head said "Don't trust her."

But his heart sang the truth: She was his one and only.

Chapter 21

Las Vegas, Nevada

Ellen stopped in her tracks. Asmodeus was not what she expected. He was quite beautiful. Dark skin with flowing blond locks. Piercing magenta eyes and a body to make Greek gods weep. Sure she'd heard the stories…who hadn't?

Asmodeus was the offspring of a demon mother and human father. But not just any demon. His mother was Agrat Bat Mahlat, a demon queen and succubus. And his father was King David himself.

Asmodeus was one of the Kings of the Nine Hells and the manifestation of one of the seven deadly sins…he was Lust.

Of course, she knew all this before she got there, but now that she was standing in front of him, she realized too late, she and Shane were in over their heads.

"Step forward, angel." Asmodeus stretched out his hands and two minions handed him walking sticks. One claw leg and one human leg. His one physical imperfection and it was a big one. He circled her. "You haven't done any time in jail, why play the part of the prisoner?"

"I don't understand what you mean?" Ellen fluttered her eyelashes and feigned innocence.

"If you'd been in the pit...ever...I'd know you. And I don't. That means you were born an angel and fell in this life?" He leaned in close and inhaled.

Ellen wanted to shudder, but held still. Showing any weakness would not bode well for her at this point. Her cloak held tight to her like a leather glove. "I did fall and recently came into possession of something you've been looking for." She bowed before him.

"Give it to me." He held out his hand and she rose, producing the artifact from Holy Hill.

Asmodeus turned the artifact over in his hands and then flung it to the floor where it shattered into dozens of pieces. "Keep looking." He smiled, circling her while running his fingers through her hair. "So why would you go through all this trouble? What do you really want?" He sniffed her again. "You have succubus blood coursing within you." He grabbed her by the throat and began to lift her off the ground. "How? Why?"

"Hey! Put her down!" Shane burst from behind the guards.

Asmodeus dropped Ellen who fell to the ground, coughing and massaging her throat. "Who are you? Do you claim this wench?"

Shane stepped forward. "I do. She's mine."

The laugh issuing from Asmodeus was rich and deep, as if Shane's words truly amused him. "Aw, that's cute. Two angels who fell in this life, working out their Daddy issues together. That's rich." He turned on Shane. "It takes a few trips to the pit and shitty demon lifetimes up here to go away. Until you realize *He* doesn't care!" He yelled to the heavens.

Shane helped Ellen to her feet and kept half his

hulking body in front of her. "I told you babe, he wouldn't care about the work we did for him or the fact we are willing to work for him. Let's go." He made a play to grab Ellen's hand and started to leave.

Their way was blocked by six mammoth demon security guards with Uzis.

Asmodeus stood in front of them. "Tell me, fallen angels, how is it you came in possession of that artifact and why *she* smells of my favorite succubus, Sindy." A roar issued from his throat. "Speak!" He screamed over the din of the house music.

Shane made no motion that they were in any danger. He was as relaxed as Ellen would imagine him being if he were watching a movie and drinking beer on a Friday night. She, on the other hand, knew that if they didn't get out of here soon, they wouldn't get out at all.

"We were visiting a friend of mine in the states. Named Rod. Works for you. The three of us were hiking in Wisconsin. We came upon a colony of *jinn* under a demon army attack. Yours I assume. So we played along and my lassie got a wee scratch from a *jinn* who'd jumped inside your succubus, Sindy. Rod was killed by a *jinn*. Gave me that trinket with his last breath, told us to finish the job you hired him for. Said the money was good. Take it or leave it, it's the truth."

Asmodeus paced back and forth eyeing his entourage. "I heard that. Damn *jinn*. We need to control them better," he snarled. "Look, if the artifact had what I was looking for, I'd pay you. How about in exchange for me letting you shitfucks live, you come and work for me?"

"Sounds good!" Ellen piped up. She felt an elbow in her ribs from Shane.

"I don't know. What do we have to do?" Shane remained calm, staring down Asmodeus.

Extracting an envelope from his pocket, the demon king continued. "Since Rod is dead, you've inherited his territory. Wisconsin was a bust. He was slated to search Minnesota next. Go there and bring me any *authentic* artifacts you find. They are to be passed from your hands directly to mine. Understood?"

"We'd love to." Ellen snatched the envelope and handed it to Shane before turning around and starting to make her way over the suspension bridge. Time to boogie.

"Wait," Asmodeus said. "You will stay with me. And work as a dancer. He can go. *If* he brings me back what I want, then you are free to leave."

Shane turned to his side and curled his fingers into two tight fists. "The lady stays over my dead body."

Asmodeus clapped. "Wonderful, she must be a worthy wench if you care so damn much. So I simply must keep her. Guards!"

Something clamped around her neck and Ellen screamed thinking she was being strangled. Only they weren't hands. It was a metal collar and with a swift tug, she was on her back and being dragged away from Shane. The look on his face reflected sheer violence as he erupted into action, turning on the guards. He became a blur and disarmed them all with his lightning fast reflexes.

Ellen was pulled to a standing position and a voice whispered in her ear. "I like him." It was Asmodeus with a knife tip digging in hard underneath her jawbone. "Kill my men. I don't care," Asmodeus said to Shane. "Or leave now and I won't kill your whore."

Ellen shook her head. "Go. I'll be fine."

Defeated, Shane lowered the firearm and gave Ellen a look of ferocity. "I will be back for you."

Ellen wanted to say something profound. "I love you." Or "Save yourself." But no words came from her mouth. Asmodeus handed her off to his guards and the last thing she saw was Shane making the letter "L" with his thumb and index finger before he was punched in the face and stripped of the gun.

****

Four guards tossed Shane through a side door onto the gravel outside the club. A valet stood by holding the limo door open for him.

"Are you ready?"

This was not going as planned. Not even a smidge.

Shane stepped into the limo and the driver hit the gas slamming him backward into the leather seat. He opened the envelope Asmodeus had handed him. Inside was a hand written note:

Extract all holy artifacts of significance from Minnesota.

Along with credit cards and a stack of hundreds.

Shane rapped on the window separating him from the driver. The window slid open. "Yes?"

"Where are you taking me?"

The driver pointed to the sign at the entrance to the expressway. "You have the next flight out of Vegas to the Twin Cities. I should caution you; anything you put on the credit cards unrelated to the cause, you will owe Asmodeus. And being in his debt is not always pleasurable."

The window slid shut and Shane settled into the rear of the limo.

Now what? Ellen was captive and he was no closer to knowing why the Demon of Lust was on a search and destroy mission for all religious artifacts. Or why that army had attacked the *jinn*. And he didn't give a shit. He'd do whatever he needed to do to get Ellen back.

He looked at the empty seat next to him and realized he already missed her. Not the succubus-fed Ellen, but the real Ellen. She was smarter than he was and always seemed to know what to do. What would she do in his shoes?

If only he could get word to the archangel Raphael, maybe he could help. But he had no idea where to even start looking for him.

His lifetime of emptiness settled in around him. Again. After five years with the demon Nara, concentrating on his daughter, Melki and finally getting over Calise, why now did he feel this odd connection to Ellen?

I am not worthy of her love.

He closed his eyes. Images rolled through his head…

The words of the demon in Wauwatosa: "You're my replacement?"

If it wasn't Asmodeus' army attacking the *jinn*, was it Abaddon's? Although his father-in-law was still incapacitated from his run in with Lucas Rojas, he was still the figurehead of Nara's family business. What interest did they have in killing *jinn*?

The demon, Rod at Holy Hill.

Asmodeus smashing the artifact in front of them saying he needed to control the *jinn* to use them.

Fucking demons. He knew what they were

planning.

Asmodeus and Abaddon were in a race.

To find the Ring of Solomon.

****

"Boss said you go on stage in an hour. Rest up," the demon said before tossing Ellen in a private cell in the lower level hovels of the dance club. She used the respite to rapid fire through her celestial knowledge base while struggling against the cuffs holding her arms pinned to the wall. The succubus blood must be waning faster now. She could feel her true self pushing to the forefront and chastising her for her impunities:

Agreeing to work with Shane.

Getting attacked by a succubus.

The succubus using Shane as an appetizer and dessert whenever the bloodlust needed satisfaction.

And now imprisoned by Asmodeus!

She needed to cut her losses and go back to Milwaukee to be with Cali. This was a fool's errand.

This prison cell housed only her, but there was an air of entrapment surrounding this whole structure. But what?

"Guard!" she said to the demon outside her cell. "I have to pee," she said, pulling the demon cloak as tightly around her as she could.

"Give yourself a golden shower. I don't care," the guard yelled.

"I don't think Asmodeus wants his best dancer smelling like urine. I'll tell him you sent me up there smelling like piss. What's your name again?" she yelled back.

Grunting, the guard appeared and shoved a rusty metal key in the ancient lock and proceeded to free her wrists. A circular hole in the cement floor was Ellen's only means of relieving herself. She squatted. The guard watched with a dirty smirk. "Better?"

Wrenching her skintight skirt back in place, she kicked off her heels and sidled up to the guard. Running a finger down his cheek, she mentally pushed the remaining succubus blood into her index finger. "Do you really have to keep me locked up?"

He melted under her touch. "Not really. It's not like you can escape anyway. None of us can." He pointed to the ceiling. Long lines were scratched across the cement.

A devil's trap. An inner hexagram, and outer heptagram with the ancient symbols placed precisely. An inescapable prison for a demon. No big whoop for an angel. *Goodie.* Seizing her chance, she kicked the demon in the gut, forcing him to step backward and had his hands secured in her former restraints before he could say, "Oh shit."

"I'll be right back sweetheart. You sleep." She tapped his temple and the minion's head slumped to the side. Pocketing his keys, she waffled on whether to skedaddle and find Shane or go spy on Asmodeus and see what the heck was going on.

Freedom from this sex hovel seemed prudent, but at what cost to Shane? If imbeciles like this guy were on guard duty, a little spying seemed in order. Besides, if she ran, Asmodeus would put a hit out on Shane. She wouldn't let that happen. Something about hanging out with him these last few days had given her a level of excitement and she sort of relished each new day they spent together creating havoc.

He was…fun. And sexy. And gorgeous. And her

best friend was in a coma because of him. *Let's not forget that.*

Her inner succubus screamed a tirade of reminders of their hot ass times in the sack. But besides the quick escapade in the limo, she'd erased those indiscretions from his head. Even if they meant something to her, it was no matter. He would never be able to recollect their rendezvous.

I mean, that was only sex to Shane, right? It's not like I want a relationship with him...do I?

Too bad. Because having her legs wrapped around his waist and him deep inside her was edging out for her favorite place to be on earth.

Shut up! Ellen chided the succubus.

Uh, that wasn't me talking you bad, bad girl!

Before her inner monologue ran farther amok, she made her way out of the basement and took the stairs back up to the club where she discreetly slipped inside the women's restroom. What she wouldn't give for sweatpants, an old t-shirt and sneakers. But alas, she was in a tight, leather dress and stilettos thanks to the succubus.

She needed a new outfit. And sunglasses. So Asmodeus wouldn't recognize her.

The first girl who pushed open the swinging door to the ladies room met a smack in the face from Ellen's fist. Ellen neatly caught her and dragged her into the handicapped stall. *What do I have to work with?* Jeans, a sequined tank top and flats. A bonus of sunglasses in her purse. Since she was already at the club, the human girl would be ravaged by demons tonight, so really, Ellen was doing her a solid favor to hole her up in the bathroom for a few hours.

After usurping her clothing, Ellen positioned the body in the corner and knelt down to peer out. No one was in the bathroom. Leaving the stall locked, she shimmied underneath, washed her hands, and headed back into the club.

Time to get her spy on. Rave and roll.

Chapter 22

Mont-Saint-Michel, France

Adrienne had made a choice. But a little voice kept second-guessing her decision. When it should be oh-so-simple. Go with Seamus. Go all-in with someone with honor and decency. Expose herself to loving and being loved.

Or run away now.

Run to the safety of another big city where she could be a nobody and live unbothered.

Why was this simple choice so difficult?

Her heart wanted to go with Seamus to America. To trust him and go on a noble crusade for the elusive Cup of Life in the name of true love. But she'd been fooled by men before. And like the old saying, "Fool me once, shame on you. Fool me twice, shame on me."

Pain was pain no matter which way she sliced it. Rushing back to her room to pack her belongings, three monks passed by her in the opposite direction. She bowed her head to show reverence to these holy men.

But are they perfect men of God?

Didn't they have sinful thoughts? Break rules? Break their word? Lie? Cheat? Steal?

And if they don't, does Seamus? That was the real question.

Mankind was notoriously selfish and when she'd

joined with Daevas she had only admitted and embraced the obvious. Try as they might, deep down all people were bad.

Sure there were the Mother Theresa's and the Gandhi's. But a handful of people among billions did not a trusting Adrienne make. And unless she had concrete proof Seamus was the kind of man he said he was, how could she trust him?

Adrienne's parents had always been by her side. As an only child from a privileged family, her mother had home schooled her and never exposed her to the evils of humankind. Life up until eighteen years old had consisted of home-cooked meals, online learning, and a solitary life with her family.

But all that changed once she got to Paris. She'd applied for the study abroad program after two years of living at home and attending a local college. Her parents had agreed to it on the one condition that after her year was up, they would visit her and she would show them around France.

So her family's death was really her fault.

If she'd stayed home. If she never went to Paris. If, if, if…

But she'd so desperately wanted time away from them.

Maybe that was her punishment for being selfish?

She folded each shirt and placed it in her suitcase…remembering.

When she was ten years old her parents had taken her to the State Fair. She'd gone on a ride with her father so she could write a paper on centrifugal force. It was called the Gravitron. It was an enclosed, padded circle and she got inside with her dad not knowing what to expect. In her paper, she later wrote that the spinning motion had the rider reach twenty-four revolutions per minute in less than twenty seconds. Then the floor dropped out. She was held to the wall by a force three times the earth's gravity. Screaming, she tried to reach for her father's hand or even turn her head to see him. But for the duration of the ride, she was immobilized.

That was the same way she'd felt every day since her parents' death. Like the floor had dropped out of her life and she was pinned in place unable to move.

Then when she'd found solid ground again the night Seamus kissed her. Everything had changed. And then he'd shared his blood, letting her into his world. And what a world it was.

Angels and demons walk among us unseen!

There was no other explanation for that thing in the air outside the cathedral. Black. Wings. Red eyes.

As a child, she'd gone to Sunday school to learn about God, Satan, angels, and demons. She'd been told you don't have to see to believe. Even Jesus did miracles over and over and people didn't believe.

She zipped up her suitcase and took one last glance around the simple accommodations which provided everything the monks needed.

She'd made a promise to Seamus. And if one virtue lived at her core, it was never to break her word. Seamus made her thirsty for truth. He might be the only human who could stop the downward spiral that had become her life

And if he believed in her, in the idea she could change, then for now, that would be enough.

Because she believed in him.

****

"Can you stop that?" Seamus asked.

Dean tapped his fingers on the dashboard of the car the monks had loaned them. Lucas revved the engine for the enth time. The monks had profusely thanked them, but Seamus was not sure for what.

Seamus felt terrible. With several dead, others injured, and so much repair needed to their abbey, they'd left the place a mess. But the monks did not seem to care or even share his concern. It was as if the whole ordeal had given the monks an infusion of faith. The injured had continual crowds around them as they repeatedly recounted their tales from the holy battlefield.

Seamus had watched as some prayed and others fell to their knees. Building faith in fervent believers would make them zealots. Seamus said a quiet prayer these men of God would stay safe. He couldn't say how they would fare if there was another attack.

The old monk from the basement bid them farewell at the car. "Thank you for bringing us truth. We will continue to train and know that we are in your debt and Le Mont Saint Michel will always be a safe haven for you and your descendants."

To each of them, they'd gifted vials of holy water from the high tide. Seamus twirled the small bottle between his thumb and index finger and gave a last long look at the majestic structure they were leaving behind.

"Where is she?" Dean asked for the third time.

"She's coming," Seamus assured them. *Wasn't she?* After their talk, Adrienne had said she was going to pack and be right out. Surely she wouldn't go back on her word. All Seamus had ever wanted in this world was to be left alone. But Lucas Rojas had changed everything. Made him realize isolation was really a selfish act. And dying at the end of a pointless life led solely to harbor personal safety was an act of disloyalty to yourself.

Seamus was officially done. No more wallowing in his own version of selfishness. How could he? He'd met the one woman he couldn't stand to be away from.

He had opened his heart to her in their first kiss in the alley. Let her in his soul. If only she could give him that which he held dear in return…her undying love, loyalty, and friendship.

And then there she was, hurrying down the stone stairs to their car. Seamus opened his car door and stepped out. "Pop the trunk," he instructed Lucas. Placing her suitcase in the trunk, he helped her inside. They were squashed in the tiny vehicle.

"Got all your makeup and high heels stowed safely away?" Dean asked over his shoulder, with a smile.

Adrienne didn't respond to his jab. Instead she turned to Seamus and said the one thing he didn't want to hear.

"I can't go with you to America. In de Gaulle, we should part ways."

Seamus heart caught in his throat. "But you said…"

Adrienne gave him a kind look and opened her purse. "The monks who walked me out changed my mind. And even though I'm not a person to go back on my word, they've convinced me otherwise. Give me your cell phone number. I want to stay in touch, I mean…I know I said I would go, but I just can't." She hung her head. "I don't want you to have to protect me all the time. They said I am a liability to you."

"I disagree." Lucas kept driving, heading northwest on the A84 motorway toward Caen.

Seamus was surprised Lucas spoke up. The man seemed to be of even fewer words than himself. But with his soul mate lying in a hospital bed half a world away, he probably had other things on his mind.

"The monks reminded me what I am," Adrienne insisted. "A darkwalker. That's what they called me. Out of God's light. Leading a selfish existence that amounts to nothing. What good am I to a cause like yours?"

Lucas began to speak, but Dean clapped him on the shoulder. "I got this one." He unclipped his seat belt and faced them. "Reality bites. Seriously, I married a demon. Had a kid with her even. Then in the middle of her redemption, I shot her."

Seamus was taken aback. These guys were cut of the same cloth.

"Have you seen those commercials for antihistamines where the world is foggy and gray? Then the person with allergies takes an antihistamine and the world becomes clear with magnificent colors and clarity." Dean spread his fingers. "Poof, the world is right again."

Adrienne nodded. "A fog descended on me a long time ago. And apparently I fed off of it and still do. The monks said I have a black cloud hovering over me every time I move. I can see it in the mirror now. The last thing they said to me was 'We'll pray for you, darkwalker.'"

How nice of those guys to slam her with a dose of reality on the way out the door.

Dean shook his head. "That's the cool part about people. We can choose, whenever we want, to lift our own cloud. We can walk, as best as we can, in the light. I don't see the black cloud that follows you. I see the light inside of you waiting for you to shuck off the darkness. And when you do, you will be our greatest asset because those who can viciously hate can also intensely love. Get me?"

Lucas nodded. "Well said. Fate brought the four of us together for a purpose. Let's not taunt it. I say we stick together."

Seamus slid his fingers through hers again, feeling the now familiar pulse of her positive energy underneath the dark sadness. Her hand radiated an energy so like his own he felt as if they could meld, become part of one another. Not daring to risk looking at her, he stared out the window at the rows of hedges. He was terrified he was the only half of this relationship feeling this deep of a connection.

But she squeezed his hand back. "Fine. For now, I'll stay. But if I feel like I'm hindering you or a detriment…"

"You won't be," Seamus assured her.

Their eyes met. "So the Holy Grail, huh? And you're its protector. In your life, have you ever come across something truly magical?"

"Yes," Seamus smiled. "You."

Chapter 23

En route to Charles de Gaulle Airport, France

Daevas Lerwick kept his distance behind the vehicle ahead of them holding one Miss Adrienne Perdu. Nara seethed beside him in the passenger seat. But as her family was his bread and butter, he cared about nothing more than doing as he was told and staying off Nara's long list of enemies.

The power and inordinate sums of money he made was well worth following orders—from a woman no less. When he was recruited for the job, Nara's father, Abaddon had convinced him to leave the large sect of Novum-Stellae he'd directed in Southern France and come to Paris. No matter to him. As in Nice, Parisians led a decadent lifestyle, which suited him just fine.

It hadn't been much of a stretch to set up shop on the Champs-Élysées. Recruiting Parisians had been far easier than he thought. The Godless self-centered life style was sweeping most urban communities anyway. Pay them for shitty work in pointless jobs. Entertain them with bobbles and shiny jewelry. Condemn them if they disobeyed. But always make them believe they're worth more than they are.

Novum-Stellae catered to the lazy bastards they already were, so Daevas and his organization flourished. He offered a pyramid scheme of power and wealth from the bottomless pit of Nara's family money. He pulled in a cool two million euros a year in cash plus ten thousand for each new recruit who was willing to put in writing that they would donate their assets to the organization upon death.

Even though the organization was outwardly non-denominational, the upper echelon knew better. Daevas knew what Nara and her father really were. Honest to fucking-goodness demons. Walking among humans, under everyone's noses and controlling everything happening on this god-forsaken planet. And with demons at the helm, came real earthly power to their devotees. Daevas refused to go back to the ways of his shitty youth ever again. His mother had been a weary seamstress and his dad like a worker ant killing himself in a factory every day. *Being poor sucks.*

His family had always been on the verge of collapse without enough food, money, or resources for him and his siblings.

Memories best pushed to the wayside.

"Do not lose them," Nara's eyes flashed red in anger. She tapped numbers in her cell with long, pointed fingernails and spoke in a brisk French, *"Préparel' avion. Vous avez dix munute."* *Prepare the plane. You have ten minutes.* She hung up, keeping the phone in her lap, and tapped her impatient nails on the dashboard. "Tell me what you know about the girl. I thought she was one of ours?"

"She is...I mean, was. I'm not sure. She was an easy pull. I met her after her family died in a plane crash on their way from the states. Exceedingly wealthy. Lost and alone. She took to our precepts without question, attended all the meetings, and was even on her way up the ladder. Maybe she was in the wrong place at the wrong time?"

Nara sniffed. "I don't believe in coincidence. She must have been a mole all along and you missed it. Can you control her if the need arises?"

The word "control" didn't exactly sit all neat and tidy in Daevas' mind. Could he control her? He knew a lot about her. Probably more than anyone. She'd confided in him. "Of course."

"Good," she said. "She has enough knowledge of Novem-Stellae in Paris to hurt us. I'll need you with me. If she is a mole, I want to know what she's told them before she's disposed of."

"Yes." Always the best answer to give Nara.

"They're looking for something," she continued. "Something I need for my Father. Understand?"

Oh, he understood all right. What Nara wanted, she got. Daevas hoped whatever it was she was seeking would bring Abaddon back out into the mainstream again. Daevas felt too vulnerable under Nara's rule and losing his power in the organization was not an option. All the glory he received from running Novem-Stellae in France was *entitled* to him. He deserved it for having to grow up with nothing. But dealing with Abaddon's daughter made his skin crawl. Almost as much as—

"I'm hungry, Mother." A voice piped up from the back seat.

"Of course, darling. The jet is fully stocked and you can eat as soon as we're in the air."

Nara didn't disturb Daevas nearly as much as what sat strapped into a car seat in the back of the vehicle. The little girl's eyes glinted crimson when the sun hit them just right. The blood running in that girl's veins was ice cold and more heartless than the vilest villain Daevas could conjure up:

Nara's demon daughter, Melki.

Chapter 24

Las Vegas, Nevada

Ellen pushed her way up to the bar and ordered a vodka twist, again pulling her demonic cloak tightly around her. She wanted the alcohol on her breath if she got manhandled by any of Asmodeus' guards. She spotted two of them hitting on stick thin, barely-of-legal-age, human girls in the corner of the club. Nodding her head to the music, she worked her way over to the area where they were chatting and indiscreetly dumped her drink over one of the girls.

"You bitch!" The girl cried.

"Sorry," Ellen mumbled. "Just trying to get closer to that." Snatching the drink out of one of the guard's hands, she licked the rim of his glass and handed it back to him. "Damn, you're yummy."

He immediately turned his attention away from the human girl. "Aren't I though? And you're so hot if you ate bread you'd shit toast."

This was the best pick-up line this schmuck had? Cripes. Ellen mustered her best girly laugh. She lowered her sunglasses and gave him a wink. She pressed up closer to him and whispered in his ear. "I wish we could get out of here."

His laugh had venom. "This might be Vegas darling, but be careful, this club might become your

Hotel California."

"What do you mean? I come here all the time." She began to finger the squishy muscles in his bicep. Some guard.

"If I take you where you want to go, then you're here for the duration, sister. See that?" He pointed at the back ceiling where the symbols and carvings looked more like rave graffiti than ensnarement. The carvings disappeared behind the club proper and must go back into their living quarters. The viewing room where Asmodeus sat and a few steps into the club was the furthest the resident demons could venture.

"You can't be serious. A demon club with a devil's trap?" She tried to act surprised, like she had no idea it was there. "You poor thing. You really can't leave?"

His lips brushed against hers before he whispered in her ear. "Don't worry, my boss has a plan. Won't be long now."

Her inner succubus had one more good run. No time like the present. "Well good luck with that." She turned to leave, knowing the succubus' searing touch had already ensnared him.

The goon grabbed her arm and pulled her back to him. He dove into her mouth with his tongue like a leech looking for blood. She gagged, pulled away and slapped him hard across the cheek. Her plan was working.

Laughing, he threw her over his shoulder and headed to the back of the club and up the stairs. Ellen kicked and screamed the whole way.

****

The chauffer handed Shane a slip of paper but said nothing when he slipped out of the limo at the airport.

The paper said, Flight 362, United Airlines and had a printed ticket with Rod's name on it.

Shane found himself pushing past the lost souls. In Vegas, there were only two types of people at the airport, the hopeful and the hopeless. The ones arriving who were dying to win the jackpot and living on a dream of money-will-make-it-all-better. Then there were the ones leaving who had to go back to their useless daily grind, now poor, and with the thrill of success lingering in the cigarette smoke of the now not so glittery city they were leaving behind.

How long could Ellen make it there? He'd seen the devil's trap. Two more steps forward and he would have been eternally stuck in the club with all the others. So this was why Asmodeus had to have others do his bidding.

The Demon of Lust was trapped.

At least Ellen was not.

But if he went back to try and save her, he might end up damning them both.

A few hours later, he hopped off the plane in the Twin Cities. He created an illusion for the human who checked his ID seeing as he looked nothing like Rod. Having played a few gigs in the Twin Cities back in the day, he hailed a cab and headed for the one place he knew would be a good start...the cathedral of Saint Paul.

The only problem was a demon couldn't enter a consecrated church. So he'd have to hire, threaten, or trick someone who would break in, go up to the altar, find the little square stone with a cloth on it and then smash the altar to remove the relic—without destroying it, of course—and then pack it up and move on to the next church. He googled the Catholic Directory on his phone. Oh goodie, only 744 churches in the state.

This gig should only take him about a zillion years.

Besides the fact that probably only some of them had first or second class relics in the Roman tradition. He was looking for first class relics, the preserved human body parts of martyrs or other saints kept beneath church altars. Once placed, the altar was dedicated and the church consecrated.

Most of the relics in altars were bones of the saints. Is that what Asmodeus was after? Deconsecrating the churches of the country would allow all demons access, but for what? Shane couldn't exactly walk into the next church he spotted and ask the local clergy to divulge their secrets. He thought of another tactic: the local library. Asmodeus wasn't after just any relic. He was looking for the Ring of Solomon. Could it be in Minnesota? Time to research the churches. Maybe he could narrow his search.

A gas station attendant pointed him in the direction of the closest public library after he grabbed a candy bar and a soda. He walked three blocks in the direction the attendant pointed before hitting Saint Anthony Park on Como drive.

Taking a bite into the candy bar and letting the chocolate melt on his tongue, Shane felt an overwhelming tsunami of guilt washing over him.

Guilt always managed to sneak up on him at the most inopportune times.

For all he knew, Calise was dead. Ellen was being ravaged by a pack of asshole demons. And his daughter had already forgotten him.

The pain of being a fallen angel was like a cement

wall constantly pushing on him, threatening to cut off his airways. Every day, he wanted to give up.

A bum covered in newspaper was on the bench outside the library taking a mid-morning nap. A little girl, about Melki's age, pranced out of the library with a sagging backpack slung over her shoulder holding her literary loot, her mother behind her, hurrying to catch up.

Shane bent down to tie his shoe.

The little girl tugged on her mom's arm and pointed to the bum. Shane eavesdropped on their conversation.

"God, they need to clean this place up," she said before addressing her daughter. "That's nobody, honey."

Shane nodded. Nobody indeed. The nobody people tried to ignore, wish away, and were grateful wasn't their problem. This kind of bullshit had always infuriated him about human beings. All of them made in the Father's image. Given the choice to help those less fortunate, humans never seemed to choose properly.

He'd gone through his childhood unnoticed by most and yet watching everyone. Holding out hope for mankind that never ceased to let him down. First, his human parents, telling him he was a freak. An odd child. Pushing him into the care of others, which ultimately put him in charge of himself. Alone and abandoned by humans only to discover his true origins as all angels and demons do when they reach adulthood.

Always a fun surprise when you turn eighteen. *Oh yeah, I'm an angel of the Lord living my one human life because I was desperate to experience the magic that is free will.*

Then Calise let him down. Hard. Told him he was too good. Hard to be around. That it was too hard to live up to his expectation. She too, left him alone and abandoned.

Then he'd let himself down. Sucked into Nara's world. Done horrible things. Hurt innocent people. Had a child with a demon thinking it would end his loneliness. Boy, was he wrong.

Free will was a curse. It was much easier upstairs when someone told you what to do and blindly, you followed orders. This free will shit tested your core. And that's when he'd realized neither angels nor humans were really made in the Father's image.

Father was perfect. Omnipresent and harmonious with all creation. Bathed in light and love and able to flow like water from one realm to the next. Humans and angels may have physical similarities to Him. But that is where the similarities ended.

His brain hurt.

Poor Ellen. She probably wasn't sitting in a car in the sunshine eating a candy bar. He needed to get a move on, find whatever Asmodeus might deem useful, and go get her. If any demon filth at that club touched a hair on her head, he'd rain down a one-man apocalypse on them all. He needed her to be safe. To be back by his side.

He wasn't himself without her around. Or maybe he was himself, but with her he was who he'd always wanted to be.

Waiting patiently for the librarian with ice blue eyes and crabby eyebrows to finish with another patron, Shane took in the familiar surroundings of a library from years of pretend studying with Calise while she was in pharmacy school. He heard the click-clack of keys on the public computers, the flipping of paper, the murmurs and occasional bursts of a coughing jag or the thud of a dropped book.

Like most libraries, the rooms were kept warm and dry to limit the books' exposure to humidity. The arid temperatures increased the woody smell from the millions of pages inked with the facts, lies, hopes, dreams, successes, and failures of so many people. Libraries made Shane jumpy. Too quiet. He hadn't liked them in college when he'd been an angel, let alone now that he'd fallen. The metallic twinge of the humming overhead fluorescent lights didn't help any either. More like the buzz of an angry swarm of bees telling him to leave this holy realm of words.

Too bad he hadn't stopped to purchase a tweed jacket and nerd glasses. The librarian he was next in line to see might find that a turn-on. And he needed to connect with her in some way so she'd divulge more information than a snub-nosed point in the right direction.

Her hair had a twinge of red. And her name…Shannon.

He could do a killer Irish brogue. Maybe that would get her.

Smoothing back his long locks, he leaned on the counter after the other patron left with a stash of romance books.

She did not look up at him. "Can I help you?"

"I hope ye can, Shannon," he said, enunciating her name and allowing his Irish brogue to flow from his tongue. "Ahh, the river you be named after is the longest in Ireland. Did ya know dat?"

Her ice blue eyes melted a bit when they finally met his and her eyebrows lifted from their scowled mount.

His brogue tended to do that. He stuck out his hand. "I'm Shane O'Grady and I haven't much time, but if ye wouldn't mind, I need yer help in looking somethin' up."

Reluctant to leave her post, she called in another librarian to fill her place and stepped around the counter. "Of course, Mr. O'Grady."

He wrapped her hands in his and led them to the stacks. "I'm a Dub here with me band for the week, but I promised me Ma I'd look up her Uncle in de church. He's clergy in Minnesota but all she could remember was he was at one of the holiest places in the state with some kind of important relics from the old country. I don't want to go-a-knocking on every church door and ask for him."

"My grandparents are from Dublin. I've been there to visit. It's very beautiful."

Shane gave her hand a little squeeze. "Next time you visit, you look me up and we'll go hiking near me where my parents retired and bought a B&B in Connemara." He needed answers and if his fake charm would get them to save Ellen, then so be it.

"I'd love that. Now what kind of church are you looking for?"

Chapter 25

Mid-air over the Atlantic

Lucas couldn't wait to get his feet back on American soil. This whole trip had been an utter waste of time and taken him away from Calise's side. Besides, what he was seeking had been in America the whole time!

Dean hadn't put down his computer since they got in the air. Seamus and Adrienne were both sleeping a few rows back and Lucas was ready to punch himself in the face.

He couldn't fight death. He couldn't fight destiny. "Found anything? Even a start?" Tick-tock. They'd wasted so much time. After they landed at O'Hare it was only a two hour drive until he was back at Cali's side. This whole thing had been a wild goose chase and he was no closer to saving his wife's life than when the whole thing started.

"Hey," Dean piped up, "I think I got something, thanks to my good Old Catholic upbringing and what Gabriel said about Galahad. If his aunt was a nun, I may have found her order. Listen to this. At the time Sir Galahad allegedly lived, there was a Benedictine abbey near his castle in Northumberland, the Hexham abbey. I would bet money his aunt lived there. If the aunt came to America and hid the grail, that leads us to the

Federation of Saint Benedict. Guess how many of those houses there are."

Lucas shrugged. "Tons?"

"Nope. Listen to this. According to the Saint Benedict's Monastery website: : 'The Federation of St. Benedict was established in 1947 by the Sisters of Saint Benedict, St. Joseph, Minn., to give moral, spiritual, and inspirational support to each monastic community and also to strengthen the Benedictine charism around the world.' From what I can find, there are ten independent monasteries included as members of the Federation outside of the original one in Saint Joseph, Minnesota. Nine of these members were founded by the Sisters of Saint Benedict. Six are in North America and three of those are in Minnesota."

"Where are the others?" Lucas asked.

"Kansas, North Dakota, and Washington state. I say we catch a flight from O'Hare to the Twin Cities. Who's interested in fifty-fifty odds?" Dean chuckled at his own ingenuity.

Lucas was impressed. This was the first ray of hope he'd heard in days. If they could hit the three monasteries only one state away from where Calise was, it might be worth a chance. "I'll call Cali's mom when we land in Chicago. If she thinks we still have time, then as long as Seamus is with us, we should give it a try. We'll start at the original monastery in Saint Joseph. I do need that cup. We've come this far. I'm not giving up now."

He could not lose the love of his life. "I'll go back and tell Seamus that from O'Hare, we'll catch the next flight to the Twin Cities. Can you book them on your laptop?"

"Can do, bro," Dean said, and starting typing.

****

Nara settled back in her seat on the private jet. Melki was napping soundly in her lap after her gourmet feast of chilled shrimp, fresh breads, cheese, grapes, and sparkling apple juice. A text rang through from one of her contacts. "They have booked a connecting flight to Minneapolis/Saint Paul in Minnesota."

"Daevas," she spoke softly, so as not to wake the child. "They've booked a connecting flight. We can beat them there. Go tell the pilot to divert us to the Twin Cities in Minnesota. Then call our people and have a car waiting."

He nodded, with an awkward little bow of his head and headed for the cockpit.

Doing her best not to snarl at the human, she turned her attention back to Melki, rocking her gently and stroking her hair. "I have a good feeling about this, my sweet. Your grandfather will be back at the helm again in no time."

And with Nara grooming Melki to take charge of the family business, all was set in motion for her family to continue with their real plan:

Abaddon must regain control of the *jinn* and take his place as a powerful leader who everyone will bow to in fear.

****

Adrienne rubbed her eyes listening to the whisper of Seamus' voice. "If this is my great-great whatever Aunt's abbey, that would be right. It makes sense. She would have been in the Order of Saint Benedict. What do we know about this monastery in Saint Joseph?"

"I'm working on it. You two just get some rest.

Looks like your family heirlooms might be in Minnesota. Funny, hey? I was starting to think this was a no-win situation."

"I don't believe in that, Dean. Both winning and losing are an illusion. Being a winner isn't success. Both are only temporary states of engagement."

Adrienne yawned. "Are we there yet?"

"Almost. You're almost back home on American soil." Seamus pulled her close and gave her a kiss on the head.

Home.

It was a long time since she'd dare utter that word. Even though they weren't actually going to the town where she grew up, Minnesota was her home. Seamus snoozed next to her and she memorized his face. Was it the airspace she was about to enter or the man sitting next to her that gave her this warm, fuzzy feeling she'd long forgotten?

Closing herself down after her parents' death, she'd lived a life without purpose or motivation. A life of feeding her every desire and wanting for nothing. Well, wanting for nothing material.

She always wanted a partner in crime. Not rob-a-bank crimes but someone she shared code words and secret jokes with. Someone who knew where she was ticklish and someone who could make her laugh. Seamus probably had ten years on her, not that Europeans ever cared about that. And she didn't either. He was a regal-looking man, like a forgotten king time had aged gracefully, with purpose.

Strong hands.

Soft lips.

He carried with him an air of deep knowledge and

human understanding beyond her surface-like tendencies to judge people based on the wrong things. Case in point…Daevas.

What had she seen in him? Wealth and power? Arrogance misconstrued as confidence? Her inner voice chastised her and wondered if she'd been wrong before, maybe she was wrong now.

"Where are you, so lost in thought?" Seamus' voice roused her from her self-analysis. She loved his accent. She could listen to him talk all day.

"Nowhere."

"Hey," he said. "It's okay. You can tell me."

And she really felt like she could. "I haven't trusted anyone in a long time. I'm sorry." And she was. Living her carefree life in Paris had fast become a means to an end. She was trying to fast-forward her life. And, having Seamus hold her hand over the Atlantic Ocean, she finally wanted time to slow down so she could relish it.

"I understand," he said, "It's not like I have a long list of people in my circle of trust. I don't even trust Gabriel. And he's an angel. Who knows what kind of plans he has that have nothing to do with me? He may have left us to help us, or to thwart us. He's gotten worse over the years. Besides my necklace, I have no idea where my family relics are now. So if you think *you* don't trust humanity, have a chat with him."

Adrienne recalled Gabriel's charm and wit while he tried to woo her in the courtyard and later over dinner. For what purpose? To sleep with her? To save her? Either way, he'd rubbed her the wrong way since the moment they'd met.

"And yet…" Seamus continued, "His heart is full

of compassion. That I do know. Why else would he have sacrificed so much for humanity for all these centuries?"

Adrienne didn't want to burst Seamus' bubble, but didn't angels have to follow orders? Maybe Gabriel wasn't so much full of compassion as he was following a directive he could not break. "I'll try to give him the benefit of the doubt. But it's been a long time since my inner optimist told me the cup was half full."

He laughed. "The cup, my dear, isn't half full. The cup isn't even filled with water—it's surrounded by water—and hidden in plain sight. The truth has always been there for you and everyone else. It's just conveniently ignored."

Adrienne could wake up every morning for the rest of her life and have discussions on the meaning of life with this man. His intellect was crazy sexy and his now stubbly beard made her want to brush her cheek against his. "Aren't you the clever one?"

"I'm not clever, Adrienne. I use logic. I wield weapons as well as the other seers, but my indispensable weapon, is my logical mind. But my logic crossed long ago into the abstract. I can see the peace in chaos. I look at things from a multi-dimensional perspective. It's not that I'm creative. I don't believe in creativeness, only higher forms of logic. I believe intensely creative people simply use a higher form of logic."

"So you 'think outside the box?'" Adrienne rested her head on the headrest. The depth of his words were something she would like to lie in bed with every night and dissect. She'd start tonight.

"More than that. My box is scatterbrained.

Predictable unpredictability. Once you climb outside the box, you can examine every angle and see beyond what *is*. True logic is the ability to see beyond what you are looking at. Don't you agree?"

All she wanted to look at was Seamus.

He laughed. "Too much? Sorry. I'll let you get some rest and go see what Dean has come up with. Do you need anything?"

You. "No, I'm fine."

Seamus unclipped his belt and went to converse with the others.

Her head was spinning. His intensity enthralled her and something about the beauty in his words made her want to show him tenderness. She wanted to love him. Every day from now until forever.

"Dean booked a connecting flight to the Twin Cities." Seamus leaned an arm over her chair. "You still in?"

She nodded. Their purpose was set and anything she felt for him would have to be put on hold until this mission was accomplished.

And whatever Seamus' mission was, was now hers. No matter what.

Chapter 26

Las Vegas, Nevada

Ellen made a show of fighting the demon who'd slung her over his shoulder and was carrying her toward an elevator. Truth was, she *wanted* inside the devil's trap. Unceremoniously dropping her to the ground once inside the elevator, she scooted backwards and pressed herself up against the wall, panting. "So that's it? I'm trapped here forever?"

He gave her a sly smile. "True that. So you might as well loosen up and let's go have some fun."

Did chicks really fall for this b.s.?

Heaving a sigh and blowing the hair off her face, she held her hands up in surrender. "Guess you're right. What's done is done. Where are we going?" The elevator slid open to reveal a narrow hallway of doors. She needed answers.

The demon stumbled a bit on his way down the hall before he rustled a hand in his pants pocket for his keys. "My place."

They must be in the demon's living quarters behind the club. The ceiling was wrought with intricate designs from the interior of the devil's trap. She wondered how many demons were ensconced in different parts of this building and for how long. He was probably on his umpteenth lifetime on earth so he had no care for death or the devil's trap. Anything to be out of the pit for a century or so.

He tumbled through his now open door and she stepped in behind him taking a quick glance around. A black couch and giant TV filled the living room. A narrow hallway led off to the right. Likely to the bedroom and bathroom. The kitchen must be behind the wall to her left. Nothing in the small entrance area except…a baseball bat.

Score.

Good thing demons didn't trust each other.

She grabbed the bat and swung at his head as he was turning around with a dumb look of "what-the-hey" on his face. The bat connected with his skull making a cracking sound and he went down with a thud. She checked his pulse. Alive. He'd have a killer headache, but he'd live.

Debating whether to tie him up and question him or get going, she decided to find Asmodeus before bidding this place a final adieu.

Slipping out of the goon's room and walking back to the elevator, she hit the "P" button for the penthouse and rode the elevator up. Odd. There was no key code needed or anything. The regular demons had baseball bats behind their doors, but the penthouse was wide open? Probably because no one dared enter Asmodeus' nest without permission.

The doors slid open to opulence. A foyer with a marble table set with fresh flowers met her. A peek around the corner found Asmodeus himself in a library snoozing in a reading chair. He opened his eyes and extended his arms. "I've been expecting you, Ellen."

Uh, oh.

"An angel in my lair. How lovely. And one that was cloaked and has the blood of a succubus still coursing through her veins."

"How did you know?" she asked, approaching him with caution.

"This is Vegas, my dear. There are cameras everywhere. Now come, sit. We have much to discuss."

Heading to a black leather loveseat the farthest away from him, she took a seat. "What did you send Shane to find?"

"Solomon's Ring or the Cup of Life, whichever turns up first is fine with me."

She scoured her memory bank. Solomon was a king of Israel and son of David who was a prophet and built the first temple in Jerusalem to house the Ark of the Covenant. To build the temple, angels gave him a powerful ring to control demons.

The Ring of Solomon was engraved with the Name of GOD and contained four jewels, which gave Solomon power over the winds, birds and beasts, earth and water, and the *jinn*. He'd wore it always and wielded its powers to construct his temple.

To the best of Ellen's memory, Asmodeus had been under King Solomon's command because of the binding spell of the ring. That was until he stole the ring and usurped its power. At long last, the angel Raphael was able to bind Asmodeus. And this century, he happened to be trapped in Vegas.

"It still exists?" She asked.

"The ring? Oh, yes. And it is near to being found. Raphael hid it, but this time, he was sloppy. My sources found out that Solomon's ring has long been bound to the Cup of Life. I believe they are hidden together. We have tracked them to America. Raphael's devil's trap has held me hostage for too long. But with the ring and cup in my possession, I will be free and all who have wronged me will feel my wrath. Raphael is foolish thinking he can free Anna from hell. Lucifer will bow to no one. Abaddon's daughter wants the Cup to bring her father back to his former glory. But I will find it first."

Ellen thought of Shane and Lucas. Smack in the middle of a power struggle between Asmodeus, Raphael, and Nara. If Asmodeus possessed the ring, he'd have power over the *jinn* and the earth. He'd also be released from his prison in the club. Catastrophic for humanity.

"Poor Raphael," she wondered aloud.

"Indeed. His paired essence was lost to him. He looks to a futile reunion and that clouds his judgement."

Shane was in serious trouble and she needed to get to him. Fast.

"Let me go. I will go to Shane. I can help him bring you what you want. He'll need an angel to get close to it. He won't succeed without me."

Asmodeus roared with laughter. "Who says I want him to succeed? I need him gone and you here, by my side." His smile turned dark. "Let you go? I think not, beautiful. You remind me of someone I once held precious. I'll never let you out of my sight again." He snapped his fingers. Six burly bodyguards appeared and surrounded her. "But this time, I won't chain you to the dungeon. You'll be chained to my bed."

****

Shane wanted to give the stuffy librarian a kiss but opted for an enthusiastic thank-you instead as he rushed out of the library. He had a location to hit first and foremost:

St. John's Abbey in Collegeville.

According to the librarian, the Benedictine monks in this area were highly secretive. Of the hundreds of churches in Minnesota, it seemed much more likely that a group of cloistered monks would have a juicy artifact instead of the highly trafficked churches in busy neighborhoods.

If this bet paid off, he'd have something of value and be able to spring Ellen from Asmodeus' lair before tomorrow. Hoping she was faring better than he was, he rented a car and sped out of the Twin Cities northwest on US-10 toward St. Cloud.

As the miles to his destination lessened, a massive headache hit him and voices began in his head. *Turn around. This isn't the right place. Go back. It's not safe. You'll never get close. No demon will.*

Good, he thought pushing the warnings aside. The place was booby-trapped and cloaked. That must mean he'd found the right place.

From the photos in the library, he'd learned the location was a complex in the middle of nowhere. In the 1850's, five Benedictine monks from a monastery in Pennsylvania were sent to minister to the German immigrants of remote Minnesota. They settled outside of St. Cloud in a place they named, *Schoenhal* or beautiful valley. Their community grew to include their Benedictine sisters as well. In 1865, they relocated near Lake Sagatagan and the following year, they qualified as an abbey and elected their first abbot.

The librarian had snickered at the old photos of the monks. Especially at the one with a tuft of hair on his balding head, small, circular glasses, and a curly beard twisting down his chest.

A little over an hour later, he reached the tree-lined street leading to the massive complex. The pressure in his chest wasn't from last night's pizza. It was sheer, overwhelming panic. His heart pounded, his headache pounded, and he began to hyperventilate and sweat profusely. He couldn't go any further so he pulled the car to the side of the road and shut off the engine.

The whole damn complex was consecrated! He needed a rest. Then he'd have to find a way to overcome the pain and push forward.

There was no other choice. He had to do it for Ellen.

Up ahead, he could see the abbey church, a modern architectural construct resembling a beehive protected by a giant letter H structure holding the bell tower.

The whole place had an Ivy League feel to it, but as a demon, he could no longer pull off the "I'm a college student" thing. He'd have to find another way in.

He turned the key and the car revved back to life and Shane hit the gas, bypassing all the buildings on 159 and looking for another way in. Turning around, he drove north and followed Fruit Farm Lane away from the complex until he felt the tension lift, where the consecrated ground came to an end. This place was huge. Like a compound. A sign pointed him to the Episcopal House of Prayer. Shane pulled the car off the road and parked among the trees unseen.

Night was falling. He'd catch a few hours' sleep and then find a way in first thing in the morning. He closed his heavy eyelids, crossed his arms, and leaned the seat back.

He didn't know how long he'd been dozing when he jerked awake. It was still dark. He checked his watch: five a.m.

He grabbed a coat and headed out on foot to check the perimeter of the House of Prayer before everyone got up. Picking his way around the brick sided retreat building, he realized the place was empty. No mission groups here for a bible retreat. No church groups for a seminar.

A path led from the house into the woods. He could see the abbey across the lake. This side was not consecrated ground although with each step, the blinding pain in his head got worse and his body threatened to collapse on the spot. He was getting too close. Faint hues of pink and lavender were beginning to dot the eastern sky, but that is not what struck him. It was the man picking his way along a worn path on the opposite side of the lake. He wore a monk's black tunic and his head was bowed reverently as he made his way across a footbridge. To Shane's left was a small sign reading "Stump Lake."

From the other side of the road, where the abbey was, this bridge would have been completely hidden.

Shane kept low and behind a tree, the monk maybe fifty yards in front of him. He was praying, in German from what Shane could tell. Extracting something from his tunic, he knelt near the shore and filled an object with water from the lake. His back was to Shane, but when he finished drinking the lake water, he turned for a second and Shane could see his face.

The face was that of a man who should have been dead: the librarian had even chuckled when she showed him his picture. Shane recognized his circular glasses and fuzzy beard. The man held a small ceramic cup in his hands. If that man was really the abbot, and he held a cup and found a reason to come and drink from it at five a.m.—

A jolt of electricity jarred Shane. The monk in front of him may be holding the cup Jesus drank from on the cross. Some called it the Cup of Life.

Shane must have pulled in a breath. The monk turned his head in Shane's direction. He pointed at him. *"Ich sehe dich, du Dämon."* I see you, Demon.

Shane had one chance and he took it. Taking a deep breath and holding it, he charged at the monk who fled, running back on the bridge he had crossed screaming "Help me!" in German, *"Hilfe mir!"*

With a surge of speed, Shane overtook him and tackled him around the waist. They both fell to the ground. The cup in the monk's tunic slipped out and rolled to the side. He writhed and kicked like a man half Shane's age. The fight in the old man was surprising especially when Shane got clocked in the face. He needed air, so he took his elbow and smashed the old man's knee.

Bone protruded from his flesh and the monk cried in pain, clawing at the ground and crawling toward the cup. But Shane beat him there. Just as the man's fingers were about to wrap around the precious object, Shane kicked it away, back down the path to unconsecrated ground where he'd have the advantage.

Taking deep breaths, Shane bolted down the footpath and snatched up the cup. He made it two more strides before he was attacked from behind and his feet swept out from under him. The monk, tall and fierce, stared at him with unrelenting determination.

His compound fracture was healed.

Jackpot. This was the right cup!

If the guy wanted a fight, Shane would give him a good one. So he grabbed the monk by the beard and pulled him down on top of him. With a clump of beard in one hand and the top of his head in the other, Shane executed a snappy, violent twisting motion, and broke his neck. He threw the limp corpse off to his side.

With another deep breath, Shane lurched forward and picked up the cup. But a swift kick to his back knocked the wind out of him and left him flat on his back, gasping for air that would not come. The monk he'd just left for dead stood over him.

The monk gently picked up the cup, put it back inside his tunic and wiped off his hands before placing a heavy boot on Shane's neck. *"Der Becher gehört mir! Und es wird nie deine sein." The cup is mine. And it will never be yours.*

Without oxygen, Shane's vision tunneled.

Everything went black.

Chapter 27

Minneapolis-Saint Paul International Airport

The faster Daevas could return to Paris and get back to his job, the better. Being number two to Nara was less than pleasurable. Damn, that bitch was demanding!

After the plane touched down on a private landing strip outside of the Twin Cities, Daevas picked up the devil child so Nara could collect her belongings, which consisted of her designer purse and her attitude. She watched impatiently out the window as the plane came to a stop. Daevas knew his power came with a price, but acting alone and in charge was one thing. Having Abaddon's daughter bossing him around emasculated him.

He wanted her gone.

Nara took care her heels didn't catch on the staircase that the airport personnel pushed alongside her private aircraft. Waiting below was a black sedan where a man wearing a chauffeur's cap held the door open. She paused as Daevas was about to climb into the car with her sleeping child.

"Give her to me!" she snapped. "This is where I leave you. I have other family business to attend to. I'll be in touch. Manuel is an expert tracker and will find your Adrienne. When you do, call me. If you can't get answers from her...*I can.*" She enunciated the last two words.

Daevas held back a shiver. Poor dumb girl. He idly wondered if Adrienne really was in the wrong place at the wrong time or truly a turncoat to his regime. Either way, he detached any feelings he held for her because she'd be eliminated very soon. One way or another.

"Of course. I am at your family's service."

"You mean mercy," she said, walking away from the sedan.

Daevas always thought he'd hit the big time. More money than he could spend. Powerful friends. *This is the life.*

A tiny piece of brain that he usually kept cramped in a dark corner piped up: *Sure it is. Keep telling yourself that.*

****

The puddle jump flight to Minnesota was a quick up and down compared to the trans-Atlantic flight they'd endured.

As soon as the prop job touched down in her home state, Adrienne felt an overwhelming sense of adventure. Time to turn the page. Although she missed her morning café au lait, it actually felt good to be back on American soil and knee deep in some Indiana Jones-type adventure with cool demon hunters.

Her life had never been better.

She'd given her word to Seamus to stay with them on this quest-adventure, even if she was a hindrance. So she was bound and determined to be some kind of help to them. After all, she did know a lot about the state, and maybe the monks would be more willing to listen to her than the hard-ass guys who were in a rush. She might be able to reason with the monks, make them understand. Or hell, maybe their information could be bought.

"Stay here, I'll be right back," Seamus gave her a soft kiss. "I have to go to the toilet. Promise me you'll stay right here?"

She nodded and he left for the men's room. They needed a car and a driver. And for Lucas' sake, they needed to get moving. Deciding to be helpful, she thought she could go to the service area and hire a driver before Seamus was back.

Lucas was busy on a phone call to his mother-in-law about his wife's fragile condition and Dean was playing on his phone.

"Hey Dean," she said. "Tell Seamus I'll be right back and I'm sorry."

"Okay, sorry for what?"

"That I'm not a girl of my word." She intended to wink, but Dean didn't look up from his phone.

"What are you talking about?" he called after her. But she was determined to do something nice. Something to help Seamus. So she made a dash for the exit, pulling her suitcase. It would only take a minute to hire a car for them. And she had the money to pay for it. It was the least she could do to help.

This fight to save Calise had become her fight as well. She felt her heart breaking watching the anguish on Lucas' face while he paced and talked with his mother-in-law. Even the ever-sassy Dean seemed to have less pep in his step coming home empty handed.

After what she'd seen in the last few days, she now believed in miracles. This cup would surely save Lucas' wife's life. Hopefully this monastery in Minnesota was not a fool's errand.

The man at the service counter gave her a ticket and told her to talk to the limo driver at stand five. Once outside, she inhaled a lungful of the not so fresh air. More like stale and exhaust-ridden. Glancing over her shoulder, she watched the belt inside the building where suitcases followed a motorized river home to their owners.

One abandoned paisley print suitcase with a bright pink rope tied around the handle made yet another circle.

With no one there to claim it, she knew it would get snatched and put in a room with other unclaimed luggage waiting for an owner to call. Maybe that was her. She was the lone suitcase, snaking through a motorized life, forgotten and alone. She'd been waiting all these years for Seamus to pluck her up and claim her as his own. For someone to see the girl she used to be and wanted to be again.

The feeling of truly belonging with another person filled her up with love.

She was sick of being adrift and so was Seamus. In the sea of humans, they'd finally found each other after snaking aimlessly through the wandering river of life. She caught a glimpse of her reflection in the long window behind her.

There was still a faint dark shadow following her.

She hadn't broken the cycle. She was still a piece of shit and needed to remind herself of that every day. To wake up every day and try to be better. To be worthy of Seamus.

Tears welled up in her eyes. She was still a darkwalker. Still a selfish person. But from this moment on, she vowed she would be better. Try harder to shake off this yoke she'd burdened herself with.

Seamus should always come first.

Finally crossing the street and finding stand five, she came around to the driver's side of the limo and tapped on the window, which slid down. "We need a ride for four to Saint Joseph."

Before the driver could answer, a car screeched to a halt beside her. Daevas hopped out. "Miss me?"

Shit.

She had nowhere to run, pinned between the two vehicles. Daevas grabbed her and shoved her inside. She bit down hard on his hand.

"You bitch," he said, letting go and spinning her around.

The last thing she felt was his fist connect with her jaw.

****

Seamus couldn't convince Lucas and Dean to wait any longer.

Adrienne was gone. Really gone. She told Dean she'd be right back and split.

A sinking feeling came over him. Like the rug of his life was pulled out from under him. His heart was sliced in two; he sank into the back seat of the rental. Who was he fooling? No one wanted to be with him. And especially not someone as amazing as Adrienne. She probably hopped in the first cab she found and zoomed as far away from them as she could. They'd busted in on her private meal at a restaurant. He'd kissed her to save his own ass. But as soon as his lips touched hers, everything had changed. At least for him. That kiss had meant something. To him.

Then her Darkwalker group had kidnapped her. Turned on her, called her a spy. And it was all his fault. Not that he could have left her there to be tortured. After that, he'd tried to let her go even though everything inside him screamed to keep her by his side. Given her the *sight*. Given her other options.

But *she* chose to meet him on the train, fulfilling her mom's unrealized dream of visiting Mont Saint-Michel. His heart rejoiced at seeing her even though he knew every moment they spent together put her at risk.

Maybe she was sick of the danger. Maybe she was sick of him.

Then he'd asked her to join him in the States to find the Cup of Life so they could heal the wife of a man she—and he—barely knew! The whole thing was over the top. No wonder she ran.

"Tell me again what she said," he asked.

"I told you verbatim. She said she'd be right back and was sorry she couldn't be a person of her word. Then she practically bolted outside. I saw her hail a car and then she was gone. I'm sorry, man. I really am. But can we go?" Dean's arm was draped over the bench seat of their rental. "Lucas called Milwaukee while you were looking for Adrienne. My sister hasn't improved, so I vote for a quick looksee through this abbey and then we have to go back to Milwaukee. Dig?"

"That makes no sense. Fine. Let's go," he said. Honestly, he barely understood how Lucas could be away from his ailing wife this long. The only thing keeping him going was the slim possibility they'd recover an artifact that might save her life.

Seamus felt like his life was over before it even began. He hadn't even had a chance. He was born a seer of the true line of Joseph of Arimathea. But now to find out they'd never really been protecting the Cup anyway.

To find out Joseph entrusted it to his brother-in-law who passed it to Lancelot's son, Galahad.

And now *his* artifact—the most powerful item Jesus had ever touched—was protected by some monks or nuns in Somewhere, U.S.A.

He felt like his whole life was a lie. A farce. A façade.

And Gabriel had known the whole time.

The bastard.

Maybe that's why he was never very interested in anything except Seamus producing progeny. He needed to maintain the lie.

Oh yeah, he was interested in one other thing. The reformation of gorgeous, earthly Darkwalkers of the female persuasion. Gabriel had made that clear years ago when he disappeared on his little escapades to shine his divine light on the ones who walked in the darkness.

Worthless angel.

And now, when Seamus could actually use his help, when the artifacts his forefathers had entrusted his line to protect were needed to save a seer's soulmate, where was he?

Trying to thwart them? Trying to help? No, just gone.

Whatever. Seamus had preferred solitude. Before he met Adrienne.

He missed her. She was the one person he, like Lucas, would have protected above all others. He'd given her his vow of love, words of honor and oath of loyalty.

But now she was gone.

It seemed the love, loyalty and honor Seamus held in high esteem was a thing of the past. He'd given his word to Lucas to help him find the Cup. And he would not go back on his word.

Ever.

The countryside wound on either side of them, flatter than the rolling and hilly expanses outside of Glastonbury.

They stopped at one of the hideous fast food establishments Americans prided themselves on. Seamus choked down a tasteless hamburger and fries that were no more French than toast or yellow mustard.

He stared at the minivans with cute, chunky kids devouring Happy Meals while mom illegally texted and drove. Is this how all Americans lived? In their cars...racing from place to place. Work to home. Carting their children around and stopping for the unhappiest of meals he could imagine.

In that moment, he vowed if he ever had a child, he would walk the town of Glastonbury, educate them in manners and chivalry, and never let them walk the selfish path of darkness. He'd let them explore their world to pass the time, not entertain them to pass the time for them.

He'd rather be dead.

Lucas and Dean discussed the advantages and disadvantages of different routes. Dean napped for a bit and Seamus continued to stare out of the window as the sun fell behind them and they headed northwest, away from the airport and any connection he'd had to Adrienne.

"I say we find a hotel and try to meet with the

monks at St. John's abbey first thing in the morning," Lucas said. "I've decided that if nothing pans out tomorrow, I'm driving back to Milwaukee, Seamus. I can't be away from her any longer. If I've failed her, I will be at her side to admit that before I lose her."

Neither Dean nor Seamus said a word. There was nothing to say. There may be a few monks who may or may not meet with them, and may or may not have answers.

And then what?

And I'll go find Adrienne. To say good-bye if nothing else.

Then Seamus would return to the doldrums of his life in England, a failure to Lucas and his ancestors. But worse of all, a failure to Adrienne.

****

Lucas hadn't had a cigarette or a beer in forever, but he was craving both right now. Seamus seemed lost and Dean was edgy. A few hours at this seminary college and then he was speeding back to Milwaukee. Across from their cheap motel was a gas station where Lucas paid for a soda, matches, and a pack of smokes.

He went behind the motel and hid in the small row of trees that did nothing to diminish the noise from the passing freeway. He tapped the unopened pack of smokes in the palm of his hand and lifted the paper cover before pulling off the small piece of foil holding the smokes. Extracting one, he rested the cigarette between his lips while he struck a match and lit the end of the cigarette.

The first inhalation burned his throat and lungs before the welcome zing of nicotine hit his system. He launched the entire rest of the pack into the brush in front of him. Just one cigarette. That's all he wanted.

Then she was there next to him, holding the pack of cigarettes. "Those will kill you, you know."

The voice of his guardian angel was a relief. Her angelic presence was warm and calming. He breathed her in with his next drag. She smelled like a mint mojito, which would taste really good about now.

"Am I a fucking fool? Am I wasting my time?"

A hand rested on his shoulder and the warmth coursing through his body from the touch overwhelmed the nicotine high by a thousand fold. He rested the back of his head against the cool brick wall behind him.

"I have come to tell you this: your path is true. Tomorrow you will find what you seek."

Lucas tried to speak so fast he choked on the smoke he'd just inhaled. "What? We found it? Are you sure?"

"I have scouted the place," a broad smile opened revealing pearly teeth and an adorable dimple on her left cheek. "And yes, you have the found it. Retrieving it will be the issue. These holy men have long protected the Cup after it was passed to them and will not give it up so easily to anyone, even the true heir. Beware. The road you walk will be fraught with lies and veils. Look to the truth and allow Seamus to show them the light."

"But how—"

"I could use one of those, too." Dean's voice came from the darkness as he rounded the building. "Who are you talking to?"

Looking to his left, she was gone, choosing not to show herself to Dean. But on this short visit, she'd given him the one thing he really needed:

Hope.

Chapter 28

Las Vegas, Nevada

Scarlet-colored satin sheets, a black metal headboard carved with the screaming faces of souls lost to the pit. Lit candles dripping wax in puddles on every flat surface. The red privacy curtains of the four-poster bed were tied back. Ellen was chained, spread eagle at the center of the bed.

Demon gang rape, here I come.

She needed to get out of here. And fast. Get to Shane and warn him.

She pulled at her wrists and ankles knowing it wouldn't do any good. At least she still had clothes on. But for how long? Asmodeus was not a patient man and her clothes weren't going to be a huge deterrent. The last vestiges of her inner succubus were jumping for joy while Ellen herself relived her indiscretions of the past few days. Still fresh in her mind.

Shane. My every thought comes back to him.

Squeezing her eyes shut, she couldn't erase the visage of his gorgeous face, neck craned back in the ecstasy of their lovemaking.

That was not love-making.

Her sane mind was back front and center with the succubus blood fast becoming the tail end of an echo down an empty hallway.

Sounds in the hall. Asmodeus was coming. And he wasn't alone.

She let her mind roar through her vast knowledge of Asmodeus, looking for a weakness to exploit.

He was one of the Princes of Hell. There were seven, one for each deadly sin, and she was lucky enough to be chained to the Prince of Lust's bed.

He was the most charming of the seven. She remembered each of them before they fell. All obsessive angels. Punished for eternity stewing in their own vice.

As she recalled, he hated water and birds as they reminded him of the Father. Loved to incite gambling. Fitting then, that Raphael imprisoned him here.

They were right around the corner. Men's laughter. And not the "ha-ha" kind.

Think! What else could she use?

He had seventy-two legions under his command.

Walked with canes and a limp due to the cock leg.

But what had Asmodeus said about her reminding him of someone?

Bingo. I've got it.

Asmodeus had "loved" a beautiful, young human virgin named Sarah. He even slayed seven of her husbands on their wedding nights to leave Sarah a virgin. Then, an ingenious human named Tobias, slated to become her eighth husband, conspired with the angel, Raphael who was able to tell Tobias how to trick Asmodeus so Raphael could bind him in various earthly hellholes. Right now, that happened to be Vegas apparently…

But how could she use this against him?

The door to the bedroom blew off its hinges and

Asmodeus appeared to her in his true form: one rooster leg, one human leg. The tail of a serpent swished behind him. But it was the three heads that made her stomach turn. A human head that breathed fire, the head of a ram, and the head of a bull. All six of his eyes staring at her with undisguised hunger.

His posse followed behind him, laughing and looking far too ready to have fun. And not the kind of fun she was looking to have. She steeled herself for his reaction to her. Thank Father the *sila jinn* had showed her a few tricks besides cloaking herself as a demon. She had also learned other forms of disguise.

When Asmodeus turned his head to find her eyes, he saw his beloved...Sarah.

"Sarah?" The bull and ram snorted as the human head spoke. "Is that you, my love?"

"Free me so at last we can be together," Ellen said.

The other demons began to mumble and crowd Asmodeus, knowing he was being duped.

"Leave us!" Asmodeus bellowed.

"She's a sorceress," said one, trying to keep their master from the illusion.

"That's not your Sarah, my King," said another, trying to point out the truth.

With a flick of the wrist, Asmodeus set one naysayer on fire and ripped the body of the other in half before her eyes. The rest of the underlings grabbed what was left of their brothers and scurried from the room.

"At last. At long last, my dear." In the blink of an eye, Asmodeus reverted to his handsome human form and climbed on top of Ellen, cradling her head in his hands. His lips were like blades of ice, slicing hers like knives when they touched.

Hiding her disgust, she lifted her head to meet his touch and rocked her hips against the demon. "My love." Reaching for him, she found her hand and legs were no longer bound. *He's buying it!*

In sheer power, he could still dominate her but Ellen had one more trick up her sleeve.

"I know what you are doing, Angel. And I don't care. I love it," he whispered in her ear. Mounting her, he pushed his massive erection between her legs.

But Ellen had planned on this and anticipated his arousal. She had given herself a form of vaginismus—a condition that prevents a woman any form of vaginal penetration due to the spasm of the PC muscle—effectively clamping herself shut. No way in.

She gave him a tight smile. "What's wrong my dear? Will you never be fulfilled by me?"

A look of agony came over his face as he tried to shove his way inside her.

To no avail.

He screamed in agony, after all this time, still unable to gain entry to the one thing he most desired, even though he knew her pretending to be Sarah was an illusion. In that one second reprieve, Ellen rolled out from underneath him, rushed to the window, and flung it open for the dozens of birds she'd mentally summoned moments earlier.

Asmodeus' mingled look of horror and defeat filled her with compassion for her long lost heavenly brother. "I am very sorry," she said before jumping out of the window. She spread her arms in a free fall, which became feathery wings that she flapped furiously until she gained the needed altitude. Thanks goodness for the gift of wings from the *jinn*. The glittery expanse of Las Vegas spread out below her. Echoing on the wind, she heard Asmodeus crying out the name of his beloved... "Sarah!"

****

Shane awoke on the concrete floor of a jail cell.

What the fuck?

The monk from the bridge sat on a folding chair outside the cell just out of Shane's reach. Next to him sat a much younger monk, hands folded in his lap.

Trying to get to a seated position, Shane found his hands bound by barbed wire. The more he tried to wrench them apart, the more they gashed his flesh. Still, he managed to pull himself to a seated position.

The man asked a question in German. Shane looked to the younger monk who interpreted, saying, "He asks, 'How did you find us?'" The older monk reached under his robes and brought forth a small item. He unwrapped it and put it in his mouth, sucking on the small candy. More German words.

"He asks if you'd like one?"

Shane shook his head.

"The sisters in Iowa make the best caramels. You really should try one," the young monk reached under his robes and extracted a piece from his own stash. The popping sounds of the caramels breaking apart in their mouths plus saliva grossed Shane out and made his stomach growl at the same time.

The words the older monk spoke this time sounded more serious. Shane waited for the young monk to interpret: "He says we can do this the easy way or the hard way. How did you find him?"

Rendered speechless, Shane shook his head. The

man in front of him was from the library photo. Was he the man who had founded the monastery and should have been two-hundred years dead? Sucking noises from the two men echoed in the underground prison.

"I plead the fifth," Shane said, twisting his hands behind him, looking for a small release from the pressure of the barbs.

The young monk shook his head at the old man who shooed him away with a wave of his hand. Soon, the young monk returned with a small basket.

Shane wondered where he was being kept. He would have had an anaphylactic reaction if he was being imprisoned on consecrated ground. So he couldn't be at the monastery. Someplace close by, for sure. But where?

All at once, eight more monks appeared and entered Shane's cell. They lifted him onto a chair and Rupert entered the cell. Shane could now see the contents of the basket the young monk had retrieved: a bible, holy water, rosary beads, a crucifix, a scapular, a medal of the Virgin Mary, the Blessed Sacrament, and the Roman Ritual of Exorcism.

Great, they think they can cast me out of myself.

Exorcism worked on the *jinn* and the *jinn* only.

The old monk circled Shane, speaking in German and flicking holy water at him. It left burn marks on Shane and stung him like bees. "Ouch."

He opened the book to begin the rite when more monks appeared outside the cell, interrupting him. "There are three men here asking about the Cup who refuse to leave. They claim to be seers, descended from the old lines."

The older man's eyes grew wide. He asked a

question which the young monk asked to the others, "What are their names?"

"Lucas, Dean, and Seamus," one replied.

Shane jerked up in his seat. Lucas was here! They could save Calise! "Give them the Cup! They need it. It's a matter of life or death."

The young monk gave Shane a level stare as they left him in the cell. "We certainly will not trust these humans now, demon. We know you only speak rich lies and dirty tricks."

Shane sank back into the chair, welcoming the pain of the barbs in his skin. He'd spoken from his former angelic platform. And by forgetting these monks only saw a demon before them, had he just killed Calise?

Again?

Chapter 29

Minnesota

"Why did you betray us?" Daevas sat in the backseat of the sedan with Adrienne, resting his hand over her tied wrists. "I always told you the truth: walk the simplest path and you will find pleasure waiting for you."

He needed to break her. Tailing the three musketeers was fine and dandy, but he wanted to know where they were going and what to expect.

"I forgive your indiscretions, my love," he continued. "We can go back to how things were. Remember? You and I? Strolling through Paris by day and making love by night?"

Her acidic glare said it all. She'd tried to forget their past. Good thing she was gagged. Wouldn't want the dumb bitch's spit on his nice suit coat. Daevas despised bodily fluids. Women were filthy whores and drank lies and ate praise like greedy maggots on a corpse.

He channeled his sickie-sweet singsongy voice. "Pretend the whole world is a series of people holding umbrellas. I am holding yours. Under it, you are safe and taken care of. Not a drop of water can fall on you and everything familiar is within my protection. I understand why you stepped outside, but the world is dark and ugly. I am happy to welcome you back into the fold."

Adrienne turned away from him.

"All right, we can go this route as well, my dear. But I'll have to kill those three buffoons you've been hanging out with."

That got her attention.

"So now you are willing to talk?"

A vehement nod allowed her gag to be loosened.

"Speak," he ordered. "I need to know everything you've told them about my organization."

"They don't know anything, I swear. Don't hurt them."

Daevas disliked the fact she'd bonded to the men. Why protect them? No matter. He had more cards in his hand to be played than she did. "You can tell me where they are going and they will live to reach their destination, or the driver can pull up alongside them and the last thing your friends will see will be your pretty face and the barrel of my .357 Magnum. Your choice."

Slumping, she looked defeated. He'd gotten to her. "They are going to some monastery on a treasure hunt. A fool's errand. If you turn the car around right now, I'll return to Paris with you, pledge my fealty and begin recruiting in earnest."

Words he'd been hoping to hear. "Done." He punched a number in his cell. "It's me. They are on a treasure hunt to a monastery. She has chosen to remain aligned with me. I'm asking for permission to withdraw and return to Paris."

Nara barked her commands.

There was no arguing with her. He clicked the

phone shut.

It was now his turn to ignore Adrienne and her questions.

Their orders were clear. Let them find what they are looking for, then steal it and kill them.

All of them.

Including Adrienne.

His favorite Rolling Stones song played in his head, "You Can't Always Get What You Want."

****

Seamus led the group into the abbot's office. He could prove to them who he was, and if they had the cup, there would be no choice but to hand it over. Then he could be on his merry way to find Adrienne. That was, if she wanted to be found.

"Let me do the talking," Lucas said.

Seamus couldn't believe what he was hearing. "No, they'll listen to me. The cup was my family's relic. I'll talk."

From the back of the small office where Seamus had taken the right chair and Lucas the left, Dean piped up. "You two will scare them to death. I'll talk."

Then they were all arguing at once. Seamus telling the others how he was the rightful owner of the cup. Lucas trying to talk above him and demanding he had the most at stake. And Dean trying to convince them both they sounded like crackpots.

When the door to the office opened, they all clamped their mouths shut. Seamus recognized the monk who had welcomed them to the abbey. At first the monk had been excited in their interest, maybe thinking the three of them would be new recruits. He was eager to launch into background of the property and its history. Then Lucas ruined everything and blurted out, "We need the cup. With us is Seamus Bron, the descendent and rightful heir to his family heirloom."

Now the monk was back. With others—and one older man in ancient robes, different garb from the others with horn-rimmed glasses and a shaggy beard. The other three holy men surrounding him looked more like burly bodyguards than men of God.

The glasses-wearing monk shuffled toward them with a bow. He took the seat of honor behind the barren desk. His chair squeaked loudly when he pulled it forward. "*Wer bist du und was willst du?*"

"I—" Lucas started.

"We—" Seamus began to say.

But Dean's voice was the loudest. "*Mein name ist Dean und dies ist mein schwager Lucas und unser freund, Seamus.*" Who knew the guy could speak in fluent German. He continued speaking the monk's language, ignoring Lucas' glare. "We are all seers and know angels and demons walk among us. Lucas and Seamus are descendants of Nicodemus and Joseph of Arimathea. We come here seeking the Cup of Life that came to you through Joseph of Arimathea. Seamus is the cup's rightful heir."

Seamus' German was rusty but he was able to catch most of it.

The monk looked between the three of them then back to his men, shifting uncomfortably in his chair.

"You speak German?" Lucas asked.

"Four years of high school German to get to go study abroad where drinking beer would be legal. What can I say?"

"What did you say to him?" Lucas asked.

Dean told him.

The monk bid the other men leave and leaned forward on his elbows. Dean interpreted his words for the others. "I was warned you would come and ask for it. An angel of the Lord preceded you. And now I have a serious predicament. I have a demon in my cellar begging me to give you my Cup. So I can see everything the angel foretold has come true. I will never give you the cup. It does not belong in your hands. You can leave quietly or I can have you forcibly removed."

So it *was* here!

"I understand demons lie," Seamus said in his best German. "But if the angel Gabriel told you to hand over the Cup, you should do just that."

The monk's eyes went wide at the mention of Gabriel's name. What had the angel told him to do? Help them or kick them out?

Seamus continued, "Whatever you have in the basement, let us talk with it before we terminate him. Lucas and I can prove to you who we are."

Lucas removed one of his necklaces and laid in on the table in front of the monk. Picking up the small splinter of the cross neatly ensconced in glass, the monk began to tremble.

Seamus hadn't seen the necklace up close before. He thought his family had a unique way of carrying the slivers with them, but Lucas' family design was also nice. Twisting the family ring on his right hand, he loved how his bloodline had made golden rings with the wood lacquered into the inlay of the ring itself. He not only never took it off, he really couldn't anymore without a healthy amount of olive oil or soap. He was wearing one of his family's rings and the other two were safely ensconced with his family's other artifacts in England.

And how many times had he examined what he thought was his family's cup among the relics before he took it to the monastery at Mont St. Michel? And now only to find out it was a fake all along. He twisted his ring again. What else was a fake?

If Gabriel had sided against them, he was officially no longer in his circle of trust. First, the angel had tried to seduce Adrienne. Then announced the cup was a fake and the real one was here in the States. But above all, he'd left them. No good-bye. No explanation. Whose side was this guy on anyway?

The older monk sighed heavily and motioned for them to follow him. Through the high traffic tourist parts of their new abbey, past the visitor's shop, and finally down three flights of stairs and behind a steel door, they entered a basement under a basement.

A dungeon, dark and dreary, but brand new. Walls neatly poured of concrete that Seamus rapped his knuckles on. As secure as the Tower of England.

They passed through two more steel, reinforced doors before coming to a cell where a bedraggled demon stared at them, red-eyes glowering.

"Hello, Shane," Lucas said, approaching the demon.

"Lucas. Dean." The demon inclined his head. "Who's the new guy?"

Chapter 30

Ellen reached out with her mind to find the one angel who could help...the archangel Raphael. With one of the seven archangels by her side, she had a chance.

Gulping in the night air, she flew northwest honing in on Shane's whereabouts. The succubus blood had left her so Ellen could no longer ignore the truth that had snuck up on her.

Shane was her everything.

Her paired essence.

The only being in the universe she was inextricably tied to, for better or worse. And she'd have it no other way. Steeled in her love, she knew that come what may, she would stand by his side to the end. Even if it meant losing everyone and everything else she loved.

Why couldn't she fly faster? She could hear his heart beat, smell his sweet scent, and feel his pain. If they'd been apart any longer, she didn't know if she'd be able to find him. But for now, she flew across the country on pure instinct, hoping she wouldn't be too late.

A streak of light flashed through the sky toward her, like the sparkling tail of a comet, then reaching her, solidified into an angelic form. *Raphael!* "Thank the heavens you found me," she said, flying full bore over South Dakota. "Asmodeus is near to finding Solomon's

Ring and Nara and her family seek the Cup of Life."

"That can't be!" he exclaimed. "Stop."

"There not time. Shane—"

Before she could utter another word, he latched on to her waist and wrestled her in circles as they plummeted toward the earth. A second before they would crash, Raphael stopped them and placed her gently on the ground.

"Tell me everything." It hit her that Raphael did not look the same as she remembered him. His blazing aura of enlightenment had been replaced with a pulse of stress and a fog of desperation. He was desperate for Anna and would go to any lengths to get her back.

And for the first time, she understood his pain. She burned with the same desire to reunite with Shane. "I have no time," she told him. "I have to get to Shane. He was sent on a dangerous mission to Minnesota. Asmodeus seeks the ring of Solomon. And Nara seeks to heal Abaddon with the Cup of Life. Shane is in the middle of both conflicts."

"As am I," Raphael replied. "The ring must never touch Asmodeus' finger and Nara cannot be allowed to heal her father. Do we agree on that?"

Nodding, Ellen intended to take flight again but Raphael held her by the shoulders. "It is imperative I get to the ring first. Will you stand with me?"

His words confused her. She had stood by him before, why would he ask her now? Then she understood. He was asking if she would choose to stand with the demon, Shane, over him. Her heart told her she'd never leave Shane, but if summoned by the Father to stand with Raphael, would it even be in her power to refuse?

"I always have," she said, choosing her words carefully. The truth was, she didn't know the answer to his question.

"Then as you said, we have no time to waste. Lead on and know I have your back. I will be in your debt if you help me retrieve the ring."

They launched themselves into the sky once again.

Hang on, Shane. It won't be long now.

In her subconscious she heard his reply, *Hurry up, El.*

****

Lucas turned to the monk who'd led them to the dungeon. "This demon is why we are here." He motioned for Dean to start translating. "He tried to kill my wife out of jealousy and now seeks to hinder my search for the Cup of Life. If he couldn't have her, he wanted her dead. Kill him, with my blessing. I'm sure the devil is waiting for him."

The German monk inclined his head and headed back upstairs with the others following.

"Lucas, wait!" Shane yelled after him. "I'm working with Ellen. I've been trying to help."

Even though Lucas was already on the staircase leading away from the dungeon, he turned and headed back to the cell. Shane leaned his head against the steel rods of the door, arms secured behind his back.

"Leave us." Lucas spoke these words to the others as more of a command than a request.

"Uh, oh," Dean said on his way out.

"You are a liar!" Lucas hissed once they were alone. "You lied to Cali, you may have managed to fool Ellen, but you can't fool me. You are a piece of shit, Shane. You deserve to have fallen. Die and rot in hell, you fuck." With that, he grabbed Shane's shirt and extracted a knife from his boot in one smooth move. He stabbed Shane in the shoulder and twisted the knife.

"Die slowly and painfully and I hope Lucifer eats your guts for breakfast tomorrow." Lucas extracted the knife, knowing with the tip dipped in the myrrh, Shane would suffer in pain before he expired. "You know what? Fuck all of you angels and demons. We don't want you meddling in our lives. Jealousy is all you know because God loves us best. You'll never be human. You'll never know love. Die every day for a thousand lifetimes and you'll still never know what pain I'll feel if I lose Calise. If I have to, I'll come to hell itself to punish you if she dies."

Working his way back up the stairs once again, he found the only angel he would consider dealing with right now: his guardian angel, Asmoday. She wrapped a protective arm over his shoulder.

"I'm here now, Lucas. I can help you with the monks and there is still time to save Calise. But we must hurry." She whispered instructions in his ear on how best to reclaim the Cup from the German monk. "You did the right thing down there. Angels and demons are a jealous bunch but I am different. I am allowed to guard my one human and love you through everything. Guardian angels have no jealously as we are assigned only one human to care for. Our mission is fulfilling enough."

Back in the office, the men stood arguing in German and English. When Lucas and Asmoday entered the room, they all fell silent. A sliver of hope pricked at his broken heart. They would see Asmoday and believe. They'd give him the cup.

And Shane deserved to die. Ellen would never be working with him. That much Lucas knew. Besides, he knew the truth. Angels were a pissed off lot ordered to help humans when all they wanted was to *be* human. And demons were hideous failures who God had tossed in a fiery garbage can.

The monks pressed themselves together like a school of fish, reaching for their crucifixes and muttering words of disbelief. Asmoday's aura shined like the noonday sun.

"Men of God," Asmoday's words perfumed the air. "I was allowed to show myself to you for this is part of God's holy plan. I am a guardian angel of the Lord." At this, she switched her glowing aura on high beam and the monks all dropped to one knee in submission. "You have carried this burden for too many years. I know Gabriel came before and told you the same thing." Laying a hand on the old man's shoulder, he began to weep. "I now absolve you of this responsibility. You may find comfort and peace knowing the Cup will be back with its original owner and be well-protected until this world comes to an end."

Tears streaming down his face, he seemed almost happy to extract a small cup from his robes. He handed it to Asmoday who showed it to Lucas. "We need to hurry. This is the Cup of Life and your wife will wake after one sip from it."

Lucas began to shake. They had it!

Asmoday held the cup for Seamus and Dean to see. Each one touched it as if memorizing the bumps and ridges in the drinking vessel. Lucas still couldn't believe it. In a few hours, Cali would wake up and things would be as before.

He put his hands together and looked up. "Thank you."

The monks all gathered around the angel. She gave them each a blessing and then a firm admonishment to speak of this incident to no one.

"We need to hurry," Asmoday said to Lucas. "I don't have much time to remain visible to you, but I want to be with you and make sure you make it to the hospital."

"This wouldn't have worked without you. I am in your debt," he replied.

Asmoday brushed off his thanks. All at once, they heard a commotion, like an earthquake coming from the dungeon. The door burst off of his hinges and there was Shane, blood running down his shirt from the stab wound. Behind him were two angels, swords of fire blazing in their hands and destruction in their eyes.

Lucas had time to recognize them as Raphael, his own pitiful excuse for a relic guardian and Calise's best friend, Ellen, though he'd never seen her look so fierce before.

Shane pointed at Asmoday. "Lucas, don't trust her. That's Nara. She's cloaked."

Chapter 31

"You're a damn liar," Lucas said. Shane watched him inch closer to the cloaked Nara. "You are the only one who is my enemy here. This is my guardian angel and she'd done more to get me here than anyone!"

"Look at her," Shane insisted. Ellen and Raphael flanked him in a show of solidarity.

Nara's cloak flickered ever so slightly before she tucked the cup under her arm. "He's your enemy, Lucas. You did the right thing trying to kill him," she said.

Shane had precious little time left. The knife might not have hit a vital organ, but he wouldn't be breathing by morning. Lucifer was probably already rubbing his hands together envisioning a millennium of torture for a former angel.

So if Shane had one last act in him before he was lost to the earth, he'd take his bitch of a wife down once and for all.

"Show yourself, demon," he spat. Holding his side, he pushed off Ellen and Raphael and limped toward her.

"Shit," he heard Lucas say when he passed.

Shit, indeed. How could Lucas have been duped into giving *Nara* of all people the Cup of Life? Calise would die and Abaddon would rise again. He held out his hand. "Hand it over and I'll let you live."

Shaking with rage, Nara lost hold on her cloak, fading in and out between that of a pristine guardian angel dressed in white and the dark-haired demon with whom he'd sired a child. All at once, she dropped the cloak, maybe finding the veil too difficult to hold with her anger seething through her bones. Her eyes once again glowed red. There she stood in front of him.

The black-haired bitch.

"Over my dead body, sweetheart," she laughed, backing her way to the door leading out of the office and back into the foyer.

Overconfidence was always her issue. Here she was, taking on angels, seers, and a host of bouncer monks. How the hell she thought she was going to pull this off was beyond him. But he didn't want her all dead. Mostly dead would suffice otherwise he'd never find Melki, and his daughter would be lost to him forever.

He needed her alive—for the time being—to get answers.

"Come on sweetheart. You're hopelessly outnumbered and might break a manicured nail." He took a step closer. The sneer on her face was less than reassuring.

"Why do you always forget I have more tricks up my sleeve than you, darling?" she batted her eyelashes. "At least Melki got my brains."

His daughter's name was like a knife to the gut. The only reason to let this bitch live was to get to his daughter. But the angels behind him might not have that agenda or be so kind. If he didn't stop her, they'd kill her.

He lunged forward to grab the cup as she moved

just out of his reach to the main entrance.

"Get the cup!" Raphael yelled. The surge of people behind him was going to ruin this! Ignoring the pain, Shane followed her outside.

Hordes of winged demons swooped overhead. Abaddon's demon army. The same army that had attacked Effrit and the *jinn*. Nara *demonstrated* and spread her leathery wings and took to the air. With a surge of adrenalin, Shane followed, his wings whipping at his hair. He sped right at her, slamming into her mid-flight and knocking the cup out of her hands seconds before she reached her army who was waiting to envelop her and usher her to safety.

Shane watched as the cup fell to earth. It was as if time stalled and the world moved in slow motion. Lucas and Seamus ran toward the Cup while Ellen and Raphael, already in the air, changed course to catch the precious relic.

Like seagulls nose-diving to a floundering fish, everyone descended on the cup at once. It was in Raphael's hands, then Ellen's, then Seamus leapt into the air and had his fingertips on it.

Then the worst happened.

No one had the cup, except the cement sidewalk, which broke it into several pieces and scattered in every direction.

"No!" Nara screamed, flying in zigzags and loops in a fit of rage and horror diving at the scattered shards. Her waiting army surrounded her and whisked her away. Shane could still hear her screams of agony as he hovered in the air, watching her escape.

Now he knew why Abaddon's army had attacked the *jinn*. The *sila* had given Nara the same training as

Ellen. And wings as well. She couldn't let them live lest they tell anyone, so she ordered the attack on Effrit's *jinn.*

He'd gone and royally screwed everything up again. Even though Nara had lost the Cup and the hope for her Father's recovery, now Calise would die, too. That much Shane knew. Once again, he'd failed.

He touched down near the despondent group. The monks began to gather up the pieces. Shane picked up a shard and stuffed it in his pocket as yet another reminder of his consummate failure. Raphael turned the base of the cup over in his hands when a small, round object fell out and clinked when it hit the ground.

"Lord, have mercy." Raphael picked up the small object and held it up in the sunlight.

"Is that...?" Ellen peered over his shoulder.

"The ring of Solomon. Indeed it is," he answered, tucking it in his pocket. "Now I have what I need to free my Anna."

Shane took his place by Ellen's side. "Are you sure? There's no proof it will work." The archangel was still obsessed with freeing Anna from hell. *The crazy things we do for love.*

Ellen moved in like she might try to fight him for the treasure. "It's too risky. I can't let you go. If you fail and Lucifer gets the ring again..."

With a roar, Raphael lunged at Ellen, in an attempt to rip the skin off her face.

With his last scrap of energy, Shane pushed Ellen out of his reach. The blow that was meant for her hit Shane square in the chest, hurtling him backwards until he slammed into the base of the nearest building.

Raphael took to the air in a flash of brightness and

was gone.

Oh El, you are always thinking the best of people. How could you forget that love sometimes brings out the worst in people? I should know.

"I heard that," she said, her head snapping in his direction.

The wound began to throb and burn and his vision tunneled. He fixed his gaze on the most beautiful being in the universe, Ellen. She was running toward him. Kneeling next to him. He struggled to make out her words while he squeezed her hand. "Hang on. Please hang on."

But that decision was not his.

****

Seamus couldn't believe it. Any of it:

Lucas duped by a demon.

The archangel Raphael out for himself and ready to go against God's will.

And this demon, Shane, who'd in essence, done everything to *help* them after committing the atrocity in the first place!

And then of course, the old monk, who sat with his legs crossed, back braced up against the bricks of his prayer house. Already he looked older. How long would it take before, without the Cup to sustain him, for him to deteriorate into sand and return to the earth, his too-long life finally at a bitter end?

The monks finished gathering the shards of the cup and put them in a small sack and handed it to Seamus. He nodded in acknowledgement before turning to Lucas, "I'm so sorry, my friend. I will find my own way home. Go and be with your wife."

Lucas said nothing, still staring at the ground

where the pieces of the Cup had been strewn moments before.

Dean shook Seamus' hand. A firm, honest handshake from a man of loyalty and honor. If there was anything Seamus could do to fix this, he would have. But with the Cup in pieces, there were no words left.

"Thanks for everything," Dean said, his voice cracking. "You did everything you could." Then turning to his brother-in-law, he said, "We should go, bro." He tried to lead Lucas away.

It was really over.

The female angel hovered over the limp body of the demon, whose fading colors and shallow breaths meant he only had minutes to live.

"Miss?" Seamus walked toward her. "Is he still alive?"

Lucas wheeled around and came back to life. "Ellen, leave that filth. If he's dead, good riddance. Come with us." He offered his hand for her to take.

"No!" She swiped at the gesture. "I said NO!" She let out a heart-wrenching scream of agony. The angel's tear-streaked face caught them off guard. Her pain over the demon's death was more than despair. Her agony was palpable in the tight space surrounding her, as if she'd managed to create a cocoon of protection around the corpse with her sadness.

Sounds and voices became inaudible to Seamus' ears. He saw Dean and Lucas' lips moving, but only a dull hum soaked his ears. He moved away from the group, not out of fear but his intuition told him something major was happening here.

That's when the sky opened.

With a crack of thunder that would have woken the dead, a sliver of sunlight pierced a cloud-covered sky. A beam of light directed at the angel, lifted her into the sky. Her appendages dangled like a rag doll and her eyes rolled back in her head. She ascended into the air as if an invisible cord was attached to her belly button.

The next words were spoken so clear, they might have come from inside Seamus' own head:

"Sardis, I know your deeds, that you have a name that you are alive, but you are dead. Wake up, and strengthen the things that remain, which were about to die; for I have not found your deeds completed in the sight of My God. So remember what you have received and heard; and keep it, and repent.

Seamus knew the passage well. A verse from Revelations. Could this female angel be one of the chosen Seven Archangels of the Apocalypse?

With that, her body began to shimmer from where the cord attached her to the heavens. The light spread through her and new, delicate wings grew from her shoulder blades. She was indeed more beautiful than before and Seamus turned his head away from her glory.

Then her form was next to the demon again, crying and clinging to his body. Lucas and Dean continued their tirade to get her to leave now and go with them to Milwaukee.

Had no one else seen it?

Her body glowed once more, so bright in fact, that Seamus covered his eyes. Squinting, he watched as her brilliant form rested her lips on those of the dead demon.

Dean and Lucas jumped on her, trying to pull her

off the corpse.

The light from within her was transferred to the demon corpse. It spread through him like a river as Seamus watched on.

Suddenly, his head twitched to the side and his eyes flipped open, staring right at Seamus.

He blinked twice, blood-red eyes sending a chill down Seamus' spine.

Then in the blink of an eye, both the angel and the reanimated demon...

Vanished.

****

"What in the holy fuck was that?" Daevas had a death grip on Adrienne's arm.

"The angel was lifted in the air and her body...changed. Beautiful." Adrienne's fear moments before had turned to awe watching the whole event, her body all but rigid, frozen.

"What are you talking about?" he said.

Hadn't he seen the angel's transformation? The ascension of her body, the heaven sent supercharge of light and gentle return as some kind of altered being with a new set of wings. How many more times could she, a mere human, have her world turned over anew?

First the loss of her parents.

Finding out the Novum-Stellae were run by demons.

The fact she had chosen the path of a darkwalker. The realization that her years of selfish living, her years of puttering out a day-to-day existence of empty material happiness was an entirely erroneous path. Not a misstep on the road of life. Not a jaunt down a side street that reconnected with the main road. But a giant leap off the difficult uncut path toward spiritual growth to opt for the glittery paved road leading to nowhere.

God *was* real. The battle between heavens and hell—good versus evil—did go on unbeknownst to the human cattle cluttering this fine planet. Her place in the universe was secure, did matter, and her actions would be held accountable by a supreme being that wasn't green and made from paper.

A hand connected sharply with her cheek. The sting took hold immediately and she lifted her unsecured hand to caress her smarting cheek. Slapped back to life. The words "thank-you" were on the tip of her tongue, but Daevas spoke first.

"You dumb bitch. Are you hallucinating? Those two on the ground just up and disappeared! We need to get those fragments and get out of here. Are you going to help me or do I need to use this?"

He bumped his hip against hers, reminding her of the revolver at his side. No doubt he'd use it. But now, everything she came here to accomplish took on a new meaning. Before, she hoped to save Seamus. Now, if she died in the process, she was suddenly at peace with her path, even if at the moment, she couldn't find a hint of a trail in the uncut forest. At least the glittery road she'd been on for so long, now showed its true colors.

All lies. Deceit. Roads to nowhere paved with gold and silver.

The real treasure was on the path she'd walk with Seamus. When he saw her, would he remember she gave him her word? She hadn't defected.

She was still "all-in".

Not able to get the vision of the ascending angel out of her head, she allowed the beauty of it to be replayed again. The angel's essence, lifted out of her body into the air, secured to the heavens by a gilded wire, and infused with heavenly power. The words spoken were crystal clear and imprinted on her soul. Only one other person had also been a witness.

One other head had looked skyward. One other human was privy to the whole thing. And nothing was going to stop her from being next to that one person, even if it was her last time standing by his side before Daevas killed them all.

Seamus.

Daevas unsheathed the revolver and scratched his head with it before he cocked it with his thumb, released her arm and gave her a push. What had she ever seen in this guy? Lack of a receding hairline and a stuffed wallet was so low on her list of priorities right now, she wanted to laugh.

If Seamus had a comfortable cardboard box the two of them could cozy up in together that would suit her fine.

"I've had enough of this bullshit, let's get the scraps for the boss and get out of this God-awful country." Another strong push to her lower back led right toward the three seers.

"Adrienne!" The joy on Seamus' face was replaced with fear and anger when he saw Daevas and moreover, the weapon now pointed at her head.

Holding up her hands to keep him at a safe distance, Adrienne shook her head and mouthed the words, "I'm sorry."

"Sorry to interrupt your little soiree boys, but I'll have Adrienne collect your scraps of the cup and we'll be on our way." He made a motion to Seamus. "Throw the bag on the ground if you want your lady friend to keep breathing."

Adrienne knew his orders. Steal what was left of the cup and then eliminate everyone. If she handed over the bag with pieces of the cup, he'd kill them all. Of that, she was sure.

Seamus wasted no time, tossing the small linen drawstring bag on the ground. "Take it, it's useless now."

"Back away and let Adrienne do what she does best: service me on her knees."

She shot him a dirty look. Of course he'd say something foul like that. Shame wouldn't allow her to lift her head and face Seamus. What if this was it? What if Daevas killed Seamus? Killed them all? Or worse yet, let her live and took her back to Europe. She'd much rather die a noble death at Seamus' side than face more earthly hell knowing the truth. Scrambling forward on her hands and knees, she snagged the sack and hurried to Seamus' side.

Daevas was right behind her with a hand on her elbow. "Give me the bag!"

Seamus spun around, grabbing the gun and Daevas' wrist. They struggled. Adrienne heard a crack. Seamus now had the gun, but blood oozed from the side of his shirt. He'd been shot!

She'd let go of the bag in the commotion and Daevas backed away from them, hands up, clutching the bag with the pieces of the broken Cup.

Seamus wrapped his free arm protectively around her and buried his face in her hair. "Are you okay?"

She nodded. "Are you?" How could he be worried about her when he was the one who'd been shot?

Hitting a release, the gun's magazine dropped to the sidewalk with a thud. "Those relics are mine asshole, and so is she. You want either of them, fight me like a man." Seamus tossed the weapon into a nearby bush.

Lucas and Dean had a curved sword in each hand. Seamus stepped back with his left foot, and held up his hands as a practiced fighter.

"Is this really fair?" Daevas held up his hands. "Three against one?" He took a step backwards. "And swords and fists?"

The rat bastard was going to run! "Drop the bag and get the fuck out of my life, Daevas." Adrienne kept her tone cool and hoped her acidic words carried daggers. "You're nobody. You're less than nothing and work for demons. Rot in hell."

He took one step forward like he might engage them then turned tail and ran like a little girl.

"Should I chase him?" Dean asked.

"What can he do with a broken cup?" Lucas and Dean placed their swords back in their scabbards. "I'm glad you're okay Adrienne, but I have to get back to my wife. Empty handed."

Adrienne went to give him a hug but he held up a hand, keeping her at arm's length. "Seamus, if you need anything, know I am in your debt. What about your wound?"

"The bullet grazed my rib, I'll be fine. I'm so sorry. I wish I could have done more."

They understood each other. Lucas and Dean turned to leave.

Adrienne had Seamus all to herself. Did he still want anything to do with her? Ever so slowly, she reached her hand to his face, exhaling with relief when he pressed his scruffy cheek into her palm. "I am a piece of shit, Seamus. But I never will be again. I'm ready to be all-in. If you'll still have me, that is."

"I've been waiting for you to say that. Because I was all-in the moment I saw you sitting next to Gabriel at the restaurant. Speaking of that useless angel, I wonder in all of this mess, where the heck he went to. I could use a little dose of his healing powers right now."

"Speak of the angel." Adrienne couldn't help but laugh when she saw him. He was fussing with his hair and straightening his silk shirt when he pushed through the double doors exiting the monastery.

Waving, he sauntered up to them. "Miss me? Sorry, I figured you'd never find it. And then when the ring turned up, well. I've kind of got my own issues to handle right now." He tossed Seamus a small sack which he caught with one hand, his other arm wrapped tightly around Adrienne's waist.

"What's this?"

"I've always had the artifacts on me at all times. Sorry, never really trusted you. But with the cup shattered, you might be hard-pressed to find me. Especially with another archangel being called up."

Stepping forward, Adrienne had to ask. "That female angel. What happened to her?"

"You saw that?" Seamus asked.

Gabriel inclined his head and an old monk shuffled forth from the monastery. He pointed at them, "*Die Zeugen.*"

Gabriel gave the man his arm. "Who would have ever thought it would be a lightwalker and a darkwalker would turn out to be the witnesses? I expect from this point forth, you will never leave each other's sides. What you both saw was the second of the seven archangels—Gabriella—being summoned for the end of days. The time draws near and the days of truth are upon us. It is now, we part ways. Spread the word of what you have seen. I'll see you in Kashmir."

With that, he vanished as quickly as he'd appeared.

Adrienne turned to Seamus. "We are the witnesses."

Seamus nodded. "I guess I've always felt it. I wonder what's in Kashmir."

"No matter. From this day forward, we tell of what we have seen standing side by side. Truth from this day forward." Adrienne knew any moment spent apart from this man for the rest of her days on this earth would cause her unbearable pain. She loved him as if she had always been with him. Standing on her tiptoes and clasping her hand behind his neck, she pulled him close. "I love you, Seamus. You are my everything."

Their lips touched and for a split second, Adrienne felt the earth shift. As if their finally finding each other put the universe in a more harmonious alignment. For this moment on, nothing could ever separate her from him ever again.

Chapter 32

Milwaukee, Wisconsin

Lucas couldn't understand why no one was answering their phone. And now even the hospital switchboard couldn't find Calise on their list of in-patients.

Am I too late?

When Lucas and Dean arrived at the hospital less than six hours later, he paid no attention to parking, but left his car near the front entrance as he and Dean raced into the hospital.

Reaching Calise's room in the ICU, they found a freshly-made bed, linens tucked neatly. The room was made up awaiting its next occupant. "We're too late," Dean said.

Reaching the nurses' station, Lily jumped when he slammed his palm on the counter. "Where is she?"

The nurse stood up and walked around the nurses' station and gave Lucas a big hug. "I'm so sorry about what the hospital did. It's terrible, really."

"What did they do?"

The nurse began to cry, her voice cracking, "…Asked them wait…pulled the plug…horrible…"

No. No. No. No. No.

She is lying. There is no way. She can't be gone. Impossible!

Lucas didn't even remember how they got back to the car. The next thing he knew, they were sitting in front of Calise's mother's house.

"I can't believe they did this. You weren't even here," Dean slid out of the car and Lucas followed him inside Calise's family home.

Her mother greeted them with a hug. "Do you want to see her?"

See her? "How is that possible?"

She took his hand and led him to her daughter's childhood bedroom where she lay a la Sleeping Beauty, her beautiful chest rising and falling on its own.

"But how?" was all he could say, tears clouding his vision.

"The hospital board made an executive decision to pull the plug. No one could get a hold of you. But she's still breathing, Lucas!"

The words infused him with a false hope. Maybe if he'd gotten the cup. But he hadn't. God knows he'd done his damn best, but the cup was in pieces and no good to anyone. Gripping her cool hand, he spoke to the love of his life, "Cali, I'm back. I'm so sorry I'm not back with the miracle to cure you. I tried, I really did." His voice cracked. "Please don't stop fighting. I know you can wake up. Wake up for Michael. For me."

He could barely feel her life force and Cali had one of the strongest ones he'd ever felt. She looked so different, with her gaunt frame and sunken in face. The horror of what still lay ahead of him made him hyperventilate.

His emotions were too much. He laid his head on her shoulder, careful not to put too much weight on her fragile bones. Counting her breaths, he managed to hold it together. After all, she was still alive. Weren't there stories of people being in comas for years and then finally waking up?

"Hey, Daddy!" Michael bounded in the room, unaware as young children are, of the gravity of the situation.

The tight grip of son's arms around his neck made Lucas cough and laugh. "I missed you kiddo. How are you doing?"

"Good. I'm glad Mommy's home."

Home. Physically, maybe. Lucas wanted to go back to that day at the park. He should have offered to buy the bread. Should have let her stay with Michael.

Should've. Could've. Would've.

Fuck.

"When is Auntie Ellen coming? I'll bet Mommy will want pizza tonight."

The expression on Michael's face puzzled him. Of course he knew his mom was in a coma. That she wouldn't be eating pizza tonight. Yet, the boy seemed almost giddy. It was easy to see him as a child, not an angel of the Lord. What did Michael know that he didn't?

Hopping up on the bed next to his mom, Michael let his legs dangle off the bed and bounced up and down like a kid with the enthusiasm of Christmas morning. His skin was still tanned from summer and he was all boy—a bundle of muscle and energy—always wanting to do something risky. Had he noticed how long Lucas had been gone? Or had he played with his cousin and been spoiled by his grandparents not realizing his Mom might never wake up?

"She'll wake up, Daddy. When Auntie comes with

her boyfriend."

Shaking his knee, he didn't know if Michael was psychic or crazy. "What are you talking about?"

Instead of answering, Michael jumped down and bolted out of the room. "They're here!" he cried.

Lucas chased him. Ellen stood at the front door. The chime of the doorbell never even sounded.

"Hi Auntie!" Michael threw open the door and launched himself into her arms.

Sinking to her knees, she enveloped the child. "I've missed you!" Bringing herself back up to eyelevel with Lucas, there were more than angelic changes about her. Her glow could be compared to only one other angel…the archangel, Raphael.

"Ellen?" He held open the door and she stepped into the house. "What happened to you?"

"I have remembered who I am," she said. "I am the archangel Gabrielle. The time grows closer for the final battle. It's time to choose sides." She leveled him a stare full of sadness and desperation. "I am asking for a favor. There is someone I need to fight beside me. There is someone who needs forgiveness to be saved. I am asking for your help."

That's when Lucas saw a fully alive Shane step out of the SUV parked in front of the house. *He lived?* "No way! Anyone but him! You should be dead," he pointed a finger at the demon who with slow, deliberate strides made his way up the front sidewalk. "Get out of here. I will not let you in."

Lucas felt a tug on his pants. Michael's voice was pleading. "You *have* to forgive him, Daddy. Let him in. He can help. You always say, 'If we don't forgive, we are no better than the sinner himself.'"

Always great when a five-year old uses your own words against you. "Michael, you don't understand. He's the one who hit your Mother with his car. We can't trust him. Ellen, *you* shouldn't trust him. My answer is no."

"But, Daddy…" Michael started.

"I said, no."

Pushing the front door shut and locking it, Lucas watched in horror when Michael walked right through the closed door. "Wait!"

Wrenching the door back open, Michael had taken the demon's hand and was leading him up the front steps. "Michael, I forbid you!"

Michael's whole being began to diffuse white light and Lucas found himself mute and his muscles tensed. Unable to move or speak, Shane kept his face averted as he pressed past his enemy and followed Michael into Calise's bedroom.

Lucas went numb, one foot in front of the other, following them, unable to stop whatever it was that was about to happen.

Michael pulled the demon close and whispered in his ear. Shane extracted a small piece of something from his pocket. A broken piece of the cup. Michael took his mother's bedside water and crawled up onto the bed. He put his thumb on her lower lip and opened her mouth giving Shane a quick nod and angelic smile.

Shane lowered the piece so it touched her lips and Michael poured the liquid into her mouth, making sure it first came in contact with the fragment of the Cup.

Dumbstruck, Lucas wanted to scream, yell, punch Shane, punish Michael, and throttle Ellen for bringing this filth into the house.

Then the impossible happened. Calise began to react, swallow, and then gulp. Her eyelids fluttered and then she opened her eyes.

Lucas still couldn't move.

Her lips were moving. No words came forth. Michael laid his cheek against his mother's mouth and pointed to Shane. "She wants *you*."

With a tentative step, he leaned his head close to hers. She struggled to form the words.

"I…forgive…you." she murmured. It was only a whisper but still, somehow, loud enough for everyone to hear.

"And I always knew you would be the one to save me," he said, his face wet with tears.

He backed away from her and suddenly dropped to his knees by forces unseen. Like he was being dragged through invisible quicksand. Red hot heat seemed to sear his chest as Lucas watched his essence return to him. His aura wavered and flickered, transforming from black to gray to white.

Ellen rushed to his side and Calise gave a faint smile.

He was once again an angel of the Lord.

"Thank you, Father." At those words, the rest of his essence poured back into his body. He sucked in his breath as if he'd fallen through a lake of ice and just found the surface after too long without air.

And whose hand was there to help him back to his feet? Lucas could barely believe his eyes…*Ellen.*

Unsteady in his gait after straying so far from Father's warmth, he latched onto Ellen's hand and allowed her strength to course through him. Hand in hand and without looking back, they left the bedroom and Lucas heard the front door close. They left together and Lucas could almost see them in the crisp, morning air of a new day, leaving Lucas with his beautiful wife and precious child.

Forgiveness Lucas thought he'd never find, issued forth as he went to his wife's side and took in her beautiful smile once again. He sent waves of positive emotion Shane's way.

The fallen angel had paid his debt.

Epilogue

Hell

Raphael stood before the legions of demons who knelt before him. The Ring of Solomon sparkled for all to behold. All the demons of hell and *jinn* of the earth would bow to his every demand. Raphael's head swirled with unlimited power.

Lucifer bowed his head with the rest, his forehead pressed to the ground.

Raphael walked in-between their ranks looking for only one. When he spotted his paired essence—Anna—he reached out his hand and pulled her to his side.

His Queen. She smiled at him before turning a scowl to the minions about them.

They would rule together.

Everything would be better.

Raphael barely heard it at first. It was a low throaty rumble, but the sound got louder and louder. While the other demons kept silent, heads bowed in reverence, the noise coming from Lucifer was full-out laughter.

He stood and faced Raphael. "I've been around eons before you existed. You think that ring controls me, you pathetic, insolent filth. Oh no, *Brother*, I created it." With a flick of his wrist, Lucifer cast Raphael and Anna into the indigo burning light of the deepest space of icy hell.

Kat de Falla